CHROMOPHOBIA

EDITED BY SARA TANTLINGER

Edited by Sara Tantlinger

Created by Sara Tantlinger and Nicholas Day

Exterior/interior art and formatting by Nicholas Day, Scarlett R. Algee, Don Noble

ISBN: 978-1-946335-43-2

Printed in the USA.

www.roosterrepublicpress.com

TABLE OF CONTENTS

"Elegy" by Nu Yang
261

CHROMOPHOBIA

Rainbow of the Macabre
Editor's Introduction

Color can be such a joyous part of life. I love spending time outdoors, preferably by water or in the woods, and my home state of Pennsylvania provides pretty great places to do so. Our state parks and hiking trails offer trees of deep, forest green, often accompanied by striking red cardinals or sunny yellow warblers. The satisfaction of walking along a trail and discovering those first bright blooms of wildflowers, whether the moment is committed to memory or a camera lens, makes the battle against insects and terrain all worth it.

Between patches of moss sits soft brown earth, and keen foragers can find mushrooms of every color in the woods. There's something about fungi that fascinates many of us, not just because of the interesting hues, but the textures, the shapes, the almost otherworldliness of them, and of course, the fact that some, despite their pretty or even bland colors, can be quite lethal. The visual characteristics of a mushroom can be essential in deciding if it's poisonous or not, but appearances also betray. And isn't color such a clever way to deceive?

After all, despite the splendor found in nature, it holds terror, too. While the stories within *Chromophobia* won't kill you with secret toxins, they might have you doing a double-take at familiar colors. Tones that once seemed soothing or safe may morph into unsettling palettes. I can't promise returning to nature will restore any calm, especially once you read stories like "Achromatica" by Pippa Bailey and "Bluettes" by Jacqueline West where elements found in nature hold the potential to change everything these characters know to be true.

Even shades as relaxing as an oceanic blue or a happy orange tone can lead down twisted paths where shadows dwell. In Red Lagoe's "Tangerine Sky", we're certainly made aware of that possibility. Terror-stricken memories and ideas can lurk anywhere, even in the magnificent tones of a sunset. Water offers no reprieve either; the sound of a river may seem calming at first, but it's an impossible, chimerical color you must watch out for. What are the perfect conditions that can reveal the truth of an afterimage? Maybe

"Stygian Blue" by Jo Kaplan can take you away in its current for answers.

It's not just the river to watch out for though, for even days spent at the seashore do not always guarantee crystal-clear skies, pale sand, and multicolored beach umbrellas. What awaits deep in the ocean where the darkness is almost vantablack? Let "From These Cold Murky Depths" by K.P. Kulski and "Greetings from Sunny Daytona Beach!" by Christine Makepeace shed some truth as sickly green seafoam crashes to the shore.

Though, seafoam-green offers more safety than past shades of green where history has presented us with fascinating, horrifying cases of brilliant radium-green and the once-popular Scheele's green—that beautiful emerald hue made all the more sparkling with its arsenic compounds. Fear has always been a companion of color; history has made sure of that in forms of lead makeup and paint, vibrant orpiment used for yellow tints, vermilion laced with mercury, and much more.

An article titled "Killer Clothing Was All the Rage in the 19th Century" by Becky Little of *National Geographic* goes into the distress hatmakers underwent due to mercury poisoning, and the article suggests that the infamous "mad as a hatter" phrase from *Alice in Wonderland* may be darker than the already implied implications. Hatmakers in past centuries did indeed suffer neurological disorders from the highly toxic recipe of smoothing down furs for felt hats with a mercuric solution. But at least it looked nice, right? At least the colors and appearances were exactly what was needed...When you read "The Dyer and The Dressmakers" by Bindia Persaud, you'll learn how precious materials can be—how essential it is to perfect the dyes.

How do we translate those specific tints onto the page? At tornightfire.com, Chelsea Davis has a few excellent articles focusing on color in horror storytelling, particularly on how written mediums have successfully incorporated the very visual aspects of color. Davis poses the question "What color is horror?" and mentions the often well-received "pulse-quickening reds of blood and demons, the sickly greens of alien beings and rotting flesh, the hostile whites of winter landscapes" along with great analysis of Gothic fiction and more. Her question got me thinking about how the authors within *Chromophobia* have answered it in their own ways; for example, grief in horror is a feature we often see, but what color is grief itself? "Nesting" by Ali Seay tackles this idea in such a powerful way, as does "Red Light/Green Light" by EV Knight and "The Gray" by G.G. Silverman. All three stories present elements of grief, of something unstoppable, yet all accomplished with unique dynamics. While grief remains a subjective experience, there is a relatable, heart-shattering component to loss that connects us as readers, as humans, even if the color of our grief is wildly different.

There is often hope, too, as we learn to deal with the events life puts us through. Hope is a particularly effective feature in "Wheels" by Jeanne E. Bush, where maybe light can reach us in our darkness, after all. Though sometimes hope looks a little twisted, a little bloodied in its freedom, as we see in the kaleidoscopic "Hollow Bones" by Jess Koch and the inventive "Golden Hour" by Kathryn E. McGee, which reminded me of the colorful rooms seen in Edgar Allan Poe's "The Masque of the Red Death".

Even in stories of fairy tales, folklore, or other takes with unique monsters, aspects of humanity are often what draws us in as readers and keeps us there—not unlike how an enchanting color may lure us to observe a particularly bright green apple, a shiny penny, or a strange grayish lake—memorable traits you will discover in "Burn the Witch (Red)" by Lillah Lawson, "The Copper Lady" by Jaye Wells, and "The Color of Friendship" by KC Grifant.

Though of course, as humans we're connected by many other shared emotions. What color is love, for example, other than a cartoony pink? What color is the search for love, or perhaps the threat of what else may bind us together? Maybe self-love is a different shade altogether as one tries to find their identity and relearn what it is they love, or who they love. Or maybe it's been greed all along that has cast shadows over our hearts...Let Frances Lu-Pai Ippolito tell you more in "Hei Xian (The Black Thread)" as well as Christa Wojciechowski in "The Oasis" and Geneve Flynn in "Double Happiness" to answer some of those questions.

Perhaps someone wants to share a vibrant, tasty meal with a companion like in "Five Stars" by J.B. Lamping. Color and food do go hand-in-hand, and "Eat Your Colors" by Sonora Taylor will have you reconsidering your food options for weeks. Or possibly the hunger for life, the desperation to eat away a curse, will infect your brain after reading "Hope in Her Devouring" by Tiffany Morris.

While food possesses the ability to convert into energy, sometimes conversions can go wrong. Something else entirely may slip beneath the skin and guide us into what seems like comfort at first, but then reveals a more unsettling purpose, such as in "Gray

Rock Method" by Lauren C. Teffeau. Transformation itself, along with identity, are often big themes in horror, and "Toxic Shock" by Chelsea Pumpkins presents quite a prismatic look into such metamorphosis.

And then comes one final change in life for us all, so when "Elegy" by Nu Yang knocks at your door, don't be afraid to open it and take the hand offered as the tale beautifully wraps up the anthology in a colorful aura.

Clothing, paintings, art, grief, love, fear, and more—it's all so subjective. In *The Secret Lives of Color* by Kassia St. Clair (a book I highly recommend), she writes, "Colors, therefore, should be understood as subjective cultural creations: you could no more meaningfully secure a precise universal definition for all the known shades than you could plot the coordinates of a dream" (27). Art has always been subjective, but what if a painting of the ocean that soothes you is just a shade off for someone else? How does a person with color blindness interpret the painting? What about not seeing any color at all? The subjectivity of color goes beyond a quick assessment of whether we like a piece of art or not because maybe it's impossible to share our exact experience with color with another person. Yet, how do we resist the temptation to try?

Sharing the experience of color will always be a little different person to person, but the wondrous and weird ways we can attempt to share an experience may inspire us along the way, for better or for worse, for beauty or for terror. That's exactly what the stories within *Chromophobia* accomplished for me as the editor.

Strangehouse Books focuses primarily on amplifying the voices of women in horror, and I felt this particular submission call was a perfect theme for that. I did some research on the varied ways men and women see color, and it was interesting to read about the different vocabulary women have when it comes to color. Studies seem to show that males are more adept at "discerning detail from a distance and tracking quickly-moving objects" while women are stronger at "discriminating among colors," which might be because "males need a longer light wavelength than females to see and perceive the same shade of color" (van Braam). The science behind it seems like it needs more in-depth study, but it's an intriguing place to start. Plus, those ideas mixed with the history of how women's dresses, makeup, wallpaper, and more have tried to kill us with such toxic hues, it made all the more sense to lean into this theme for our second Strangehouse anthology by women in horror. I certainly was not disappointed with the wonderful submissions (it was difficult letting so many stories go, but I know they'll find excellent homes, too).

Editing *Chromophobia* has been such an honor—I said something similar in my introduction to *Not All Monsters,* but the sentiment remains true. It's a privilege to read submissions and be a part of an anthology's creation.

Thank you to everyone who submitted for giving me a chance to read your striking words. Thank you to Nicholas Day and Don Noble for your art, formatting, and friendship.

I am so grateful to all of the authors within *Chromophobia* for sharing their talent and their exquisitely haunting ideas on how colors can trickle deep into the mind and change an entire perspective or experience.

I am equally grateful to all who have supported, bought, and shared *Chromophobia*—thank you for journeying across the macabre rainbow with me.

—Sara Tantlinger

WORKS CITED

Davis, Chelsea. "Color in Horror: The Grim Rainbow of American Gothic Fiction." tornightfire.com, 2021.

Little, Becky. "Killer Clothing Was All the Rage in the 19th Century." *National Geographic*, 2016.

St. Clair, Kassia. *The Secret Lives of Color.* Penguin Books, 2016.

van Braam, Hailey. "Why Men and Women See Color Differently." colorpsychology.org, 2020.

Hei Xian
(The Black Thread)
By Frances Lu-Pai Ippolito

a thread binds those who share a fate

that thread can stretch, tighten, or tangle,

but will never break

– Fortune Cookie

Xing-Yun rubbed his forearm on the mahjong tiles, trying to soothe the burning itch against the smooth backs and carved ivory faces littered across the table. He sighed and closed his eyes, letting the cool tiles ease the unrelenting throb under his skin. It'd been a long day manning the gambling tables at Vinny's back room; more than once he'd wanted to rip off his sleeve and gnaw at the black mark encircling his left wrist like a handcuff. But he knew that wouldn't have been a good look for a table host who ran the games, ordered drinks, and watched for cheats.

He blew out a breath and glanced at the wall clock. Almost done. At 2 a.m., the seats were all empty save one. Regular Aspen Lin was draped across the felt table-top, far too drunk to play another round even if there had been four players. The 21-year-old loved to brag that he was a "parachute adult" dropped off by rich Taiwanese parents to party in America. It was an asinine thing to say, signaling him as an easy target for anyone looking for deep pockets. Xing-Yun did what he could to shield Aspen from the worst because the kid really wasn't a bad guy, just spoiled and lazy.

"Why bother having a name that means 'lucky,' if you never play with us?" Head slung sideways on the green table, Aspen slurred every word and let out a sour breath that easily cut through the hazy cigarette smoke hovering over the table.

"I don't gamble," Xing-Yun replied, rolling down the sleeve of his navy-blue dress shirt to cover his sinewy forearm and wrist. Then he stood and stretched, cracking his neck to loosen the soreness in his muscles. Feeling the swish of his ponytail on his nape, he reached up to check for escaping strands of his hair.

His answer and movements roused Aspen, who lifted his own head of shorter jet-black hair, to jab his forefinger into the air, as if the principles of life were etched in the smoke between them. "Wasting your luck."

"Like wasting your money?" Xing-Yun shot back, his dark brown eyebrows arching, which elongated his pale face and emphasized a dip in the bridge of his nose where a rowdy customer had scored a right hook. He was aware that gruffness wasn't the best way to handle clients, but he was particularly short on patience today.

Aspen stood up, or at least attempted to, bungling his movements and knocking over his chair. Xing-Yun grabbed his shoulder, but Aspen shook him off and scrunched his nose, revealing his many dimples under drowsy eyelids. "See these two lines—" he gestured at deep wrinkles crisscrossing on the soft, unworked skin of his left palm, "—that's wealth. I'm gonna be rich all the way through. And here— " he flipped his hand over and pushed it into Xing-Yun's face, "—family."

In the mound of skin at the base of Aspen's pinky, pronounced creases striped across his palm, so many that Xing-Yun lost count. "Bet you've never seen so many," Aspen continued. "I'm having lots of babies. That's fate."

Xing-Yun smacked Aspen's hand away. "You'd better be rich to feed all those kids."

"Let's see yours." Aspen reached for Xing-Yun's left wrist.

Xing-Yun dodged. "I don't believe in luck or fate, just work," he said and slid a full glass of water across the table. "You give that a try."

Later that morning, the mark grew wider—ripening into an inky thick band collaring Xing-Yun's wrist. Under the pelt of wet heat and steam, he'd showered and scrubbed and then scrubbed more in the sudsy foam until his skin was red and raw. Roughly toweling off, he climbed into bed, trying to forget the black line by sliding against the smooth curves of his fiancée's thighs. Both worked the same overnight shift at Vinny's—she waiting the tables and he dealing the tiles. But things between them had scarcely started, when he spied a wispy black line—long and loose—floating in the air above their naked bodies. *Was it a strand of K's hair?*

"Lucky, what's wrong?" K opened one eye, making a strange wink. On top, she straddled him with her waist-length midnight hair tightly fisted behind her head in one hand, while the other pressed his chest.

"Nothing," he lied, shifting his gaze. *I don't believe in that fate shit*, he reminded himself and tried to concentrate on the glistening sweat pooling in the partition between her breasts and the rhythm of her damp skin meeting his. Slowly, though, his gaze wandered back and he could see that the black string didn't come from her at all, but extended, separately out between them, leading a path from the circular mark on his wrist through a spot in the ceiling.

"What are you looking at?" She asked, both eyes open now, studying the space where the string dangled as if tied to a helium-filled balloon.

He propped himself onto his elbows. "Do you see it? The string?"

She froze, squinting at the air and then at him. "A fate thread?" she asked, a tremor of excitement in her voice as her eyes widened, growing round like mooncakes in her flushed face. Then the brightness disappeared, her face clouding in an instant as she glanced at her bare breasts, navel, and legs, and then pushed her hands out to palm the air. "I don't see anything." She paused to look down into Xing-Yun's eyes, "—is it red?"

He shook his head. "Black."

She gasped, quickly shuffling off his body and scooting to sit on the opposite side of the bed.

"Wha—" He went to her, but she drew her knees up to her chest and snatched a pillow, wrapping her arms around it like armor as if she were afraid to be touched by or tangled in the thread she couldn't see.

Seriously? Xing-Yun slumped heavily back into the bed, bouncing K up and down to the sound of creaking springs.

"Red for love; black for death," she whispered from a childhood story Xing-Yun also remembered.

"The old man, Laozhu, who lives in the sky and uses the sun as his spinning wheel. Blah. Blah," Xing-Yun said. He adjusted the pillow under his head and then turned on his side to look at K's shapely arms crossed in front of her, the fuzzy short hairs standing on end.

"Thread spun from clouds, dyed, and tied to those bound by the same fate in life," she added.

"Silly folktales."

Her arms tightened, squeezing the pillow. "You're sure it's black?"

Sighing, he leaned back into the pillows. "You believe in those kid's stories?"

She shuffled near enough to pat his thigh, but remained careful not to get too close. "Don't you?"

"No."

"But you see it? Tied to you, binding . . .," she trailed off.

"Me to someone I have to kill, and who will kill me," he finished for her.

She nodded.

"You know how crazy that sounds right?"

She hesitated, not meeting his eyes.

"Do you actually know anyone with a fate thread?"

She shook her head. "But I've heard the stories, we all have. A black thread leads you to...death."

"K, please." Xing-Yun had been born in America, unlike his fiancée, and it was times like these he wished she hadn't brought so much of the old world superstitions with her from Taiwan. He'd heard lots of the same stories as a child from his grandparents— the red string that tied destined lovers and the black that linked fated killers. Two people tied by a red thread would always end up together. But the black thread meant inescapable death.

"In my village, I heard a story that a man found a black thread tied to his ankle. He didn't believe in it at first and tried everything he could to get rid of the string that no one could see except him. Within a week, he disappeared."

"Ha ha, sounds like he ran away from all the gossiping."

"Far from it, he was in the middle of cooking. The rice done; the daikon and taro peeled and chopped, ready for stewing."

"Well, maybe someone who didn't like him took the opportunity to take him out. Everyone expected it anyway." Feeling suddenly too warm, Xing-Yun bunched the white comforter lower to his waist, exposing the chiseled indentations of a lean, but defined torso.

"And then there was my mother's friend, who told her about a story she heard from a friend—"

"Surely, that's reliable," he interjected.

"Hush. When the black thread appeared, the girl decided to follow it and secretly spy on the person at the other end. She found out it was a thief who was hiding in her town. That night, she knocked on the door and when the thief showed up disguised as an old woman, the girl gave him a poisoned apple, which he ate."

Xing-Yun started to laugh, sitting up to catch his breath. "Straight outta *Snow White*."

"Just listen. As soon as he died, the black thread disappeared and she lived a very long life after."

Xing-Yun yawned and plopped onto his back. "These bedtime stories are making me sleepy. I wish *someone* would give me *something* else to do instead of sleep." He gave her a meaningful look and grabbed the comforter's edge, flapping it like bellows to cool his sweaty legs. A pillow flew into his face. "Ow!"

"Are you hearing anything I'm saying?"

He schooled his expressions into seriousness. "How can I not listen to the beautiful naked woman in my bed?" His arms stretched out to capture her narrow waist.

"Wang Xing-Yun!" She slapped his hands away.

"Kong Shu-Pan!" He answered with K's full-name.

"You're impossible! Don't you understand? You have to find out where it goes." Her gaze darted about the room, sending her hair fanning and swinging, and then sticking in clumps to her damp skin. "Wh-where does it go?"

He sighed and pointed up.

She peered at the ceiling; her smooth throat fully arched. "I can't see it."

"Then I must be hallucinating. *Mei le.*" It's gone, he added in Chinese.

"You have to find the other person, and..." she stopped short and her face pinched. It wasn't hard for him to guess what she'd almost said aloud.

He lunged and hooked an arm around her waist, bringing her in. His nose nudged into the sensitive parts of her neck, smelling the soap on her skin. "What about us?" he murmured, gently stroking with his lips. "No red thread. Not soulmates? K, they're just stories."

She stiffened and pulled away a little, to look into his eyes, a mixture of sadness and pity in her expression, and then she pushed him completely away. "Red or black, it's all the same. You belong to someone else now." And she threw on her clothes and went home, leaving him alone.

Tangled in the sheets unable to go back to sleep, Xing-Yun touched the thread hanging in the air; sniffed it; licked it. It gave the scent and taste of lemongrass, which seemed to him a strange flavor for death. In his fingers, he experimented—prying, rending, kneading, and stretching. The thread yielded to whatever force applied, but never broke or frayed, always returning by elastic memory to the same persistent shape.

"I don't believe in you," he told the black thread and jumped from the bed to stride naked into the kitchen. The thread followed and lengthened to exert a light tug, ever present to remind but not hinder Xing-Yun from moving. In seconds, drawers were yanked open and left that way—tongue-like planks hanging out of their wooden mouths. As Xing-Yun's hands moved, the thread danced like a ribbon in the wind, drawing wave-like patterns in the air. Rifling through spoons, Xing-Yun spied the blue handles of scissors and the red V-stripe of a Vinny's matchbook buried underneath. He tried the scissors first, setting his left wrist on the counter, yawning the blades open to flank the black thread between the cutting edges. A stray string, he decided, like the loose threads of his pants. Nothing more, nothing less. The black thread did not appear to disagree and rested at a relaxed angle in the scissor's teeth.

Xing-Yun's thumb and middle finger flexed, closing the blades' distance but halting them partway. An unwilling anxiety arose in his chest at the seamless way the thread attached to his wrist as if wrought from his own flesh. Would it hurt? Could it bleed? Was he letting K's stories get in his head? He rolled his shoulders and forced himself to snip the string, barely daring to breathe. He missed. At the last moment before the blades kissed, the thread slipped out, gliding deftly over the sharp tips. *What the hell?* He tried again. Then again to no avail. When the cutting edges met, the strand always drifted to safety, riding on the breeze of the rotating blades. He kept at it until his fingers ached and the promise of blisters burned.

Breathing hard, Xing-Yun dumped the knife into the sink and tore a match off the book. He lit one and an orange teardrop flame was struck to life. They waltzed—the black thread with the flame—flexing, bowing, even embracing, but never singeing.

An hour later, the matchbook was empty and Xing-Yun stared at the ceiling, a cleaver now clasped in his hand. It was preposterous, he told himself, yet that little Chinese boy he hid in the deepest part of himself (the one who remembered his grandparents' stories), was uncertain if he was seeing things or if he could bring himself to kill another person if he had to. He was aware that if any of it were true, it was simply a matter of time before the guy on the other end saw the thread. *If that guy believes, he'll eventually come for me.* In the quiet room, sitting on the cluttered kitchen floor, Xing-Yun's grip tightened until his knuckles popped and cracked and the skin bleached to the white of bone.

He bought a gun. *Nine millimeters, nicely balanced, easy to keep, easy to reach.*

K didn't know he'd gotten one, but Xing-Yun thought if she did, she'd come back to him instead of switching her shift and avoiding his phone calls for the last three weeks. She'd made it clear when he did catch her after work one day, she considered him as good as dead and painful as it was to say, "there was no point in their being together."

Hearing her words in his head, Xing-Yun patted the bulge in his stretched waistband and paid for the steamed pork bun at the Chairman Bao's food truck parked outside of Vinny's. As he bit into the pillowy, sweet dough, he raised his left wrist, studying the black thread that trailed him everywhere like a leash. It'd stayed more or less the same size, shape, and color, conspicuous in its existence to him, but invisible to everyone else. Was it real? Xing-Yun still wasn't completely decided, but the truth was it didn't matter. He could see it and the longer it tailed him, the more he itched to get rid of the thread, to follow it to the other end and take care of the whole messy business. Plus, if any of the stories were true, then what of the other guy? There was no way whoever was on the opposite end hadn't seen the mark by now.

What's he waiting for? Is he watching me? The sweetness and texture of the soft dough tasted like sand and Xing-Yun tossed the bun into the trash bin.

"Hey Lucky!" Aspen called out and waved from the crosswalk.

"Hey," Xing-Yun answered, wiping his hands on his jeans as Aspen bounded down the sidewalk like a cheerful child.

"Are you leaving already? It's only 6 p.m.," Aspen asked.

"My shift changed," he answered, realizing then the last time he'd seen Aspen was the day the mark appeared over three weeks ago. In that time, life had apparently treated him well. A new glow now brightened Aspen's skin and a rosy tint brought liveliness to his plumped cheeks. Gone were the unwashed designer clothes, replaced with a button-down and pressed khakis.

"I'm here to say goodbye to everyone. No more gambling. Getting married!" Aspen held a young woman by the shoulders, one he'd taken in tow across the street. Much shorter than Aspen, she appeared bashful and shy, peeking up to look at the food truck and Xing-Yun, but then averting her eyes.

"Married? I didn't know you were dating?" Xing-Yun stared with suspicion at the petite Asian woman with bowl-cut hair and a fresh face, who looked to him to be, frankly, under-aged.

Aspen chuckled and pointed to his neck. "Red thread."

Red thread? Xing-Yun didn't hide his curiosity, leaning in close to examine Aspen's wheat-colored flesh, almost breathing on his neck. He saw nothing. Puzzled, he turned to the woman covered from head to toe in a modest high-collared paisley dress, who seemed to shrink under his glare.

"I don't see anything," he said finally.

Aspen shrugged. "Eh, I guess that's expected. Only the destined pair can. Julia and I see it fine, and we decided why waste time if you know it's fate. Right?" He grinned and familiar dimples constellated his face. She returned his smile, but kept her eyes downcast.

Some people have all the luck, Xing-Yun thought and started to congratulate the new couple, but stopped when he realized his black thread had gone slack, meaning the other guy was so close that the extra length coiled tensionless at his feet. Xing-Yun spun around, scanning the sidewalks and streets.

"Do you have one too?" Julia asked, her voice lilting like a child's.

"Hmm?" He said and stumbled when he found her face only inches from his chest. She'd sidled to his side as Aspen waited in line to order at the Chairman's window.

"You're looking for someone important," she whispered in a furtive voice as if in conspiracy. This near, Xing-Yun thought her very young, but attractive in a delicate China doll way—her face flawlessly smooth, an even honey tone, framed with blunted bangs and bobbed hair.

"I...I'm looking for someone, but—" Xing-Yun hesitated, unwilling to speak out his fears. With the thread pooled at his feet, the other guy had to be watching, listening, waiting.

She nodded in understanding, placing a fingertip coated in bubblegum polish on his forearm, and tapping him with the lightest beat of dragonfly wings.

"The red one led Aspen to me. Now," she paused and blushed, "we're expecting." Another of her fingers twirled a knotted tassel cinching the waist of her wrap dress. "I haven't told him. It's a surprise. Shhh." She touched the finger to her lips.

Xing-Yun looked down at the tassel and fell back, ramming into the rear of the bun truck.

"Dude!" The Chairman yelled as he held onto his dumpling-shaped hat that threatened to topple off his head in the rocking truck.

"You ok?" Aspen steadied Xing-Yun while balancing his paper plate of pot-stickers.

Xing-Yun heard them speak, but his vision had blurred and funneled to nothing but the black thread that fed right into Julia's gut, into the place where babies are cradled and made. His fingers twitched, and unconsciously, his hand drifted over his shirt, right above to where the butt of the gun stuck out from the waistband. *5 feet, maybe 90lbs, to my 5'9", 170. It'd be easy to shoot her, like slaughtering a puppy.* His breath hitched and his eyes squeezed shut. *Only the baby.* He made his hand still, willing himself to open his eyes and drop both arms to his sides. *Not here. Not in the open.*

Aspen cleared his throat and let go of Xing-Yun's shoulder. "Lucky," he said with uncharacteristic solemnity, "you've always taken care of me, like an older brother." He patted him on the back. "Thank you." He held out his hand. Xing-Yun took it, hoping Aspen couldn't feel it trembling.

Aspen cleared his throat again and let Xing-Yun's hand go. As soon as he did, Julia reached for Aspen and pulled him close.

He kissed her on the head. "Why don't you head home and rest?"

She beamed at him. "Ok, I'll walk, it's not far."

"Do you live in the Cooke building on Wilshire?" Xing-Yun asked just as Aspen started to leave.

"How'd you know?" she replied without looking at him.

He forced a strained smile. "I'm on the third floor."

"I'm on the sixth."

"That's perfect!" Aspen slapped him on the back. "We're getting married and she's still too embarrassed to ever let me in her apartment." He chuckled and tweaked the bridge of Julia's nose. "Xing-Yun's the best, he'll walk you home for me."

A glimmer of something flickered in her dark brown eyes, disappearing before Xing-Yun could decide what it was.

"Ok, walk with me," she said directly to Xing-Yun, her voice now strong, unwavering.

"I love you," Aspen said, kissing her again before heading up the stairs into Vinny's.

Xing-Yun and Julia walked in a viscous silence through downtown blocks lit by street lamps. To others, it may have painted a romantic picture, the man and woman strolling in unhurried quiet under the prismatic bands of a setting sun's sky. But all the way, Xing-Yun's heart hammered unrestrained in his chest and he wondered if Julia could hear it pounding from the outside.

He broke first and asked, "How long have you known Aspen?"

"Almost a month," she said in a thin voice that required effort for Xing-Yun to hear.

"So not pregnant for too long?" He knew it was an extremely intimate question, but then again, she'd offered that intimacy at the start.

She hummed a response, which he took as "yes."

Was it even Aspen's? Xing-Yun wondered at the timing and the urgency of courtship. Perhaps, it was someone else's child and she found Aspen an easy sucker to pin it on. And if he were to do away with it, wouldn't that be helping his buddy out?

Slowing his pace, he intentionally let her amble ahead, watching her profile in the reflections of glass building panes, scrutinizing her figure, and pondering how to find and aim at a woman's uterus. Abruptly she whirled around, confusion splayed over her face. Engrossed in watching her movements and learning her form, he didn't notice he'd stopped walking altogether. Her gaze slipped to her shoes, a pair of ratty brown Nikes that Xing-Yun thought might have started out white.

"You're protective of Aspen. He's told me you made sure he ate, slept, stayed off drugs, and never spent too much at the tables." She lifted her gaze back up to Xing-Yun's face, biting a lower lip that was the color of peaches. "Red thread or not, I adore him and those magnificent dimples." Fat tears rolled off her cheeks and stained the concrete.

Around them, the streets were full, but the gun's muzzle prodded at Xing-Yun's skin. Meaning only to adjust the gun's position, his hand snuck under his shirt on its own to touch the grooved metal in an unhidden motion that Julia's eyes saw and easily followed. A harsh expression seized her face and the teary softness in her eyes calcified into stone.

Does she know? But before Xing-Yun could take out his hand or the gun, Julia swooned and would have hit the ground if he hadn't instinctively grabbed her arm and leaned her into his chest.

"I haven't eaten in a long time," she murmured. Xing-Yun sighed and picked her up. She weighed nothing, giving him a moment of fresh hope—*maybe she'd miscarry and it'd die all on its own. Maybe he could wait, just a little while to see if he even needed to worry. What would K think about killing a baby?* With some bitter amusement he thought the thread might as well have been red judging the way he carried Julia bridal style the remaining three blocks back to their building, up the elevator, and to the threshold of Room 66.

"Please, come in," she said when he set her down.

"I don't th—"

"Until I feel better," she insisted, palming her flat belly.

He nodded, curious to see where she lived and whether she was fragile and irresponsible enough to lose the kid on her own. She shut and locked the door right after he stepped into a room as dark as night.

"Do you use blackout curtains?" he asked.

She giggled.

She sounds strange. Is she lightheaded? Xing-Yun's fingers fumbled along the wall until he found the panel and flicked the switch. The ceiling light shined on Julia standing in the center of an unfurnished room.

"Minimalist," he observed.

She said nothing, staring intently at him.

He tried again. "What's that?" He gestured to the windows covered by a bumpy fibrous plaster.

She gave him a twisted grin, raising the hairs on his neck and sending prickles down his spine. *This felt wrong. She felt wrong. Have I made a mistake?* It was in that moment Xing-Yun appreciated how little he actually knew about this strange woman he'd never seen and who'd locked him inside a completely empty apartment. He felt the creeping vines of quickening fear and wanted desperately to leave.

"I'm pretty tired." He headed for the door. Two steps in, he was yanked back by the black thread on his arm, the force so strong that it flung him around to face Julia, who stood in the same spot, her head cocked to one side. She watched him as her hands unbuttoned the clasps at her neckline to her chest and then untied the tassel at her waist. The flaps of the wrap dress opened like flower petals, and the entire garment loosened and fluttered off into a puddle at her feet. In only a white cotton bra and bikini panties dotted with pink hearts, she continued to grin as she thrust out her hips, squatted, and spread apart her knees, exposing the thin rectangular strip covering her crotch.

What the hell?

That white strip bulged and pulsated from undulating pieces shifting underneath. From the edges of the cloth, shiny, obsidian tips emerged, lengthened, and grew into four pairs of jointed legs, climbing out. As the eight legs poured forth like birth, Julia's skin and the rest of her undergarments sloughed off and collapsed—unboned from the inside. The clawed tips of eight legs clicked on the wooden floor in frustration as a bulbous hairy body struggled to free itself from Julia's fleshy skin, the head apparently stuck.

Run, dammit. Xing-Yun forced his legs to move, able this time to get to the door while the dog-sized creature fussed with taking off its human husk. He grabbed at the doorknob, turning, pulling, but it was jammed shut. Taking a deep breath, he raised his foot and kicked the door, banging the hinges. The creature shrieked and wrenched the black thread, slamming Xing-Yun to his knees.

"We're famished." It spoke in Julia's voice from Julia's China doll human head. That head being all that remained while the rest of her laid in a pigtailed sheet like curled banana peels on the floor. The head now watched Xing-Yun from atop an arachnid's abdomen perched on eight thick, hairy legs. "It's so nice to stretch," she said with a happy smile, flexing her feet and kicking aside the molted skin.

Then she scuttled closer and Xing-Yun pressed his back against the door, keeping his eyes on her, because all he could do was stare with the terror freezing his mind. "You wanted to kill us." She laughed a tinny, metallic sound and plucked the black thread, strumming it like a guitar string, sending the vibrating waves that struck Xing-Yun's arm and rattled his teeth. "Humans believe whatever shit we spiders spin." She cackled with uncontained mirth and rolled her eyes. "A spider's story is how we lure you in. Though, Aspen has been too sweet to eat just yet." She inched nearer, lifting and lowering each foot slowly one after the other.

"Stay away from me, you monster!" Xing-Yun finally found his voice and drew the gun, shooting rounds that ricocheted off her back and legs.

She yawned and twitched a toe, catching the black thread that connected Xing-Yun's wrist to a spinneret at her rear. She began to wind it around her foot like a spool, shortening the thread and compelling Xing-Yun to lie prone on the floor as she reeled him in. The pull was uneven and as she dragged, he felt splinters in the wooden boards tear and scrape at his chin.

Struggling to hold the gun, Xing-Yun rolled onto his back and saw from that angle the spider's middle legs were snugly folded across a silky belly, clutching protectively to a white sac. There were hundreds of eggs, if not thousands, all carrying the same type of creature, but smaller, every one with a human infant head affixed to a squirming spider body.

"Go to hell!" Xing-Yun screamed and emptied the rest of the magazine directly at the egg sac.

Julia howled in pain as a yellow liquid squirted out of her underside. The egg sac fell to the floor and she charged, colliding straight into Xing-Yun's head with a force that blossomed instantly into blinding pain. She wasn't done and soon reared up on back legs to plunge a foot into and then out of his chest, shattering his ribs and leaving a gaping gash that quickly filled with blood. He collapsed on the floor, holding his torn flesh, trying to push it back in. She flailed and thrashed, but couldn't right herself or staunch the flow of yellow blood that rushed out of her, mixing to orange with Xing-Yun's red.

In mere moments, she began to shudder, struggling to breathe. Xing-Yun could tell she was dying, but then again, maybe so was he. When a final breath hissed out her sides and at last, she stopped moving, Xing-Yun closed his eyes to rest and wondered if he could stand and still kick down the door. Seconds passed and a sound like pebbles tumbling from stairs broke through his rhythm of panting and wheezing.

They'd hatched. The surviving newborns scurried to encircle Xing-Yun, skittering their toes against the floor. *Babies look like their fathers*, he thought as he recognized their familiar thumb-shaped human faces filled with Aspen's dimples. He should have run or tried to escape, but hesitated, stunned and horrified by the sheer number of the growing horde that swarmed him. By the time he tried to crawl away, the children had already cast out thousands of silk threads, all black ones that bound and secured Xing-Yun in place.

Stygian Blue
By Jo Kaplan

Think of the river.

Think of the river's current, fixed and unrelenting. Implacable in its refusal to stop or turn. Think of its movement, its unidirectional flow. Like time. You can't push back through time like you can't push back through a current.

Think of the river behind the Mapletons' farm, bordered on its far bank by the forest. Beyond the chicken coop and the pasture. The river made a natural boundary for the farm, more permanent than any fence. It was a river without a name, and none of the Mapletons had ever followed it far enough to see where it went, or where it came from.

One can imagine the animals that lived on the farm, as they went grazing, discovered the river and thirsted. They must have drank its cool lifeblood. This was probably what precipitated all the strangeness with the cows.

First, Mr. Mapleton discovered one cow upside-down.

Not lying on its back, but occupying the same patch of space it would had it been standing up—floating with its hooves in the air and its ears nearly grazing the grass. Mr. Mapleton said he found it on the far end of the pasture, and it reversed direction after only a second or two, so that it once again stood upright.

How do we know that's what he really saw? It's possible his eyes were only playing tricks on him. He'd been drinking heavily of late and had just recently turned to hair of the dog to ease his hangovers. His drinking was starting to spill over from one day to the next, poisoning his wife and daughter by proxy.

But it wasn't just the upside-down cow. The Mapletons claimed they found another cow split in half down the middle, its two parts separated by no fewer than fifteen feet. They saw cows presenting impossible abilities.

Cows that disappeared and reappeared. Cows that seemed to move backwards. Cows that briefly doubled before snapping together again.

They tried to convince their neighbors, but it was a hard sell.

Who would believe in interdimensional cows?

At least that was the theory Mrs. Mapleton favored. She trusted her intuition. On the other hand, Mr. Mapleton thought they'd been cursed or were being somehow haunted. Which is why Mrs. Mapleton grew fascinated by the cows while Mr. Mapleton grew ever more irate the more she talked about them. She didn't care that no one believed them. She only wanted to be with the cows, examine them, understand them.

He only wanted to escape.

A kind of falling away is what happened. Not an argument. Mr. and Mrs. Mapleton simply turned away from each other.

None of them really knew what was happening.

Not until Anya went for a swim.

Anya, seventeen and moody to a fault, escaped to the river to breathe out the emotional pollution in every place her parents touched. She toed the water, chilly even in the dead of summer. The sun touched her straw-colored hair done back in a braid and her scattering of freckles.

She watched the cows, which were generally behaving like cows again now that her father had begun actively keeping them away from the river. They seemed unharmed by their jaunt into the infinite.

She couldn't decide how she felt about it. On one hand, she was defiantly uninterested in comprehending what had made the cows behave so strangely, unlike her obsessed mother. On the other, she refused to be frightened off like her father.

Maybe that was why she put on her swimsuit and went out to the river.

Her feet seemed all right, so she took another step into the water.

Current against her ankles. Cloud occluding the sun. All ephemeral and in flux.

Then, a voice: Her father calling her name the way he did when he was drunk and unhappy. Anya imagined him ripping her away from the riverside with frantic admonitions. Accusations of her listening too much to her mother. Fear knotting into anger.

Silently she slipped into the water—its shocking cold—and swam down towards the riverbed, wondering how deep it went.

Anya Mapleton never hit the bottom.

Instead, when she thought she must be getting close, her hands broke through into open air, and she bobbed to a new surface, wondering if she had somehow turned around without realizing it but feeling deep in her wary heart that this wasn't possible.

Before the current could take her away, she swam to shore. Pulled herself up the muddy bank, wiping grass from her swimsuit. Looked across at the forest.

But it wasn't a forest. Or, it had been, once—a long time ago. Now it was only a blackened graveyard of burnt trunks, petrified on an otherwise barren plain.

When she looked behind her, she saw the ruins of a farmhouse in the distance. Recognized it even in its state of decay. The wind had battered it near to splinters. No one could possibly live there. No one could possibly have lived there for many, many years.

Fighting a rising panic that she had emerged from the river somewhere *else*, Anya noted the reddish cast of the sky all in haze.

Unable to stop herself, she again looked at the farmhouse, which was the Mapletons' farmhouse. The severe neglect haunted her with its *wrong*ness. She had grown up in that house; she knew it as she knew herself. What lay at the end of the field, however, was long abandoned. Nothing more than a relic.

Upon a second look, something appeared to be moving. Emerging from the house. A figure. A very tall, thin figure. Walking towards her.

What might be living in that ruined house in this ruined world, Anya could not bear to imagine. She turned and dove into the icy water.

All she had to do was swim straight down, and eventually she would re-emerge back home. She decided she would laugh about this someday. She would begin to question whether it had all been her imagination. She would think of it as no more than a dream.

All she had to do was swim down.

She came up sputtering, blinking water from her eyes, jaw chattering with cold, full of relief and trepidation, one of which would become the other as soon as she was able to get a clear look around.

Relief won.

There stood the verdant woods. There stood the farmhouse painted blue.

Breathing, sighing, Anya looked for her towel but found it must have been blown away. Dripping she crossed the pasture, eager for the comfort of her bedroom. For warmth and dryness and familiarity.

She must have been on the other side long enough for Mr. Mapleton to stop calling for her as she heard no voices. Her swimsuit clung, cold, to her torso.

Through the cluttered living room and up the groaning wood staircase until Anya stood in the doorway of her bedroom but made no move to enter. Because she was already in the room.

There was the back of her as she sat on the bed facing the window. Sunlight streamed in around the gold edges of her hair. Then Anya on the bed turned her head and looked straight at Anya in the doorway, their cornflower eyes locking.

"What are you doing here?" asked Anya on the bed as Anya in the doorway walked backwards, away from here, something terrible lurching up from the depths of her. She stumbled as she approached the stairs, not daring to take her eyes from the doorway as Anya stood from the bed and came around to watch her.

She turned and fled down the squealing stairs. She threw herself out the front door. She ran.

To the river.

And, not hesitating, dove in. Swam down.

There were more surfaces of the river and more worlds beyond them. There were more Anyas. There were places without the house or the grass or the trees, places where something white like snow but not cold piled up around the riverbank.

None of them was home.

She started opening her eyes in the water, attempting to spot the moment when she was no longer swimming down but up. She tried to stop herself at that moment and swim back to the previous shore, but it was impossible. If she stopped too long halfway down (up) the current threatened to drag her away, sending her in a new direction entirely. In was in these moments she forgot which way was up and which was down and found herself halfway between the two, in a place where the dark danced strangely around her as waves formed in the current.

Maybe that's how she would get home. By following the dance of the blue on the black. But still she was afraid to give herself over to the current at the center of the river. The conduit.

Finding herself grown too clinical as she experimented with understanding the river, Anya reminded herself not to become too much like her mother, who was so cold, so uninterested in her.

She remembered, then, to feel fear.

For a time, this fear consumed her. She wavered at the edge afraid of the churning endlessness of the river but also afraid of the uncanny world that was not hers. Not knowing whether to stay in this strange place or leap into the unknown down ever more diverging tributaries.

Then she reminded herself not to become paralyzed by fear like her father.

Anya jumped.

She next emerged beside a ring of proselytizing cows. They bowed before the cow at their center, who seemed to glow. A line of cows with pails in their mouths carried water from the river to the central cow which elicited a series of gentle moos in what seemed a meaningful pattern.

Anya crawled out from the water ignored. Mud caking her feet. The glowing cow pulled her vision to it like a magnet, wonderful and terrible. It drank from the pails set before it.

Then it turned its black bovine eyes to her and stared with an alien intensity.

Its next moo sounded like a hello.

Each cow turned its head to stare at Anya, over a dozen impenetrable gazes fixed on her. She felt scrutinized but not judged, for it was by something other than human intelligence.

The glowing cow blinked and said, *You have come from the river.*

"Where am I?" Anya finally shouted. "What the fuck is happening?" She felt she could not swim anymore and fought back the burn of her eyes, the exhaustion of her body. Bits of wet grass in her hair.

You are here, said the cow unironically even as Anya thought how unhelpful an answer it was.

"What *is* it?" she asked, staring into the blue water in constant motion as an evolving wave expressing itself differently at each point in time. Always moving but impossible to navigate or control.

The river is like an artery, said the cow.

"The fuck does that mean?"

Think of it like a nerve in the cerebellum of the universe, said the cow. It drank from the pails, taking the river into itself, into the rivers of its brain. Making more and more of itself the wave that moved the river.

"How do I get back home?" Anya asked while pretending to ignore the absurdity that she was conversing with a cow.

I do not know the way, said the cow. *The river does not move backwards.*

"I don't need to go backwards. I just need to go..."—a frustrated shake of her head— "... through."

Through, contemplated the cow as it emptied a pail. Its eyes seemed to effervesce a strange dark hue and its flesh rippled or vibrated. *Through. Ah, yes. You go through. All the way through. And what do you see?*

Now the cow seemed to be speaking gibberish, or at least in phrases Anya could not follow. She shook her head again. She didn't know.

STYGIAN BLUE! The cow shouted or mooed in something resembling a shout. *STYGIAN BLUE! STYGIAN BLUE! STY-*

Then the cow burst into a billion glimmering pieces that burned themselves out on the air.

Having witnessed this dissolution, the rest of the cows fixed their black stares upon Anya as she stumbled back into the water, glided to the middle of the river, and swam down.

And down.

And down.

The river seemed deeper here. She reached a layer of midnight divorced from the sun at either or any side of the river. She wondered what might happen if she turned and swam along that layer of darkness, turned away from up or down and towards a new direction. What if she kept going forward but there wasn't another surface for her to find? What if she drowned in the endlessness?

The current pushed her gently to that deeper darkness but she resisted, swam forward. And up.

She coughed and gasped at the surface, her limbs trembling with fear and cold and exertion. Sunset promised twilight in its rosy hues.

Here the woods encroached on either bank of the river. Barefoot she crept among the trees for sign of life, stepping on nettles, swatting the buzz of mosquitoes. Darkness thickened under the canopy.

She thought of her parents.

By now Mr. Mapleton would have realized Anya was no longer there. His calls would echo empty on the wind, unreturned. Maybe he would find her towel and shoes and jean shorts folded in a neat pile beside the river and he would know where she had gone. But he would be too afraid to go in after her.

Perhaps he would tell Mrs. Mapleton and she would decide to leap in after her daughter. Would she follow the same path as Anya or emerge from other surfaces even stranger? Would she become irrecoverably lost, never to find her way back home?

She tried not to think of these things and soon she came upon an angular hut set crooked between trees. Rough, simple, built by hand. Leaf-laden branches shivered above it. Orange glowed from the solitary window, the kind of orange that shivered.

Like a witch's shack in a fairy tale, Anya thought. But it was this, alone among the trees, and nothing more. Nowhere else to go. Nothing but ever-darkening forest and the river behind her, always rushing, always moving.

She knocked on the door.

When it opened, she felt the dry heat of a fire which turned the woman in the doorway to a dusky silhouette.

"I can smell the river on you," said the woman. "Come in."

Grateful and ashamed, Anya followed her into the hut to sit beside the crackling fire. Animal hides hung on the walls. A small skinned creature roasted on a spit above the flames. Smelled of bubbling fat and sweet meat. Her stomach grumbled.

Only when she felt the deep ache of cold begin to recede did she look up at the woman who lived here.

The woman had no eyes.

Anya's heart lurched up her throat but she could not tear herself from the fire to return to falling darkness and icy water—could not allow herself to be frightened off so easily from warmth and light.

The woman regarded her with gaping holes in her freckled face, hair hanging stringy. She tore a piece of meat from the spit with soot-blackened fingers and chewed, swallowed.

"What is this place?" Anya asked.

The woman considered. "I don't know. It's only where I washed up. The forest goes on for miles and miles. I think maybe it goes on forever."

Anya shivered. Wind creaked through cracks in the hut and the trees outside rustled with the voices of multitudes.

"You've been through the river," the woman said.

Realizing the silence of her nod, Anya said, "Yes." Then: "What happened to you?"

"I went through the river too," the woman said. She tore off another piece of meat and handed it to Anya, who could not help but take it. She bit. It was tough and chewy. "Years ago. I went for a swim. But I got lost." The woman's mouth hung open like the wounds of her eyes where darkness danced. She stepped closer. "Stay here. Don't go back in."

Anya recoiled. "What? I can't stay here."

"It's no use," said the woman, every bit of her gaping open so that Anya felt she could see too much of her insides, too much of what ought never be shown to the world. "If you go back in. You'll tire. You'll be swept away." Her mouth trembled. "Don't look at the river's bottom."

Anya frowned. "I thought it had no bottom? Since you always come out another side?"

"Oh," said the woman, chuckling, "it has a bottom. The river is deeper than you can imagine, but it has a bottom. If you swim long enough."

Despite herself Anya felt her mother's curiosity prickling through her. "What's at the bottom?"

The eyeless woman pulled a chair beside her and sat, reached forward to touch Anya's hands. Brought her mouth close to Anya's ear. Whispered, "Stygian blue."

Anya tried to pull away but the woman's grip tightened on the bones of her wrist. "What's stygian blue?"

The woman's lips pulled into a grin around rotting teeth. "A forbidden color. Something we're not meant to see." Then she laughed. A mad sound, like the shouting cow.

With an almighty tug Anya pulled herself away, overturning the wooden chair which cracked against the floor. She rolled free of the woman's reach, trying not to look up into the darkness swimming in her empty sockets, dark and blue, and with splinters in her stinging feet she stumbled back against the wall as the woman turned one way and then the other, searching for her.

Then as if she had forgotten Anya altogether, the woman turned away, stoked the fire, took the roasted creature from the spit, ate more meat. Humming to herself all the while.

Anya stood silent in the corner, watching.

By turns the woman added words and odd cackles to her humming. Anya recognized the tune as something she had listened to as a child, but she did not recognize the lyrics the woman added.

"I can't see me and I can't see you," she sang as she walked around the hut with her hands out, feeling her way to the table where she set down the meat.

Observing her from the corner, Anya realized the woman could not be much older than herself. She even had the same straw-colored hair.

Gazing about with her black sockets, she sang:

"All I see is stygian blue, stygian blue, stygian blue."

Anya took a step but her shifting weight made the floor groan. The woman stopped singing.

"Who's there?" she called sharply.

Holding her breath, Anya took another step. Another. Slow. Ghostly.

The woman turned her face this way and that.

"I can smell the river on you," she said, voice flat.

Three more steps to the door. Anya wanted nothing more than to be out of this hut and away from the woman with no eyes.

"You'll see," the woman muttered as Anya reached the door, though whether she was talking to Anya or herself, Anya couldn't say.

Night had fallen. Blue gloom shrouded the clicking, rustling sea of trees. Anya did not want to find out what creatures roamed the eternal forest, so she picked her way over brambles and roots until she saw the rippling river gleaming silver in moonlight.

She sat on the bank, hissing at the chill when she tested the water. A chasm of melancholy opened up inside of her. She wondered what was the point of continuing to swim from one surface to another. She wondered what was the point of even trying to get home, to a home where she was ignored or berated. She wondered if her parents were even missing her or if they were simply going about their lives growing ever more remote.

Perhaps she ought to leap into the river and simply let it take her away.

Stop fighting. Stop fearing. Stop trying to figure it out.

She stood and dove into the sparkling water, and when she reached that no-man's land between up and down, she drifted with the current, let it pull her away from up or down and into the deeper dark. Let her limbs float and her body tumble. Became part of its movements.

When she had attuned herself to the rhythm that guided the river, she added her own movements and started to swim.

Not up or down or even sideways but *deeper.* Towards the bottom.

She opened her eyes. She exhaled a tiny stream of bubbles that disturbed the dark.

Then she saw it: The blue.

The blue as dark as the black. Like seeing color while blind.

Figures crawled and swam at the river bottom like scavengers, figures of stygian blue which morphed and twisted in the current, *with* the current, part of the river or maybe its natural inhabitants.

She decided she would not be afraid.

The figures found her, took hold of her. She was not supposed to be here. Her presence at the bottom of the river violated the universal wave. Her lungs burned and she saw the shape the river made as if from above, the same shape the waves made in the water, a shape that turned in on itself again and again like a Möbius strip.

Lungs ached, could no longer hold back. She breathed in. Icy water filled her chest. She was on fire. She felt the blackest blue, the bluest black, race through her arteries like ink.

The police fished Anya Mapleton's body out of the river six miles downstream. The coroner declared it an accidental drowning.

The one thing no one could explain was how her body had vanished from the morgue. One moment it was there and the next it was gone. Just before it disappeared, the diener who had been cleaning the autopsy tools glanced over at the corpse and saw its blue eyes open and staring.

He came closer and Anya Mapleton who was definitely dead looked right at him with pupils that expanded and expanded, black into the blue. He leaned closer, mesmerized by those eyes, by the way some deeper darker blue was dancing in the black. Her gray lips moved slightly, a song whispering between the tiniest possible breaths. He leaned closer. Listened.

"*All I see is stygian blue,*" the corpse sang, almost inaudible, "*stygian blue, stygian blue.*"

After the body disappeared, the diener quit and supposedly has not been seen since.

EAT YOUR COLORS
BY SONORA TAYLOR

Angela assured her it'd be easy. She gave no impression of anything else on her Instagram feed, one that Eve followed with keen interest in her seemingly never-ending quest to eat better. She didn't want to diet, and she didn't want to starve. Nor did she want to spend a lot of money.

"You can give a big middle finger to the diet industry," Angela said as she held up a bowl of oatmeal dotted with the freshest blueberries Eve had ever seen. "While giving your body the big hug it needs."

Angela promoted clean eating and whole foods, a way of eating so rooted in common sense, Eve didn't understand why it was so hard for her to follow. But for every one day of eating the right thing, she'd follow it up with two or more of candy and French fries punctuating the salads and grains. She wanted to know Angela's secret—so much so that she was willing to pay for one of Angela's one-on-ones over Zoom to get on the right track.

"So how are you looking to change your relationship with food?" Angela asked. She sat on a beautiful pillow with her legs crossed. She wore flowing white capris and a matching long-sleeved t-shirt, and her blonde hair fell out of a swept bun in delicate swirls around her face.

Eve, on the other hand, sat below the bright glow of her desk lamp. She'd run a comb through her own dirty blonde hair and put on a bit of lipstick, but still felt drab pictured next to Angela on her screen.

"I just want to eat better," Eve said. "I want to stop eating so much—"

"Stop right there." Angela held out a finger towards the screen. "Your relationship with food shouldn't be about stopping or ending, it should be about adding. I don't promote minimizing. Nothing about you needs to be diminished, not even your plate."

"Not even candy or fried things?"

"If you want those, have those!" Angela laughed as she tucked a strand of hair behind her ear. Eve waited patiently for the catch.

"But have them *as well as* healthier things. Add the colors of the rainbow to your plate, and you'll see how much better you feel even when you eat artificial stuff."

"I've tried that. I eat salads and whole grains and—"

"Do you eat your colors?"

Eve furrowed her brow. "I mean, I eat foods *with* color."

"Eating your colors means eating food that shares a color with every shade of the rainbow. Red, orange, yellow—"

"I know the colors of the rainbow." Eve softened her expression when she saw anger flicker across Angela's otherwise serene face. "Sorry for interrupting."

"Hey, no sense going over what you already know." Angela smiled again. She was always so happy. Eve wondered if the food she ate was why she was so cheerful. "Well, that would be my advice to you: each day, eat all the colors of the rainbow. Red apples, oranges, yellow peppers—"

"Greens, blueberries—"

"Exactly! It's so easy."

"What about indigo?"

"Let's make a deal with ourselves." Angela held her hand towards the screen. "Let's make a pact to our bodies, right here and right now, to eat our colors and bring a bright rainbow into our souls."

"Sure, okay," Eve said with a nod.

"Come on. Put your hand on the screen."

"Why?"

"Because we can't touch palms in person, silly!" Angela giggled, and Eve tried not to show her discomfort at how bubbly Angela was acting. She wanted professional advice, not silliness.

"Come on. It'll be like a virtual pinky-swear to our bodies," Angela prodded.

Fuck it, Eve thought, and placed her palm on the screen.

"Okay. Repeat after me," Angela began. "I, Eve Middleton—"

"I, Eve Middleton—"

"Love my body so, so much."

Eve hoped that Angela wasn't recording this. "Love my body so, so much."

"And I will add to its loveliness by eating my colors and helping it shine!"

"And I will add to its loveliness" —Eve held back a snort— "by eating my colors and helping it shine."

Eve felt a shudder pulse through her body, one that made her twitch and remove her hand. The sensation soon became warmth.

"That was great," Angela said with her brightest grin yet. "You're great, Eve. I know you'll feel amazing!"

Eve certainly hoped so—if she'd paid $100 to touch a laptop screen and recite inspirational words, she was going to pitch a fit.

Eve spent the next day grocery shopping. She tried to find food in every color, which was harder than she thought. Some were easy, like the apples and greens that she and Angela had discussed. She didn't like bell peppers, so carrots and oranges would be her best orange bet. She was glad she liked blueberries. And what exactly did count as indigo? Eve found some dark blue plums next to the purple ones and hoped for the best.

Still, Eve had to admit that the bounty of colorful produce in her cart was much more appealing than the usual frozen meals. She made herself a salad with almost every color of the rainbow, and finished off the one missing color with a snack of plums before dinner. "That wasn't too hard," Eve said to herself as she threw away the pits.

The days went on, and she made sure to eat the rainbow. Her plate looked incomplete if she didn't have at least three colors of the rainbow on it. Eve felt her mood improve and saw an extra bit of dewiness in her skin. For all her woo-woo talk and the money she charged, Angela had helped her—Eve couldn't deny it.

Towards the end of the week, Eve noticed she was out of purple plums. She was also waiting for her paycheck to deposit. She supposed one day without every color of the rainbow wouldn't kill her. She ate her food with diligence, though a nagging feeling of guilt at not following instructions today wouldn't leave her mind.

The next morning, Eve woke up incredibly sore. She stretched her arms, then gasped. Her arms were covered in large, dark bruises. Eve whipped off her blankets, then cried out when she saw her legs were spotted as well. "What the hell!" she cried. She looked like a fricking Dalmatian.

She went through the possibilities in her head. Maybe she'd been sleepwalking. Maybe she tossed and turned too much the night before, even though she didn't recall having any nightmares. She poked at a large bruise on her forearm, one that seemed to glow and throb like a purple beacon. *Maybe if I ate my arm, I'd get my purple for the day*, Eve thought to herself with a smirk.

She chilled a little at the memory of missing the one color of the rainbow. She then shook her head. Missing one day of plums wouldn't cause bruising.

All the same, Eve searched her cupboards for something, anything that might be purple—to start the day fresh with a new rainbow, not because of the bruises. She saw a carton of forgotten raisins in her cupboard. Grapes were purple. Raisins had been grapes. They counted, right? Eve's heart thumped as she sprinkled the raisins on her cereal. She hoped it counted. She didn't want to slip two days in a row.

She took one bite, then another. Eve glanced at her arms. She saw with relief that they were beginning to fade. A blip—nothing more.

While the bruises may have been a blip, Eve found that eating her colors was difficult in other ways. She was getting bored with some variation on salad every day. The foods she did like in certain colors were starting to get tiresome. But when she thought that maybe just this one day, she didn't need her greens or didn't have to eat a bowl of pineapple chunks with organic cottage cheese, she saw Angela's face looking at her in disappointment, as if Eve were betraying her by going against the simple obligation to be kind to her body.

One day, though, the mere thought of salad made Eve nauseated. She decided to skip her greens. The ones she'd bought were starting to wilt anyway, and she was going to the store the next day. She'd have a salad then. She didn't need every color every day.

The next morning, Eve woke up barely able to breathe. She lifted her head from her pillow, then felt suction in her nostrils as a small gap formed in whatever had stuffed her up. Sticky liquid seeped over her upper lip. Eve wiped her nose and looked in disgust at a thick, slimy trail of bright green snot across her palm.

Both sides of her nose leaked. She clamped her hand across her nose and darted towards the box of Kleenex. She blew and blew, but the snot would only start to trickle again once she was finished.

What the hell! she thought. It wasn't allergy season. Eve's stomach grumbled, and her heart sank when she remembered the lack of salad the day before. Had her body gotten so used to salad that she was having some kind of allergic reaction?

She raced downstairs and searched through her fridge. The only green item in there was the remains of her wilted spinach. It had even developed a slimy sheen overnight. Eve moved to shut the door, when another torrent of snot bubbled out of her nose. She grabbed a paper towel, blew her nose, then stared at the fridge.

Eve cooked the spinach with eggs. She hoped that sauteing them and adding salt would reduce the slimy taste. The final product was only somewhat palatable, and Eve felt her stomach lurch with every bite—but she also felt her nose run less and less. She finished the eggs and spinach with one last painful swallow. Her nose stopped running.

Within the hour, Eve had vomited up her semi-rotten breakfast. But at least she'd had her greens.

Eve's next trip to the grocery store was a challenge in not only finding all the colors of the rainbow, but finding them in varieties to ensure she wouldn't get bored and skip a color. Though Eve didn't understand how, she gathered that the bruises and the snot were related to her missing one of the colors. She had no intention of making the same mistake again.

She left the store with cherries, apples in three different colors, lemons, pineapples, fresh and frozen greens, berries, even her dreaded bell peppers. Eve had no intention of harming her body further. Angela was onto something with eating the colors, something her body loved so much that it was reacting when it went without. Eve wondered how she ever functioned before taking on this new way of eating.

Eve went several days without issue. Even when the bile rose in her throat at the taste of bell peppers, she preferred that to the thought of deviating from the rainbow. She could do this. She smiled to herself as she sautéed frozen spinach with red and orange bell peppers to make a fat-free stir-fry. Everything was fine.

The next morning, though, Eve awoke with another stuffy nose. Her eyes widened as she sat up and felt the all-too-familiar trickle of snot begin to course down her nose. "How—" she muttered, but stopped and gasped at the sight of her arm. It was covered in red splotches, all of which began to itch. She scratched her arms as she dashed to get a tissue. Before going downstairs, though, she had a Zoom call to make. She scrambled to her phone, DMed Angela, and wrote in all caps, *PLEASE TALK TO ME.*

"Hey, beautiful!"

Angela looked as radiant as ever. She wore a silk shell-pink bathrobe, and her blonde hair was swooped into a messy bun that looked perfectly coiffed. She looked better than ever, which made Eve feel all the worse for being on camera with a runny nose and blotchy red skin.

"What's happening to me?" Eve wailed.

Angela puckered her eyebrows in what Eve thought was a trite look of sympathy. Maybe Angela was so busy being beautiful and perfect that she didn't know how to be sad. "Looks like you're having an allergic reaction," she cooed.

"I don't have any food allergies. I ate all my colors yesterday."

"Has this happened before?"

"Yes, when I haven't eaten a color. I got bruises when I skipped purple."

"Ah ah ah!" Angela waved her finger in disapproval, though with a cheeky smile on her face. "So did you skip your greens and reds yesterday?"

Eve's mouth fell at how blasé Angela was acting. "Did you know this would happen?"

"Once the body sees what it can be, it reacts pretty harshly to not getting those good foods it needs to be perfect."

Eve dropped her gaze in disappointment. Just like she'd suspected.

"But I ate all my colors yesterday. I had red and orange bell peppers with sauteed spinach for dinner."

"Ah ha, red and orange. Your body needs a *different* red food in order to count. Otherwise it's just peppers on peppers."

Eve furrowed her brow as she snerked back a trail of snot. "Seriously?"

"Afraid so." Angela shrugged. "I mean, you get *some* benefit, but it's better when you have different colors *and* different foods. That way you're getting the best variety!"

"I guess that makes sense." Eve began to dread her next grocery store trip. How would she find so many different foods? "But I had my greens yesterday. I had frozen spinach."

Angela clucked, and Eve felt like she'd been stabbed. "Fresh is always better than frozen," Angela said. "You don't know how old that spinach is."

"I thought frozen was actually really good for you," Eve replied.

Angela's expression grew cross, and like the time Eve interrupted her, Eve shivered a little at Angela's wrath. She felt an icy pang strike her heart, one that melted when Angela smiled once again.

"Nothing's as good as fresh," Angela said. "Stick with fresh, and you'll be A-ok!"

Eve remembered the green apples in the fridge, and sighed with relief. But she soon panicked again—she also had red apples. What red item would she eat to get rid of the rash?

"It's all worth it, I promise you," Angela said as she held up her palm. "Remember what we said: I will add to my body's loveliness …"

Angela waited for Eve, palm up. Eve brought up her palm, and repeated, "I will add to my body's loveliness—"

"By eating my colors and helping it shine!"

"By eating my colors and"—Eve removed her hand to cough and wipe away more snot—"and helping it shine."

Eve's fridge became a plethora of colors that even a Care Bear would envy. Fruits and vegetables—all fresh—poured from the shelves and beckoned to be eaten.

Eve's body behaved, but otherwise, she'd never felt worse. Every time she prepared a meal, she wondered if she'd done everything correctly. She'd go to bed afraid of waking up with some sort of malady related to whatever she'd missed—and what she missed seemed to constantly change. One morning, she awoke freezing cold. She looked at her nails and saw they were blue; a glance in the mirror showed that her lips matched.

"Blueberries are out of season!" Angela chirped when Eve called her.

"I can only eat in-season fruits?" Eve asked with a shiver.

"They're certainly best! I know you'll find something. Teas help too—though only loose leaf, never bagged! Have you tried butterfly pea blossom tea?"

Eve hadn't, and when she saw the price, she knew why. But she bought it anyway, because sipping it meant she wouldn't wake up feeling like the dead of winter.

She'd easily take blue fingers, though, over what she awoke to the following week: seeping boils that blubbered yellow pus onto her skin. "I eat something yellow every day!" Eve screamed over Zoom before Angela had a chance to say good morning. "And different things too! Lemons, carrots, bell peppers—"

"Peppers are out of season—"

"Lemons aren't!"

"Have you only been eating lemons?"

"What the hell else am I supposed to eat right now? I could only find orange carrots at the store last week, and they were out of Gold Rush apples! How many of these fucking rules do I need to follow?"

Angela smiled, and for the first time, it made Eve feel dread instead of warmth.

"As many rules as your body needs to be its best," Angela said sweetly.

Eve swallowed back tears as she looked at the pus on her arms. "My body was fine before," she sniffed.

"It's better now."

"How is this better?"

"Because you're worried about it!" Angela grinned wider. "And something's only worth having if you're terrified of doing the wrong thing and losing it forever! Your despair is how I thrive, and it's exactly what I need!"

Angela clamped her mouth shut as Eve snapped her attention to the screen. "What did you say?"

"I said it's exactly what you need."

"Don't lie to me!" Every session with Angela came flooding back to Eve, with Angela's sweet smiles and glowing cheeks that only seemed to brighten while Eve poured her heart out in her quest to be healthy. All that time, Angela was feeding off of her—an appetite that grew with every new rule Angela made to keep Eve in check. Eve stared at her boils and wanted to cry.

But Eve was done crying. She glared at Angela. "Stop fucking lying to me," she said, "or I'll stop consulting with you."

Angela snorted. "I don't need your money. You know how many followers I have?"

"I'll tell them what a liar you are and what you're doing to me. You'll lose followers so fucking fast—"

Angela's face showed a flash of fear before she settled back into a sweet smile. It was enough for Eve. Finally, Perfect Angela had a weakness.

"What would you tell them?" Angela sneered. "That you can't follow a simple path to wellness? That you don't want to be your very best?"

"I just want this bullshit to stop!"

"And I want something from you: a testimonial."

"What?" Eve couldn't believe the nerve of this woman.

"A live testimonial to my followers and yours, talking about how great my consultations have been. Who knows—maybe doing a good thing for someone else will help you out, and make your body more receptive to less strict of a regimen. Maybe it'll stop rebelling against you."

Eve felt one of her boils throb. She had to admit, the offer was enticing. "Will it stop completely?" Eve asked.

"You should never stop being good to your body," Angela said, her serene smile glued in place.

Eve should've known that Angela wouldn't let her off so easily—not while she was thriving on whatever power she had from Eve and likely countless others' despair at wanting to attain Angela's perfection. The only way to break free was to break Angela. Eve sniffed again as she stared at the boils on her arms. They were disgusting.

Eve stared a moment longer in thought. They were just what she needed.

"Okay," she said to Angela. "You're on."

"Hi everyone! I'm Eve Middleton."

Eve looked better than she had in days. She'd eaten all her colors, followed all of Angela's rules, and been rewarded with clear, glowing skin and shiny hair. Eve did her makeup and put on a glittery top. She'd asked Angela if she could do her testimonial close to midnight East Coast time, so she could reach West Coast viewers after they'd had their evening meal. "Sure," Angela had agreed.

"Especially on a Friday, people will be up late and coming home from evenings out."

"And feeling like crap," Eve added. "They'll want to know how to feel better."

"Yes!" Angela's eyes lit up, and Eve imagined her thinking of all the late-night regrets she could feed upon. "You'll be thinking like me in no time! Maybe I'll make you a representative."

Hold that thought. Eve simply smiled in reply.

Now, Eve was live and making her debut as a testimonial to Angela's help. Angela had been promoting it all week, and Eve had hundreds of new followers ready to watch her live. "A couple months ago, I reached out to Angela and asked for a health consultation. She promised me assistance focused on wellness and feeling good—no restrictive dieting, no starvation, no thinly-veiled eating disorders, just listening to what my body wanted and giving it what it wants. She gave me a simple instruction: eat your colors. Every color of the rainbow on your plate, every day."

Eve saw the clock on her laptop switch to midnight. She tucked her hand under her chin to show her arm. "Easy, right?"

A comment came to her almost immediately: *Is that a bruise?*

Bruises slowly bloomed on Eve's arms. She smiled wider. It was exactly what she wanted. "Yes, it is a bruise," Eve said. "It's purple, because I didn't eat anything purple yesterday."

The bruises grew and turned shades of gray and indigo too. Her lips and fingernails began to turn blue. "In fact, I didn't eat any of my colors today," Eve said. "I ate burgers, fries, and pizza."

Pizza has tomatoes, one commenter said, behind a sea of shocked emoji faces and concerned question marks.

"Ah, but pizza has tomato sauce!" Eve chuckled, and a burst of green snot came from her nose. "And only fresh tomatoes count!"

Eve had hoped for boils as her lack of yellow began to make itself known, but instead, her skin began to turn a sickly jaundiced shade. The exclamation marks and wow faces told her the transformation was having its effect.

"Angela wants to make sure you follow her rules to be the best you can be," Eve continued. "Once you shake her digital hand, she'll be in complete control. She'll hold your hand and keep you on a regiment of color, and if the rules change—" Eve held up her hands, which were now fully yellow and slowly becoming covered in crusty orange scabs—"she'll let you know!"

WHAT ARE YOU DOING? Angela wrote in a private message. Eve picked up her phone, then used the opportunity to check Angela's follower count. It was down. #TerrifyingAngelaTestimonial was trending. Eve's viewership was going up, and Angela couldn't stop her because Angela couldn't feed off of anger—only despair. And Eve didn't feel despair, not anymore. She marveled at her colorful body, which was almost every color of the rainbow.

A salty, iron taste on her tongue told her she was almost there. Eve smiled sweetly. "So if you want to be like me," Eve said, "then talk to Angela. Because thanks to her, I've added to my body's loveliness—"

She waved her fingers, showing off the orange scabs and yellow, bruised skin with blue fingertips.

"By eating my colors—"

She wiped snot from her nose, and saw red streaked within the green. Her nose began to bleed, as did her eyes. But it was when Eve grinned that the full effect was there for all to see. Her mouth, gums, and teeth were stained with red, blood flowing over every crevice as it coated her lips and tongue.

"And helping my body shine!"

NESTING
BY ALI SEAY

"He likes you in that dress," the medium says.

I stare at her in her purple shift and pretty braids. No bangles, no headdress, no theater. Just a cute young woman in a thrift store frock with her dark hair in twin braids.

She looks like she's twelve.

I want to be jaded. I want to not offer her any scrap of information. That is how they read you. They're con artists, tricksters. They feed on hope and grief and desperation.

But I am desperate. So very desperate.

"Thank you," I say. Then I laugh. Am I thanking her or Charlie?

She smiles at me, perfectly content to let me collect myself.

"He says you're not sleeping well."

Of course, I'm not. Who would be? He's only been gone a month and somehow every day stretches out longer than the last. At night, I push my hand to his empty side of the bed, shove it under the coolness beneath his unused pillows.

I'd even like to hear the whooshing hiss of his morphine machine. Or his restless sleep.

But it's only silence now. A big yawning blank where my husband used to be.

I'd take the sleepless nights and constant care and ever-present grief at watching him die to this.

Because at least he could reach out and grab my wrist and say—

"There's my girl," she says.

I jump. My eyes fill. I twist the hem of the yellow dress I know he likes in my fingers. He said it matched my "flaxen hair". Flaxen. He was a man who used words like flaxen.

"My trophy wife," she goes on.

I stand so suddenly, I knock my chair over.

"I'm sorry. I'm sorry," I stammer, righting it. "I have to go. I—uh, I'm not feeling well." It's only been about ten minutes, but I toss sixty bucks on the table. The price of a full half hour reading.

"This was a mistake," I say.

It was. She couldn't have known that, and he can't be here.

"He misses you," she says.

I nod, a constant stream of tears flowing down my face. "I miss him, too. More than I could ever explain."

It's raining when I open the door. A heavy downpour on a gray day.

"I'm here if you change your mind!" she calls. "Sometimes people just need time."

Time.

Or therapy.

Or to crawl in a hole and die.

I'm lying on the bed in the wet yellow dress. The sky outside is steely and gushing water. The thunder rumbles and I don't react.

Storms used to scare me. Now, nothing scares me.

I run my fingernail over the seam of the mattress, trace the network of stains that Charlie left behind. Dying is messy business, and here's a map to prove it.

The brown trails of blood. Some from bed sores, some from putting in his port. Some from nosebleeds. Yellow. Yellow can be sweat or it can be urine. It's both. But I don't care. There's a pink smear from the bed sore ointment that always reminded me of calamine lotion and a weird drip of blue from the mouthwash hospice provided for his sponge bath/grooming time.

I pick at a yellow spot and it comes unraveled just a bit.

Exhaling, I worry at it.

I need to put new sheets on, but seeing these marks that are sign posts on the road to the end of my husband's life, I am hobbled.

My phone rings. I let it.

It cuts off, vibrates to tell me I have a message, then goes silent. Within seconds, it's ringing again.

I paw for it without turning over, pushing my face to his bare pillow, smelling the very ghost of him—what he used to smell like— under the forefront odor of sickness and death.

"Mom," I say.

"Andi, how are you? You didn't answer."

"I know."

That was intentional.

Pick, pick, pick. I wedge my thumbnail beneath the breach in the mattress. I dig at it until a bit of fluff emerges.

I put it to my face, smell it, hoping for a scent of him.

Maybe a long-ago scent of sex or laughter or happiness.

It just smells like bed.

After a pause, my mother goes on. "We're going to dinner in an hour or so. Just me and daddy."

By that she means no other people. I can't be around a lot of people. I tend to start leaking from the face. Once, I started screaming. My brain isn't ready for the world and the burden of seeming okay.

"Why don't you come?" she rushes on.

"Maybe next time, Mom. I'm tired."

Tired is a good excuse. Tired can't be argued with.

My body is tired, but so is my brain, my heart. My lungs from breathing, my eyes from blinking, my mind from thinking. And thinking. And thinking some more.

Wondering what if he hadn't died? What if we both had? What if he had never smoked? Drank soda? Eaten fish? Lots of mercury, you know. What if he'd never microwaved his food or gone in the sun or eaten smoked meats?

Apparently, cancer is everywhere. It's an unavoidable eating machine headed straight for most of us. Hungry and feral.

"You can't always be tired, Andi."

I snort.

Pick, pick, pick.

Another bit of fluff. I smell it. Get nothing. Move on.

"I assure you, I can."

Silence. She's worried. She's stumped. She doesn't know what to do to help me. I can read her mind.

"Will you please reconsider? Just me and daddy. We can have a nice meal. You can go right home after."

"Next time, Mom. I promise."

She says more but I zone out. I dig with my fingernail until I liberate a ball of mattress stuffing roughly the size of a cotton ball.

I rub it between my fingers. How many restless nights did he sleep on this ball of fluff? How much pain and sadness are soaked into it?

I toss it on the floor with the others.

"Next time, Mom. I promise," I repeat and then: "I have to go. I'll call you soon. Love you."

I hit disconnect before my mother can argue.

I fall asleep with my fingers in a hole in the mattress where my husband used to lie.

The garbage trucks jolt me awake. It's not even six a.m. and my arm is in a hole in the mattress nearly up to my elbow. I've hit springs while I slept. To prove it, my fingertips are raw and bloody.

I study them and then stick one in my mouth. The sting wakes me up more. Down in the kitchen I make instant coffee.

I hate instant coffee.

We hate instant coffee. But it's fast and it's enough to jumpstart me. I don't really care about flavor anymore. Or pleasure, or beauty, or life.

I stare at the wood grain of the tiny kitchen table, rub my eyes. "I miss you and I don't think I can take this much longer," I say to his empty chair.

I sip my coffee, chew my lip, taste blood again. It only takes a second to call. She answers immediately, sounding awake and bubbly. How is that possible?

"How are you?" she asks.

I stammer for a second and then say, "Not good."

"Would you like to come in today?"

"Yes."

"He's worried about you."

I want so badly to believe that. That he's telling her. That he's out there. Somewhere. Still in love with me, still aware of me, still mine.

"I'm worried about me."

I tell the medium I'll be there at noon and crawl back into bed. The TV is on just to have noise. I push my hand back in the hole, feeling the cool springs, the springy foam, the soft bits of fluff I haven't excavated.

I do the thing I do when I can't sleep, which is most nights.

"Do you remember when we went to that place in Pennsylvania? Some battleground? And I fell into that poison whatever and you had to rush me to the doctor because my thigh and ass cheek turned to fire."

I can imagine him brushing his fingers through my hair and murmuring agreement. Laughing softly.

"And then you had to spend the whole vacation smearing calamine lotion on me, and you said it was sexy. Such a pretty shade of pink. And we fucked in the claw foot bathtub and the water went everywhere and—"

The sobs are what stop me and then I doze off. Sleep is my best friend and my saving grace.

"I wish I could sleep forever until a new life with you can be born. You told me once you'd loved me before this lifetime and you'd love me again after."

Christ, I hope that's true.

She's in green today. A single braid. A large smile.

I'm not in a dress today. I'm in faded jeans and an old tee from Charlie's softball team.

My fingers tug and pluck at the hem where it's thinnest and stretched out.

"Yellow again," she says and startles me.

"I'm sorry?"

"It's yellow again. Like your dress."

It hadn't occurred to me that the shirt is yellow. It's a very faded lemon shade that almost resembles off-white in the sun.

"I guess so."

"It's the color of rebirth," she says.

"What?"

"Yellow."

"Oh."

"He wants you to know that. This isn't it. There's more to life and death and...you."

"Is he okay?" I blurt it out very fast because I need to, but I'm scared of the answer.

"Yes. He's fine. But he misses you."

"I miss him, too. I can't even explain it."

"Your grief is very dark around you. Heavy. Like dragging chains with you everywhere."

She takes my hands, and hers are young and cool. Mine look old in comparison. I never felt old until Charlie died. I always felt young and full of hope.

"It feels like it."

"You can put them down. You can let them go. You don't have to drag them."

She talks in her super soft and very sweet voice as I listen, missing Charlie, wondering what good this is. She can say anything she wants. Charlie is still dead; I am still alone.

When I pay her and thank her for her time, she says, "Please, Andi. Know that this isn't the end. It will be okay."

I nod to reassure her.

At home, I turn the TV on, lock the door, and crawl onto the bed. I push my arm in among the foam and springs and stuffing. I push my face into his pillows and inhale the scents of him. The healthy scents and the sick ones, too.

Do you know if someone dies in your bed, the undertakers will offer to take and clean your bedding? They want to strip your bed and take your sheets and wash them up and then return them as if nothing has occurred.

As if that person was never there.

As if that death never happened.

It's supposed to be if there's any kind of mess. Death can be messy.

When they offered, I gave a stunned, "No thank you."

When they pushed, I screamed at the poor man and ran him out of my house.

I kept my sheets. And I'm still sleeping on them.

But they're only on my side because his side is bare so, I can work on the mattress.

Charlie's holding my hand, swinging it, walking by a river that was near our first apartment. He's talking but I can't hear him. If I can get closer, I might hear him.

I lean in. I watch his lips.

Still nothing.

Sharp pain stabs my scalp. Hurting. Pulling.

What is that? I ask dream Charlie. *What is that pain?*

He cocks his head, smiles, says something as he runs his fingers through my hair.

Flaxen.

I wake up on a sob. My head throbbing. My fist full of something soft. Sunlight penetrates the cracks in my blackout curtains where I didn't pull them flush.

Hair.

I have a hand full of hair. My hair.

I let it go and it drifts down like filaments.

My hand skates along my head and I feel whole patches, nearly bare, raw, and tender.

"What did I do?" I ask Charlie's pillow.

I push my hand into the hole that seems to have grown and peek down in it. There's the missing hair. There's the rest of what I managed to harvest while I slept.

What is happening to me?

Without overthinking it, I push the hair that I dropped on the mattress down into the hole. I push my hand down into it, feel the softness of my own feathers.

"Nesting," I say to Charlie. "I'm nesting."

We never had kids. We never wanted them. But when we moved in together, he'd teased me as I bought pillows and blankets and comforting warm things for our home.

"Look at you nesting."

I'd stuck my tongue out and just kept doing my thing.

I pull out a few more hairs, sob at the pain on my already tortured scalp.

I shove them in the hole, push my hand deeper, move things here and there. Then goes the faded lemon-yellow tee. Over-washed and softer than anything you've ever felt.

Layering it in carefully, I wedge my arm deeper, use the strength in my elbow to push back springs.

A ragged end jabs me, makes me bleed, but that doesn't matter because yellow—lemon—flaxen is the color of rebirth.

"Rebirth," I tell Charlie's pillow.

I can picture his head there. His face young and strong and laughing. Then later. Wasted, tortured, a husk. I pat it and whisper where his ear would be.

"Don't worry. It will all be fine. It's fine."

The phone is ringing and I don't care.

When I've cut myself one too many times, I take a break and make coffee; I even take the time to do the whole French press thing and brew a real cup. Because I'm feeling hope. I'm feeling better.

Eyes shut, I sit and drink my coffee. Outside, a lawnmower hums like a busy bee. A dog barks. There is the ignorable drone of a suburban street early on a weekday.

It seems so surreal now, that it's just me. Like I'm trapped in a movie and I'm waiting for the punch line.

I pour out the rest of the coffee. Consider a bagel or a muffin. My appetite has been shit. I've lost weight. And I realize I need to keep the trimmer shape, so I skip the food.

I won't need food or coffee anymore, soon.

I'm going to transform.

There is a scarf on the back of my desk chair in the dining room. It's meant to look like a giant version of the old library checkout cards. It was a gift from Charlie because I love to read. It's a searing sunshine color and I snag it as I walk past.

"Perfect," I say to Charlie. I imagine him walking next to me as I go. One day we'll walk together again.

In our next time around.

Somewhere along the line, I have breached the box spring. It's less padded there and the hair and tee have settled unevenly.

It takes putting my feet in the hole and moving them deliberately, pushing my legs apart, forcing springs and wood and some nails and other things to bow to my will. Something punctures my foot and blood flows.

It's all fine. Nothing should be wasted. Not blood or sweat. Not hair or little flecks of skin.

My gaze goes to the pink goo smear on the remaining mattress top. I think of bed sores and bolus pumps and sleepless nights and cramps.

Endings are painful. So are births. It stands to reason that rebirths should be, too.

My arms are in the hole up to my shoulders. I push them around while keeping my legs wide. What I must look like, I think

Then a wild cackle as I imagine it.

Me and my patchwork hair, my sleep puffed face, my sorrow written on my skin in the form of time and grief.

"This is fucking crazy, Charlie. But I'm so tired. So fucking tired."

My phone vibrates and I see a text. My mom.

I TRIED CALLING. NO ANSWER. PLEASE CALL ME. I WORRY. I LOVE YOU ANDI. I WANT TO HELP.

"I wish you could."

Finally, blood slick and hair stuck to me, I have created a bowl shape in the mess of my bed.

I lay the scarf he gave me and push it into some of the gaps. I wish I had more hair.

When I peer into the recesses, I see lemon and wheat and sunshine. I see a hidden place from the world that is far too lonely and far too painful.

I stand, feet in the hole to my knee. I'll need to ball up my tiny frame even tighter. I'll need to coil in on myself and surrender to it.

I sink down and start to turn and press and make a space in this new place that is steeped in the memories and remainders of Charlie. Dead skin, sweat, semen, urine, hair, the smell of chemical cures that only lead to painful and untimely endings.

If I'm going to be reborn, I want it to be where we were. I want to start fresh with him after ending where he ended.

I'm bleeding from the springs and wood.

Who knew how many hard things were in soft beds?

I stretch, using my elbows, using my knees. Finally, I settle. Bleeding and sweating and crying and ready to surrender. I don't want to do this anymore, and now I don't have to.

I'm here and I will stay here until something happens or something ends.

Behind my closed eyelids is a soothing, shifting swirl of yellow shapes and patterns.

It is tight and hot and I may be stuck. I'm not sure.

But that's fine. I'm not scared.

Wombs aren't supposed to be spacious.

Toxic Shock
by Chelsea Pumpkins

Carrie sighed in defeat as the brown watercolor stain painted the lace thong hammocked between her knees. She shoved her hand up into the metal toilet paper dispenser and tried to unroll. Tiny bits of one-ply tore off, thwarting her attempts. Carrie had felt the leak seeping into her slacks but couldn't excuse herself from the quarterly presentation with senior management. So she had sat through the remaining presentations, bleeding out. Twenty years of menstruating and she still leaked through her tampons almost every month, tracking apps and birth control pills be damned. She could command a room full of suits, change a flat tire, and bake better cakes than her Betty Crocker mother, but she still couldn't master this part of womanhood.

In her mid-thirties and childless by choice, her period was now just a countdown to mortality. At twelve years old it was a thrill, becoming a woman overnight. Recess abuzz with whispers about Aunt Flo and TOM. That speck of blood was entry into a new club, unlocking a new understanding of the world. At nineteen it was a relief, a lucky break after a careless one-night stand. Shirking responsibility, paying no price. But these days it was a memento of the irrevocable passage of time. And that was fine.

She reached down, snagged the saturated cotton string between her thumb and forefinger, and tugged. Poppy-red blood seeped into her cuticles and trickled between the webbing of her fingers. The slick worm slithered out of her body and dangled above the toilet seat. She laid it on the paper atop her knee. As she began to roll it up, a streak of royal blue caught her eye, running lengthwise in her tampon.

Her heart skipped a beat. *Probably just some new leak protection gimmick*, she thought, the irony not lost on her. She finished wrapping the biohazard cocoon and tossed it into the stall's receptacle. At the sink, she scrubbed the blood from her fingers. Was there a tiny trace of blue among the suds? She shook her head, erasing her suspicion. Carrie waved her hand in front of the paper towel sensor four times: three squares to dry her hands and one to open the door with.

Saying goodbye to Helene at the front desk, she pushed the front door open with her forearm. *Is it true that blood is blue until it mixes with oxygen?* Theories grew like fungus in the back of her mind, self-diagnosed hypochondria spreading its roots. She tried to distract herself with grocery lists and to-do's, but as she turned the key in the ignition, the blue streak still consumed her thoughts.

Pungent fumes burned Carrie's sinuses as she stirred balsamic vinegar over low heat. She exhaled hot steam through her nostrils. As the reduction simmered, she drifted into a contemplative trance.

She came to accept that she had already realized most of life's big transformations. She got married, bought a house, and reached the top of the career ladder. She had her bunions and wisdom teeth removed years ago. Tiny threads of gray grew in around her temples, making neighbors with the faint creases around her eyes. She and Jeff decided that children weren't for them. The only thing left was menopause, then... death. Sure, there were places to see, made up milestones to accomplish. Visit all fifty states! Enjoy a three-Michelin-star dinner! Dive the Great Barrier Reef! But overall, Carrie poised on the crest of life's roller coaster. All she had left to do was throw her hands up and ride it out.

A splash of hot balsamic erupted from the pan and burned her hand. It startled her out of her reverie. Cooking was Carrie's meditation and, while the notion was a bit outdated, providing for her family with her hands like this filled her with pride.

"Ooh, prosciutto flatbreads?" Jeff's work boots clunked onto the shoe tray next to the back door. "My favorite!" He kissed her on the cheek as she spooned globs of fig jam and goat cheese onto the dough. These small acts of normalcy dragged her mind out of shadow.

By the time the oven timer rang out, the familiar dampness in her underwear returned. A warm, gooey clot slipped out of her cervix and sludged through her vagina onto her clothes. *God dammit.* She yelled to Jeff to take the flatbreads out and darted to the bathroom. She pulled her pants down. This time royal blue streaked her underwear. And was that—

"Yellow?" she whispered.

Her pantyliner was covered in a bruise, multi-colored and festering. But when blood dripped from her vagina into the toilet water, it was vibrant. The ripples spread radially as droplets sank to the porcelain—a cerulean center, ringed with canary yellow, and encircled by burnt sienna, the color of dried blood she was used to seeing.

She recalled memories of Yellowstone as remnants of her uterine lining turned the clear water into the Grand Prismatic Spring. Normally she would call for Jeff to provide reassurance. He would organize her symptoms into a logical sequence, ground her in probabilities, and hold her shaking hands until they steadied. But her hands weren't shaking. There was no way Jeff could come up with a rational explanation for this. Instead of panic, she was overwhelmed with serenity. She sat and stared at the masterpiece beneath her, a masterpiece she created. She was bleeding in technicolor, and she was utterly mesmerized.

"You okay?" Jeff asked as Carrie walked out of the bathroom, "You were in there a while."

"Yeah, just shark week."

"Bummer." He looked at her with pity.

She scarcely slept that night. Pain charged through the muscles along her spine like a roiling thunderstorm. Rumbling aches pulsated between her ribs, ratcheting in intensity until a clap of searing agony bore deep into her lower back. The storm raged inside her for hours. Whenever she managed to doze off, she was plagued by disturbing dreams. First, she dove from a stony cliff and plunged towards a dark, bottomless sea. Later, surgeons cracked her shoulder blades apart and plucked the tendons in her back like guitar strings. Strum, strum, *snap*. She awoke with a start each time. Her last nightmare was the most vivid of all.

Carrie's wrists were bound to a steel slab, and her ankles locked into stirrups. A heavy scaled egg squeezed through her birth canal and thrust through her already strained vagina. The hard, leathery surface tore through her perineum like a serrated knife, her underside like shredded red cabbage. She was drenched in sweat and soaked from blood pooling beneath her back. The egg was no longer inside of her, but Carrie was still attached to it, connected by a primal urge to protect her seed. Giant claws emerged from darkness and took the egg from between her legs. The reptilian monster came into full view as it began to tear into the egg's tough exterior. She couldn't dodge the flinging bits of membrane and viscera from her newborn's embryo. They clung to her naked body like a hug, a plea. The clawed creature tipped her egg upward and slurped all the fluids from the shell. Golden elixir dribbled down its jaw—her baby's blood. The monster sat back on its haunches and flapped enormous wings overhead. The creature was satiated. Tiny hooves hung limply on spindly legs spilling out from the discarded remnants of her egg. Carrie howled.

Carrie gave up on the notion of sleep after that final bout with terror and despair. She unpretzeled her limbs from the fetal position and sat hunched on the edge of the bed. Live wires electrified her abdomen with pain, her pelvic floor throbbing with the shocks. She gritted her teeth, slipped her feet into plush slippers, and shuffled into the bathroom. By the time she reached the bathroom door she was overcome with nausea.

She barely had time to lift the toilet seat before thick yellow bile spewed from her throat. When her empty stomach was done heaving, she lay her head on the cool porcelain. The bowl's putrid contents appeared almost iridescent, the surface shimmering like nacre. Her brain was too fuzzy to give it much mind, and Carrie chalked it up to whatever toilet cleaner Jeff probably bought. She reached for the flush handle and tried to summon the energy to call out sick from work.

This wasn't the first time that Carrie's period had wiped her out. It's not even the first time it caused her to vomit. But this time there was an undeniable stirring within. Organs twitched and shifted, rearranging inside of her abdomen. Her ribs expanded against their fleshy boundaries. They burst free of the ligaments holding them to her spine and split through her back. The bass of her heartbeat ruptured her eardrums, and pus drained down the side of her face. She hobbled to the vanity and stood agape before the mirror. She looked the way she did on any other sleepless morning: Bed head and bags under her eyes. Her physical form did not match the torment she was enduring. The dichotomy made her question reality altogether.

She ran a bath as Jeff got ready to leave for work. He fetched her the box of Motrin before kissing her forehead goodbye.

"Text me if you need me to pick you up something on my way home," he said. She didn't have the energy to tap into her cravings right now.

Carrie turned the tub jets on. As they roared to life, she prayed for relief. She peeled her clammy pajamas off into a heap. Her underwear perched on top of the pile and her sanitary pad flaunted itself from the folds, taunting Carrie in her suffering. She glared at it, squinting at the painter's palette of rich rainbow hues. It was inexplicable. It was *beautiful.*

She went light-headed and the bathroom tilted on its axis. She was an astronaut spinning in zero-G, but she wasn't afraid. She squeezed her eyes shut, gripped the side of the bathtub, and gingerly stepped over the ledge.

Steam rose from the edges of her shoulders, breasts, and knees—bobbers in the bathtub. Carrie counted her breaths in (*one, two, three, four*) and exhaled even more slowly. The walls of her uterus scraped down the sharp edges of a box grater. She held the next in-breath in her lungs and let her head slide underwater. She was warm and weightless, and for a moment she opened her eyes.

Neon green and purple lights danced across the water's surface. Bubbles of air leaked from her nostrils and caught on her eyelashes, but she didn't blink. She was hypnotized. The colors rippled with the stream of the jets and reflected off the ceramic walls. It brought her back to their honeymoon in Iceland, where they saw the Northern Lights. They had hypnotized her then, too.

She gazed beyond the colors into the ether above the bathwater. Her reflection stared back, distorted. Her eyes were more luminous than usual, brilliant even. Sharp spines peeked out from beneath her flowing hair. She tilted her head to get a better view. Her reflection didn't move. This was not her reflection.

Carrie sprang upright from the water, coughing and spitting. A frightened sob hitched in her chest, and she swept the water from her eyes. No one was there. She sat alone in the bathtub as tiny warm waves rocked against her belly. *Was I dreaming?* She combed her fingers through her hair, massaging her scalp. She felt a slight twinge behind her jaw, like the early signs of a menstrual migraine. When she caught her breath again, she saw the truth of what was in front of her.

The Aurora Borealis was not a dream; it was alive in the bathtub. Midnight blue swirled with orchid in the currents and churned with shades of lime green and chartreuse. The colors bubbled around her body, as if she were being boiled alive by the night sky.

She stood up in the tub, stoic. As the bath water oozed off her body so did her pain, melting away, dripping off her edges like rendered fat. Her hands caressed her skin, checking for an explanation. Arms, belly, behind her knees—nothing. No wounds, no makeup, no smudges or stains. Carrie grazed her fingers between her thighs and they emerged from her labia covered in a bright syrup.

A kaleidoscope. Pigments and patterns so foreign to the natural world. There was something about this that felt so right. That final jigsaw piece snapping perfectly into place. Perhaps she wasn't breaking but growing. Transcending.

That's ridiculous. Carrie knew she should be alarmed. She was feeling things she couldn't see and seeing things that shouldn't be possible. She couldn't wait any longer. She stepped out of the tub and threw her robe around her shoulders. It caught on something behind her back, but she quickly untangled it and tied the belt around her waist. She lifted her phone off the granite countertop and called for an ambulance.

"9-1-1, what's the location of your emergency?" a woman's husky voice asked.

"This is going to sound crazy."

"Ma'am, your location. Are you in a safe place?"

"Yeah. Yes, I'm at home. 1247 Fairbanks Drive. It's just that I'm—" She was almost laughing at the absurdity of it all. "I'm bleeding... colors. It's my period, there's blue and purple and—"

"Ma'am please stay on the line I'm going to send—"

A click.

"Hello?" Carrie tapped her phone screen to see if the call had dropped. Her skin prickled.

She was about to hang up when a voice cut through dead air. "I'm sorry Miss, we must have lost connection for a moment." The woman's voice sounded different: Warmer, sweeter.

Am I losing my fucking mind?

"As I was saying, please stay on the line while I send help to your address."

"Okay. Yeah, no problem." Carrie heard typing in the background.

"Help is on the way. Can you tell me when you started to transform?" the saccharine voice asked.

Did I hear that right? "Transform?"

"Your period, Miss."

"Oh, right." Carrie paused to think, her brain still in a fog. "I think two days ago?"

"Two days, that's wonderful!"

Wonderful? Carrie's mouth went dry, and her heartbeat accelerated.

"If you don't mind my asking," the dispatcher said, "can you check behind your ears for anything out of the ordinary?"

Carrie was beyond confused, but she obliged. There was something hard in the tender recesses behind each of her earlobes. A sharp, icy point poked out of her skull and through her skin. When she touched their tips, an electric current penetrated her molars, like biting foil with a filling. An eel in her head. She gasped in pain. "What the fuck?"

"And, sorry to bother, but can you examine your tailbone for me?"

With her hand quivering, Carrie reached behind her and found a stiff, fleshy protrusion above her buttocks, about four inches long. Nausea returned.

"Can you please tell me what's going on?"

"Don't worry, Miss. Like I said, help is on the way. While I still have you conscious, can you—"

"While you still have me conscious? What is happening?" Carrie begged.

"Can you please check your eyes in a mirror? Should only take a second."

Succumbing to panic, or whatever freak illness she had, Carrie began to sway, and the edges of her sight blurred in fantastic colors. She squinted through the aura at her reflection. Her irises were no longer deep brown. Her irises weren't there at all. Color had taken over the entirety of her eye. Both eyeballs were glittering gold.

"They're... sparkling," Carrie said, barely able to stand.

"Oh, wonderful. Wonderful! This is great news."

"Please." Carrie started to cry. "What's happening to me?" Aquamarine tears sprung from the corners of her eyes and painted her cheeks. Her blue-streaked face was the last thing she saw before she lost sight altogether.

The voice giggled lightly. "I told you. You're transforming!"

Carrie was lying on the cool bathroom floor now, blind and on the edge of hysteria. She was moments away from passing out, and she was terrified of what would happen then.

"Transform," Carrie's breath was so shallow and ragged she had trouble speaking. Her voice reduced to a whisper. "Into what?"

"Not to worry, Miss," the candy-coated voice assured, "you'll find out soon enough."

Carrie was too faint to hold the phone any longer. Her fingers went limp, and it clattered to the floor out of reach. A ringing took over her sense of hearing, but she caught a vague distant whirring sound, like a helicopter far above her roof. They were medevac'ing her out of here. She clung to the rhythmic whooshing, trying to stay conscious. As the sound got closer, she picked up on a strange slapping quality to it, less like blades slicing through wind and more like—

"Wings?"

Nothing was impossible anymore. Her final reserve of strength faded now. She felt a pounding through the floor. Heavy boots running up the stairs; paramedics coming to her aid. Big paramedics, with a steady tempo. They shook the whole house. Were they footsteps, or were they...hooves?

ACHROMATICA
BY PIPPA BAILEY

Lucas cradled a dewy crate of beer and an oblong box in a bag across his chest and fumbled with his key in Tiff and Iris' front door. "Girls, I'm back."

"What took you so long?" called Tiff.

Lucas kicked the door shut behind him and headed through the lounge out to the garden. Sunlight bounced across the surface of a gray inflatable jacuzzi tub, which Tiff and Iris purchased a month earlier for their summer extravaganza. Specifically, for the two glorious weeks of summer weather Scotland received towards the end of June.

Iris drained the last drops from her can and dropped it to the ground. "Yeah, where've you been?"

Lucas slid the crate onto a rusted garden table and placed the bag onto the floor beside it. "Hey— I'm meant to be the guest, you know. Aren't family due special treatment?"

Tiff shrugged. "You've still gotta pay your way, bruh."

Lucas grimaced. "Don't say bruh, it sounds—"

"But you're my baby bruh, bruh. Now beer me."

I'm going to strangle her selfish ass.

Lucas cracked the case and distributed the chilled silver cans. He slipped into a deckchair and pulled the oblong box from the bag, and turned it over in his hands.

Iris pointed at the box. "That's why you're late?"

He nodded. "Been waiting all year to get a pair."

"Let's see them."

Lucas opened the box, revealing a pair of crimson sneakers.

Tiff whistled. "Oh, those are shiny. Put em' on."

Obliging, Lucas kicked off his canvas shoes and yanked on his new sneakers. He stretched up onto his toes and twisted his feet around in circles. "Damn, they feel like stepping in clouds."

Iris rested her arms on the side of the tub, letting her body float behind her. "Worth the money?"

"Totally."

Tiff lunged across the tub, planted her lips on Iris' butt cheek and blew a raspberry.

She kicked at Tiff, spraying water across the grass. "Oi, get off!"

"I couldn't help myself; it's a juicy peach."

"My juicy peach."

"I think you'll find, legally, I own at least half of it, and right now, I'm choosing this half here." Tiff prodded Iris' left butt cheek.

Lucas stepped across the lawn, ignoring the girls' bickering. In front of his merlot sneakers lay a pure white circle the size of a basketball. The grass within, bleached of color. Scattered around the patch lay more dots of white.

"Have you seen this? I think you've burnt the grass with all that water splashing; it's like a Jackson Pollock out here."

"It's grass; it'll get its green back," said Tiff.

Lucas scraped his sneaker across the large patch, flattening the nacreous grass. "I guess."

Iris peered over the tub's edge and nodded at a collection of clementine tiger lilies. "There's lots over there."

Patches of the plant's stem missed any semblance of the rich green that lined the rest, sections of the flowers almost pearlescent. Lucas leaned over, his eyes following a trail of white that wove across the garden.

Tiff rested beside Iris. "Don't touch it, might be poisonous. There's no way we got water all the way over there."

Iris pointed to a collection of sticks on the deck. "Luc, grab that bamboo cane."

"Why?"

"Can you stick it in the ground at the edge of that big patch over there? I want to see if it gets any bigger."

"That's smart."

"I'd call it pre-emptive measures. There's something odd about this."

"You're right. It is pretty weird."

Tiff shrugged and burped. "Bruh, beer me."

Blind, Lucas stretched his arm across to the living room table and scooped the warm half beer he'd abandoned the night before. He drained the can in two gulps and attempted to part his sticky eyelids. You can never have too much beer, but beer with a wine chaser and whatever that green stuff was, is ill-advised. He dropped the empty can to the floor and pulled the blanket over his head.

I'm never going to try and drink Iris under the table again.

Warm air from the open garden door ruffled his protruding hair. *They're up already? What time is it?*

Lucas pulled himself upright, eyes clamped shut. If he could keep them closed, the world wouldn't spin, and he wouldn't spew over what he was sure was the rainbow patchwork blanket their mother had stitched Tiff when she first came out. She loved that blanket.

Lucas forced his new sneakers onto his bare feet and dragged himself to a wobbly stand, grasping the back of the sofa. He opened his eyes to face the blinding sun.

You've got this, tiny baby steps.

He teetered towards the door and out into the garden.

"Good morning!" yelled Tiff.

"Yep, don't do that, thanks."

"I think someone is a bit hungover," Iris laughed.

"Nope, I'm fine. I just didn't sleep so well."

Tiff patted the deck chair beside her. "C'mon, little one, come sit."

Lucas collapsed into the chair. "Urgh, that was a rough one."

Iris offered him the dregs of her coffee. "Here."

Lucas obliged and grabbed the warm mug. He inhaled deeply before downing the creamy brown liquid.

Iris smiled. "Better?"

"So, so."

Tiff pointed at his feet. "Damn, look at your shoes."

Lucas peered at his left foot, the previously crimson sneaker, now bleached from the sole all the way to the tongue, like he'd stepped in a puddle of white paint, leaving a ring of red at the top. "What the—? Shit."

Tiff shrugged. "Maybe they got wet? Bin them and buy some more."

"They cost me a fortune, Tiff."

Iris climbed out of her chair and crouched by Lucas' feet. "I don't think water would do that, or beer. Maybe you got some faulty ones?"

Lucas scraped his shoe on the paving slabs. "Why is it just the one shoe?" He rubbed his temples and peered across the garden. The bamboo cane he'd planted the day before now sat clearly within the circle, the same sallow color spreading up the withered cane's wood.

Wilted, bleached plants lined a fence Tiff and Iris shared with their neighbor. Giant circles of white covered the grass; new spots like tiny footprints littered the green. Any plant life within the patches lay shriveled and dead.

Lucas sighed. "It's that stuff on the grass."

"What is it?" asked Tiff.

"I know as much as you."

"I did say not to touch it yesterday."

"Are you saying this is my fault?"

"No, well, it's your fault you touched the stuff, but I'm not saying you made it worse."

Iris chimed in. "It's not your fault, but I don't think we should be out here until we know what it is."

"Do you think it's poisonous?" asked Lucas.

"I don't know, but plants need to be green to live. I mean, most of them anyway, photosynthesis and all that. They're green to absorb the infra-red light. If they can't absorb the light, they die."

"I knew I'd married a super-smart woman," said Tiff.

"Not super smart; I remember biology class. I think we should go inside."

"But it's so nice out."

"I know, love, but we should stay away from that stuff."

"Fine, if I have to stay inside and miss out on my glorious sunshine, don't expect me to be happy or sober, and Luc, you're leaving those shoes outside too. I'm not having you bleaching my beautiful pink carpet."

Lucas kicked his sneakers off. "I wasn't going to wear them inside."

"I don't care. They're not coming back in the house."

Tiff peered out of the lounge door and tapped her nails on the glass. "This is such a fucking waste."

Lucas, tucked under Tiff's rainbow blanket, shrugged and stretched his arms across the back of the sofa. "The sun is setting anyway; you wanna watch another movie?"

"No, I don't want to watch another movie. I want to sit in the sun. I want to drink too much and get sunburnt. I want my summer back."

"I want your summer back too, but you can't seriously want to be outside with that—"

Iris cut him off. "We're not the only ones. There have been thousands of searches for white patches in the last twenty-four hours."

"Thousands?"

Iris nodded and pointed at her phone. "Thousands."

"See, Tiff, we're not alone in this; everyone else is suffering too," said Lucas.

"That doesn't make it any better. How do we get rid of it?"

Iris scrolled her thumb across the screen. "Doesn't say. Lots of people asking the same questions. Well, similar questions, there are quite a few spelling errors, 'What is bletch grass?' and 'Why does not coler my?'"

Tiff pressed herself against the glass. "It's probably some fungus or something in the water that's screwing up people's lawns. It's not that bad in ours."

"People are reporting it in their houses too."

Tiff pointed at Lucas. "And this is why I said your sneakers are living outside."

"Hey, I didn't fight you on it. Come and sit down; I'll put something else on." Lucas patted the empty seat between him and Iris.

Tiff grimaced but agreed and flopped onto the sofa. She snatched her rainbow blanket from his lap and wrapped it around her shoulders. "Nothing with happy people."

"Horror it is."

A woman clung to a rope suspended from the ceiling of a black cave. It slowly frayed; each climbing motion brought her further away from the ravenous horde of monsters below and yet closer to her demise.

Tiff grasped Iris' arm; her butt pressed into Lucas' side. He didn't mind. Sometimes it was nice to see his sister being fragile, even if horror movies were the only thing to bring out that side of her. She'd spent a lot of time curating her bitchy attitude, he knew because he'd been on the receiving end of it for much of their childhood. He never could understand how she'd bagged a girl as lovely as Iris. She was sweet and kind and patient; everything Tiff wasn't. It wasn't like he had a crush on her, not really. She made him question if legitimately behaving like Tiff didn't have certain benefits.

The rope creaked and groaned, lowering the woman towards the bisected, fanged jaws of the creatures.

A dazzling light reflected off the tv screen, obscuring the movie.

Tiff jumped. "What the hell was that?"

Lucas stared at the door. "I don't know."

"I didn't expect you to actually know."

Ah, the attitude was back.

Iris climbed to her feet and moved towards the lounge door. "It's probably one of the neighbors with a torch."

Lucas joined her at the window. "It looked like it was in your garden, though."

Tiff huffed. "If it's those bloody kids from number thirty-three again, I'm going to go around there and wring their necks."

"Number thirty-three?"

"They stole people's garden ornaments over Christmas. They took Mr. Sausage," said Iris.

"Not my Mr. Sausage?"

Mr. Sausage, the garden gnome, was so-called on account of his gratuitously stuffed, purple, glittery shorts. The ten-inch gag gift had taken pride of place on the girls' deck after Lucas had given it to them as a wedding gift.

"The very same."

"Fucking monsters. In that case, Tiff, if it's the kids from number thirty-three, I'll wring their necks for you."

A ball of shimmering white light bounced across the far end garden, too low and large to be a torch beam. It skittered in circles and weaved through the flowerbeds like a dog looking for a place to leave a deposit.

Lucas screwed his eyes but couldn't make out any shape beyond the intense light. "That's not a kid. It's some kind of animal."

"What do you mean?" asked Tiff.

"I don't really know, but I reckon it might have something to do with those patches outside."

Iris pressed her nose to the glass. "I can't see it properly. It's pretty big, though. Can you tell what it is?"

Lucas shook his head.

Tiff joined them at the window.

The ball of light scrambled up a stocky juniper bush. It ran along the top of their fence until it disappeared beyond the neighbor's garden.

The rope snapped, the woman careened downwards, she screamed and struck the rocky ground. Blood poured from her broken skin, staining the dirt red. The obsidian creatures swarmed, consuming her in a sea of darkness.

Tiff gestured to Iris. "Make me wet."

Iris aimed the repurposed disinfectant bottle and spritzed Tiff with cold water.

"More."

Iris rolled her eyes.

"Please?"

She spritzed Tiff again.

"It's too hot to be indoors," Tiff whined.

"I know, love, but we don't know what's outside."

"Do we really have to keep all the windows shut?"

"They're not shut; they're on vent."

"They're not open either."

"We don't know how safe it is."

The garden, a stark white version of the green, lush place of relaxation two days prior, reflected the blinding sun back towards the house. Their flowerbed, which previously burst with color, from the orange tiger lilies to the rainbow Livingstone daisies, now resembled a patch of crumpled paper. Tones of white and gray, against more white and gray.

Lucas fanned himself with a magazine. "I'm going to catch it."

Tiff tutted and signaled Iris for more water. "That's a stupid idea."

Iris sprayed. "She's right."

"We can't stay like this. If I catch it, maybe we can find out what's happening."

"How do you plan to do that?"

"I don't know, maybe the old box and stick method? It's worked for hundreds of years."

"Truly, you're the next Bear Grylls."

Lucas sniffed an armpit of his orange t-shirt. "I don't see you doing anything but complaining."

Tiff looked at Iris. Iris shrugged and resprayed her. "You know, you are being a bit—"

"I'm being a lot; I'm aware of that," said Tiff. "Ok, say you catch this thing? What do you expect to do with it, huh?"

"I'd get it looked at by someone. You know, a vet or a scientist."

Tiff laughed. "Do you know any scientists?"

"No, but that's how it always works on TV. Someone stumbles onto a new creature or invention and contacts a scientist online, and they become a millionaire. I might not share my money with you if you're going to be an ass. What if it's like the missing link or Bigfoot?"

Tiff shook with laughter. "Pfft, you think it's Bigfoot?"

"I think he means Cryptozoological," said Iris.

"Yes, that, that's what I meant. A cryptid."

Iris tutted. "Me correcting you was in no way support for you trying to catch whatever it is."

"Aren't you curious?"

"Yes, but that doesn't mean it's safe to go out there."

"I don't care what it is. I want my garden back," Tiff whined.

Lucas rolled his eyes. "Realistically, what is it going to do to me?"

"The thing, or the bleaching?" asked Iris.

"Either, both, I don't know. I mean, if I don't touch whatever it is, and I don't touch any white patches on the floor, I should be fine, right?"

"I guess if you don't touch anything. I mean, I can't guarantee anything. We don't know what it is."

Tiff grabbed the spray bottle from Iris and spritzed herself. "How come you trust him to go outside, but not me?"

Iris mocked Tiff. "I'll stand outside, maybe I'll sit in the chairs, let's use the pool, oops, I fell on the grass."

"Since you made such a good point for me being an idiot anyway, what if I do go out and get in the pool."

"Seriously?"

"Seriously!"

Iris screwed her eyes and clenched her fists. "Stop being such an arsehole!"

Ooft, this was pretty new; not often, Iris lost her temper.

"Right, ok, both of you aren't helping. I'm going to use my canvas shoes." Lucas pointed to the entirely white sneaker by the door, its twin with a similar shade of nothing. "Since my new sneakers are fucked."

"What if you do get it on you?" asked Iris.

"I won't."

"Yeah, but what if—"

"I won't."

Lucas peeled his canvas shoes off by the door, placing them onto a dirt-covered splotch on the deck. He trailed a length of rope into the doorway and slid the door almost closed behind it. Leaving a gap to yank the cord and pull the stick free, trapping the creature under Tiff and Iris' plastic laundry basket. One of those hard plastic ones with delightful daisies cut out of the sides. He grabbed a cushion from the sofa and hunkered down beside the door, determined to catch the creature.

"You touched nothing?" Iris asked Lucas.

"I touched nothing."

Tiff sat beside him, lining herself up with the gap in the door to catch any breeze. "Are you sure this is going to work?"

"No idea, but it's better than doing nothing."

She nodded and pointed to a small blue plate that sat under the laundry basket, atop it something beige and lumpy. "Peanut butter?"

"Yeah."

"Why not cat food or something?"

"Do you have any cat food?"

"No."

"Have you ever seen a dog turn down peanut butter?"

"You think it's a dog?"

"I didn't say that. I just think it helps our chances."

"What now?"

Iris dropped onto the floor. "Now we wait."

Tiff sat with Lucas for ten minutes until she grew bored and headed back to the sofa. It didn't take long for Iris to join her. Lucas listened to their movies, later watching them reflected in the glass, as he stared out at the darkening garden, admiring the hum of blue and purple twilight before it faded to black.

Light nudged him awake. Lucas peeled his face off the glass and wiped the drool from around his mouth on his t-shirt. A large wall clock read twenty-past-four in the morning. Behind him lay Iris curled beneath her hoody; Tiff must have crawled off to bed.

"Psst, Iris. Iris, it's back."

"Yeah, that's good," Iris mumbled.

"No, Iris, the creature is in the garden."

Lucas watched the glowing light weave across the iridescent grass and towards the laundry basket in the center of the garden.

Nothing can resist peanut butter.

"Iris!"

She shuddered awake and rubbed her eyes. Lucas gestured for her to come over. She staggered off the sofa and crumpled to the floor beside him.

Lucas grasped the rope. "It's—"

Iris pressed her finger to her lips. "Shush."

The creature of light padded closer to the basket, closer, closer. It ducked under the lip and towards the plate of gooey peanut butter.

Lucas yanked the rope, the stick flew free, and the basket crashed town on top of the creature.

"I got it. I fucking got it!"

Tiff appeared in the lounge doorway. "Stop yelling."

"I caught it, Tiff, come look."

White light radiated from the cut-out daisies, creating strange patterns on the wilted grass. It slammed against the sides of the basket, knocking it back and forth.

"What are you going to do with it now? It looks like you're going to lose it," said Tiff.

"Like hell I am. Do you have a box or something? I need something to transport it anyway if I'm going to show it to a vet or a scientist."

"Not this again."

"Where do you keep your recycling?"

"You could leave it until daylight; if it's still there, it's meant to be."

Iris chimed in. "We could call Animal Rescue?"

Lucas shook his head. "I doubt they'd come out at this time in the morning for a magical, glowing beastie. Plus, I don't want them taking the credit."

The creature whined; the sound carried like birdsong, sweet and piercing. There was something unnatural and haunting about its melody. How could something be so peaceful and yet so agitated at the same time?

"Where is your recycling?"

Tiff pointed to a cupboard in the kitchen. Lucas ran to the door and wrenched it open, knocking over a precariously balanced ironing board. He spotted an old delivery box while wading through stacks of beer cans, plastic tubs, and pizza boxes. He reached it, still full of packing peanuts.

I knew I could count on Iris to save a good-looking box; you never know when you'll need one.

Lucas tipped out the peanuts and brought the box over to the sliding door. "I'm going to do this."

Tiff offered him a pair of pink marigold washing-up gloves. "Take these."

Iris grabbed his wrist. "Are you really sure about—"

"I've got this."

Lucas pulled on the gloves and slid the door open. He slipped his feet into his canvas shoes; patches of white scarred the toes. It didn't matter, now was his time to make history; he could deal with that later.

"Don't step on the white bits," Iris called after him.

Lucas waved a hand in her direction, ignoring her warning, and strode straight down the center of the garden, box in tow, towards the glowing laundry basket.

He saw a long bushy tail whipping back and forth through gaps in the plastic, light flickering and dancing along silvery strands of hair.

"It's furry."

"Like a cat?" asked Iris.

The creature threw itself at the side of the basket; it tipped but didn't fall and thudded back into place again.

"Whoa there...No, I think more like a dog or something." Lucas ran his hand against the bleached laundry basket. He was right; this thing was causing the weird discoloration. "Hey, little guy, calm down. I'm not going to hurt you. Shhh. It's ok; I just want to get a look at you."

"Careful," Tiff called from the house.

I know what I'm doing; this is it, my big break. What if this changes the world?

Lucas positioned the box against the side of the laundry basket, prepared to slip the basket up and slam the box down, over whatever it was inside. He slipped his fingers under the lip and gradually raised it. The creature cowered on the grass.

"I think it's tame," he said.

He creaked the basket entirely out of the way. "There."

It was a silver fox, its elongated shimmering tail twitching by its feet. It had four legs, like a fox, and two ears, which trembled back and forth, collecting sounds from around the garden, like a fox. But unlike a fox, it had one large, prismatic eye. The eye blinked a triangular lid, disrupting a rainbow glow, which spilt in light ribbons from the prism's sides. The eye, without any semblance of a pupil, appeared not to focus on any one thing.

"This is amazing; you need to see it!"

"What is it?" yelled Tiff.

"I don't know. Isn't that awesome?"

"Get it in the box before it escapes."

Lucas released the edge of the laundry basket and raised the box in front of him, lowering it towards the fox.

The fox released another haunting call, the sides of its furred throat quivering. It hunkered down, and with an unrelenting push from its back legs, launched into the air, its front paws hitting the top of Lucas' legs. Its back legs joined the front, pushing again. Its feet rested on Lucas' shoulders; the fox's soft body pressed against his chest, sliding up onto his face, sweet-scented fur stroked his skin. It sprung over his head and landed on the neighbor's fence before sprinting into the night.

Tiff looked at her brother. "Damn, so close."

He didn't look right. The front of his orange t-shirt had lost all color, the white radiating outwards from his center. Tiff's eyes followed up to his face, his tanned skin like moonlight, his hair once dark mahogany, now struck with patches of grey.

"Luc, are you ok?"

He collapsed to the ground on all fours. "I— I can't—breathe."

Tiff ran into the kitchen and threw on another pair of washing up gloves, chucking the third at Iris. She shoved her feet into her boots and launched across the garden to her brother.

"Don't—touch—me," he panted.

"Don't be an idiot; we need to get you some help."

"I—"

"Shut up and breathe slowly. Iris, get over here and help me get him up!"

Iris stood frozen in the doorway, gloves still in hand. She yanked them on and a pair of sneakers and joined Tiff and Lucas in the garden.

"Grab him by the arm; the bit that's not white yet, come on."

Iris nodded and grabbed him. The two of them led his wobbly frame through the house and forced him into the back of Iris' car.

"I'm so tired."

Tiff peered into the back seat from the passenger side, "I know. Just keep breathing—Iris, can't you get us there any quicker?"

"I'm trying. I'm not used to night driving."

"It's like driving in the day, but darker. Just do it. The sun's coming up anyway."

Lucas' hands and legs shuddered, achromatized further with every passing second. The seat around him faded and became paler and paler until he lay in a halo of white.

Please be ok, please be ok.

"We're here," yelled Iris.

Tiff flung the door open before the car had stopped, outside A and E. "Help, can anyone help us? My brother is hurt."

A couple of paramedics walking out of the entrance spotted the car. They grabbed a gurney and rushed towards Tiff.

"He's, he's going all—"

The first paramedic peered into the car. "Damn, Steve, it's another one. Give them a shout inside."

The second grabbed his radio. "It's Paul, we've got another Achromatica case, it's a real bad one, we're outside. Where do you want him?"

A voice grated back from the radio. "Another one? We're close to capacity. Get him in bay six; it's being cleaned down."

"Another one?" asked Tiff.

Steve pulled on a long pair of gloves and reached for Lucas. "Yeah, this stuff is nasty; it's all over the place. We've had cases nonstop for the last two days. Haven't you seen the news?"

Paul helped prop Lucas up onto the gurney. "You got this big guy, deep breaths, they're gonna help you inside."

Tiff touched Lucas' arm with her rubber glove, "You're gonna be fine; you'll be able to breathe easier soon."

His eyes rolled back into his head as he wheezed.

"What did he do, fall into a pile of the stuff?" asked Paul.

"No, he tried to catch the creature responsible. He sort of did catch it," said Iris.

Steve stepped back from the gurney. "You saw this thing?"

"Sort of, I was too far away to see it properly, but Luc said it was like a dog or something."

"He actually touched it?"

"No, the bastard jumped all over him and disappeared," Tiff wiped her eyes on her sleeve. "Is he gonna be ok?"

"We'll do what we can."

They passed through the waiting room, people squeezed onto rows of seats, patches of white covered people's hands and knees. Some wore masks and gloves. Others had bin liners wrapped around their extremities. Entire legs. Splotches of white peeking out from the pursed tops of the liners.

They'd had this wrong. When people searched online for the bleached patches, they hadn't considered that people were asking about themselves, not just their gardens.

They pulled into bay six. Nurses dressed in masks, aprons, and gloves hooked Lucas with a drip line to his left arm, filled with something that looked like painkillers. They pressed a mask over his face securing the elastic at the back.

"Why can't he breathe?" asked Tiff.

"Because—" a doctor appeared from around the corner, dressed head to toe in a hazmat suit, her face hidden behind Perspex. "This stuff drains the color from everything."

"That's pretty obvious."

"Yes, but color is a vital part of nature. Without it, plants can't photosynthesize, and humans can't transport oxygen without the red haem in their blood. It's a bit more complicated than that, but in layman's terms, if everything loses color, we die."

"What about albino people?" asked Iris.

"They still have red blood," said the doctor. "I'm Dr. Akeley. Are you family?"

"I'm his sister, Tiffany, and Iris is my wife."

"Right, we need to give him a blood transfusion. Lucas, is that his name?"

Tiff nodded.

"Lucas, we need to give you a blood transfusion. Do we have your permission to do that?"

Lucas tried to remove his mask.

"No, leave that on, just nod or shake."

He nodded.

"Do you know his blood type?" the doctor asked Tiff.

"Yes, A positive; Lucas had an accident on his bike when he was little and had to have a transfusion."

The doctor signaled to a nurse, who hooked up a blood bag to Lucas' right arm.

I can't lose him.

Tiff stared at the needle penetrating Lucas' stark arm, "Is he going to be ok?"

The doctor gestured to the edge of the curtain. "Can we have a word outside?"

They moved into a corridor beyond the emergency bays. Tiff stared down the hall, trying to focus her eyes on anything, blinking away tears. She expected to see the odd empty bed or maybe someone being wheeled to a different department. But the hallway was lined with rows of trolleys, each one stacked with multiple black bags, patches of white shimmering on a couple. It took Tiff a second, but she understood what she was seeing. Bodies, rows of bodies in bags. She shuddered.

Lucas is going to be ok; we got him here in time.

"It's not looking good," said Dr. Akeley.

Tiff grasped Iris' hand. "What do you mean it's not looking good?"

"There's only so much transfusions can do; once Achromatica takes hold, it's impossible to stop."

Tiff sobbed. "Why?"

"We can't keep up with the change. Right now, the best we can do is keep Lucas comfortable. You haven't touched the achromatic stuff, have you?"

They both shook their heads.

"Shall we go back in?"

Trembling, Tiff stood for a minute, frozen by the news there was nothing she could do. Nothing anyone could do to fix this. She wanted to go back in time and stop him from going out there. Stop him from touching that fucking creature. Maybe if she'd been a better sister, he wouldn't have tried to catch it; he only wanted to do it for her.

Inside bay six, Tiff watched Lucas' eyes fade from an ocean blue to a crisp white, like two twitching pearls.

His heart monitor grew erratic, lights flickered, and alarms blared.

Iris pointed to the IV bag; the tube leading from the bag to Lucas was white. Plumes of silver spread through the bag's liquid, smothering the crimson, turning it pink, and then creamy nothing.

"It's time," said the doctor.

Lucas wheezed and shuddered still. The monitor whined a shrill single tone.

Tiff leant as close as she dared. "I love you, I'm sorry."

A nurse unhooked the monitor and nudged the doctor, "We've just been notified a school bus is coming in, more Achromatica. Fifteen kids on a camping trip, they'll be here in ten."

The doctor hurried them away from Lucas' body. "There's nothing more we can do. You need to get out of here before you get exposed."

Iris put her arm around Tiff, steadying her. "Where do we go?"

"Go home, lock your doors, shut your windows, and stay away from anything white."

Tiff screamed and punched the dashboard.

Iris gripped the steering wheel. "It's ok. We just need to get home, not far now."

"It's not ok. It's never going to be ok."

"You did everything you could."

"It wasn't enough."

Iris pushed Tiff through the front door and locked it behind them. She pulled the curtains closed as Tiff made her way to the lounge. The entrance to the garden lay open.

Something made a noise in their bedroom above.

It's in the house.

Iris made her way up the stairs, Tiff close behind, wiping tears on her sleeves. Tiny dots of white marked their pink carpet.

They entered the bedroom.

A silver fox with one prismatic eye sprawled across her bleached rainbow blanket, which lay bundled on the bed. It twisted its tail above it like a toy, whimpered its melody and contorted atop the mantle, like a puppy at play.

Iris' phone buzzed. She pulled it out of her pocket and placed it on the nightstand. A warning blared across the screen.

ACHROMATICA. DO NOT TOUCH THE WHITE. DO NOT LEAVE YOUR HOUSE. SEAL ALL WINDOWS AND DOORS. DO NOT TRY TO TREAT FAMILY MEMBERS.
SELF ISOLATE IF YOU HAVE BEEN EXPOSED.

Tiff launched forwards and grasped the edges of her blanket, bringing them together and trapping the fox inside. The creature howled and struggled against the cloth. Tiff screamed and slammed the bundle against the floor.

"Tiff, don't!"

It thudded on the carpet, something crunched. Tiff spun around and smashed the bundle into the wall, again and again. Limbs crunched and twisted, their celery snap of broken bone through flesh filled the air. The howling stopped, and so did her screaming. The blanket dripped with a crystal substance; Tiff knew it had to be blood.

"Open the window."

Shaking, Iris did as told.

Tiff launched the bundle outside; chunks of fur, flesh, and bone tumbled loose and splashed into the hot tub.

Two months later

Light creaked through masking tape holding newspaper across their living room windows.

Tiff grabbed Iris' plate and made her way into the kitchen. "Do you want anything before I start on the washing up?"

"Just a glass of water, please."

Tiff dropped the plates into the sink and filled a glass from the tap, setting it down beside Iris. she stole a kiss and went back to the kitchen. She turned on the tap to fill the sink and peeked out through a gap in the taped window. She couldn't tell what anything was anymore. Houses were primarily white, although some patches remained, showing hints of duck egg or cream.

She scooped the washing up liquid bottle and squirted a blob into the sink. As it struck the water, the lurid green vanished. She sprayed again; it disappeared.

In the lounge, Iris retched.

Tiff rushed through.

The drinking glass lay empty on the floor, its liquid spilt across the carpet, bleaching the pink. Iris gripped her stomach and vomited; red pasta sauce turned white mid-air before it struck the table and spilt over the sides.

No, no, no.

"No!"

Tiff rushed to hold her. Iris trembled; her mouth stained white. More white vomit poured down her chest and splattered Tiff. She shuddered, then grew still. Tiff gazed at her dying wife's china doll face, the unpainted emotion of a deathmask. She propped her against her favorite pillow.

"I'll see you soon, my love."

There was nothing left.

Grief-stricken, Tiff stripped off her vomit-soaked clothes and walked, naked, to the garden door. She twisted the key in the lock and wrenched the door open, tearing tape as it moved.

Tears coursed down her face and struck her chest. She stepped out of the door, planting her feet on the crystalline ground. She stared up at the blinding white sky and decayed trees, disgusted by the unfettered destruction Achromatica had wrought, and walked. Strands of white crept up her legs like milk smothering tea tannins; further, cupping her breasts, neck, and face. Until she was no more distinguishable from the cruel barren world of white around her.

HOLLOW BONES
BY JESS KOCH

Far away, the aviary burns, and Margaret—Mags—sits at the bar and flicks a lighter open and shut, open and shut until the woman next to her grabs her wrist and pins it to the damp bar top.

"Cut it out. You're driving me nuts."

Mags clicks the lighter closed one more time, for effect, and then places it next to her half-drunk whiskey sour. She shrugs her colleague's—her friend's—hand away.

"Dan loved birds." Mags twirls her glass. The ice cube slowly melts into the piss-brown, watered-down excuse for a drink. "Loves," she corrects herself.

"Probably not those birds."

Mags smiles. She can't help herself. "All birds," she says. "He was always smug about it, too. He thought birds were so much better than other pets." Mags drinks, wipes her mouth with the back of her hand, drops the glass down too hard. "I just wanted a cat. But can't have birds *and* a cat. But he never got any birds, either."

"I know." Sahra nods. "I hate him too."

"I don't hate him."

"Well, you should. He's living in your house with your things and that pretty new wife of his."

"You really think she's pretty?" Mags looks up at herself in the wall-length mirror mounted behind the bar. Even in the dirty low light she can see her dark, sunken eyes, paper skin, dull hair. Colorless.

"I meant it disparagingly. He only cares about looks."

"Beautiful things."

Sahra sips her wine. "He's shallow, is what I mean." The Malbec leaves a pink stain on her upper lip. "And anyway, we're supposed to be celebrating. Forget about Dan for a minute." Sahra raises her glass and tips it towards Mags. "To the end of another biological horror."

Mags clinks her glass with Sahra's, and they drink.

"That one seemed different than the others," Mags says as she swirls her finger in the circle of condensation where her glass had been.

"How so?"

The smell of burnt feathers clings to her clothes. She can't get the screeches of dying birds, dying half-birds out of her head. In her mind, she rewinds to early that day and sees the aviary standing, the great glass dome reflecting back a low golden sun. And then she is inside again. And there are the birds, perched above her head on high branches with their blue and yellow plumage. Colors so bright they almost look like they give off their own light. There's a woman sitting in the garden. But she's not just a woman. She stretches her arms—no, her wings—out wide to either side of her. She hears the click of the lighter again, feels the heat of the fire. Mags reaches out toward the woman as her feathers catch the flames.

She opens her mouth to scream.

But then Sahra's voice cuts in. "Mags, what do you mean?"

And Mags is back in the bar, rubbing her temple. She takes another sip of her drink, buying herself a moment. "I don't know. All the others were...disturbing. Wrong. But this one was..." She wants to say *beautiful*.

"It wasn't any different. Illegal and messed up is what it is. What they all are." Sahra downs the last sip of her wine and shakes her head. "Besides, we're not paid for our opinions. We're just the muscle." She taps the lighter with her index finger, then digs into her pocket and pulls out a twenty. "This one's on me. I'm gonna go home." She turns her head to sniff the collar of her coat and crinkles her nose. "And take a shower."

Mags watches her leave. The bar is mostly empty now, except for the bartender and a couple sitting in the corner booth giggling flirtatiously, maddeningly while the screaming woman's voice still echoes in the hollows of her mind.

Her reflection stares back at her from beyond the wall, a mocking patron, as if she's saying: *This is all you are, all you'll ever be.* But Mags ignores her and takes the last sip of her drink.

She leaves, coat pulled close, a secret in her pocket.

Far away, the aviary smolders, and Mags stands in her bathroom looking at the same reflection in a different mirror. The toilet runs, the shower head drips through the duct tape, people yell somewhere in the distance, sirens follow.

Harsh white light casts shadows on her face from above. Limp, uncoiled curls stick out at odd angles from her head. Her eyes are a weak shade of brown. Her nose is too wide, her smile too crooked. No wonder Dan doesn't love her anymore. She looks old. Old and ugly.

There's a pill in her hand. The capsule is half blue, half yellow. She places it on her tongue, and it seeds her mouth with bitterness. She swallows it.

She pushes her bed up against the window, so she can watch the city from her tenth-floor perch. She crawls up and props herself against the pillows. She likes being so high up, where the people are small, but the sky is big.

She scratches an itch on her shoulder that burrows up from under her skin, where her fingers can't reach.

All night the itch spreads across her skin like the fire through the aviary, and Mags rubs her arms and stares down at the midnight people as they wander clumsily, drunkenly from bar to bar. As if their only purpose is to numb themselves so they can forget. She wonders if Dan is down there, forgetting her, or if he's sitting up in bed waiting for her to come home.

Far away, the aviary is smoking rubble, and Mags wakes on wet sheets soaked through with sweat and blood. Evidence of change. Her body hums, her skin burns, her temples throb.

In the same bathroom mirror, in the new morning light, Mags sees color where gray skin used to be. Plumes of soft feathers cascade in layers down her arms. Her eyes are a soft yellow, her cheekbones and nose sharper. She feels lighter.

Her phone buzzes next to the sink with a text from Sahra, but Mags ignores it.

She smiles.

Far away, police walk through the ashes of the aviary, and Mags is standing outside Dan's townhouse—her old townhouse—in a long coat that hides her wings. It's still morning and the streets are mostly empty. But on the way, she passed an elderly woman walking two dachshunds. The dogs barked, the woman stared, but of course they did. She is beautiful now.

Mags knocks on the yellow door. She picked out that color, painted over the ugly pea soup green that was there before. Dan hated yellow. But he never changed it. Not even after the divorce.

No one answers. Mags scratches a single talon along the face of the door, peeling back a strip of honey paint. It curls and falls, revealing the ugliness underneath.

The door opens. Dan adjusts his robe around himself in the dark doorway and squints outside. He isn't wearing his glasses.

"Mags?" His voice scratches out like he just woke up. He can't see her yet, not clearly. "Jesus, it's early. Why are you here?"

"Can I come in?"

"Uh, sure." He lets the door swing open. "Let me go grab my glasses, hold on."

Dan rushes down the hall in his socks and slips into the wall, knocking a framed picture off it. He swears, and then disappears into the kitchen.

Mags steps into the foyer and looks up the stairs. She wonders if the other woman is even here. If she still warms the left side of his bed or if he made her leave, too.

Rummaging sounds come from the kitchen. Papers tossing, chairs being moved. Dan swears again. He can't find his glasses. That's so like him.

Mags admires herself in the oval mirror that hangs by the door. It's the one with the heavy gold frame that she found at an antique store downtown. Dan was so mad that she bought it because they had to carry it down to the subway and then six blocks back home.

She shrugs off her coat and lets it fall to the floor. This is what he wants. This color, this beauty.

Dan reappears in the hall and walks toward her.

He unfolds his glasses as she unfurls her wings. Pushes them up the bridge of his nose.

He looks up. Stops.

He looks at her. Really looks at her for the first time in years.

She stretches her wings to their full width. The tips skim the walls on either side of the entryway.

He does not smile. "What did you do, Mags?"

Right here, Mags is sitting on the edge of her open window. The phone buzzes in the bathroom again. For the fourteenth time. Someone is trying to call her.

And then, for a little while, there is silence.

Dan told her to leave, told her to never come back, told her to get help. But she doesn't need help. She *is* beautiful, even if he can't see it. Can't understand it.

Someone rings her apartment. The box on the wall chirps, lights up. Then a sound fills the space, harsh and static. A voice calls out from the speaker.

"Mags? Mags are you home?" Sahra's voice is strained, worried, on the edge of cracking. "Dan called me. Why aren't you answering your phone?"

She looks around her apartment, at the peeling wallpaper, the warped floorboards. This was always a place for leaving. Maybe she just needed a push, a reminder that she could never go back, she could only go—

Mags clutches the windowsill. The wood cracks and splinters under her talons as she leans over the edge and looks down. She isn't sure if she would fly or fall. She isn't sure if it matters.

"Mags! Please answer me."

It's a long way down but the cold wind rustles her feathers. An invitation.

She spreads her wings, holds her breath, feels the air catch, falls.

"Mags?"

Silence.

The phone buzzes again and again and clatters to the bathroom floor.

Far away, a bird flies over the remains of the aviary.

THE GRAY
BY G.G. SILVERMAN

When the gray comes, people shutter their windows and doors, and call in their children and loved ones. The first warning is the mass of clouds that gathers at the horizon, streaking the sky with melancholy. Then the ocean grows dark as a broken mirror. Fishermen and women bring in their boats, families pull in their linens. Boys and girls tug kites down from the sky or scramble from forts in the trees. The animals are left out to pasture, because the gray never comes for the animals.

Thick rolling mist creeps in from the water's edge, delving down the road, slowly enveloping everything. It rolls over the docks, down Main Street, swallowing white-painted shops and faded salt-box cottages. It blankets the schoolyard and the churchyard and the gravestones, sifting toward the woods, where it filters through the trees in ribbons. It only ever comes in summer, though no one can predict when. And that's why in summer we're never truly at peace. Even on the brightest of days, the winds might change at any time and bring the gray.

Many who've gotten lost in the gray never return, and those that do are altered and forever silent—like Pa, a shell of his former self, a shell that hides something or someone else. It's been ten years since Pa got swallowed by the gray, only to reemerge ten days later; though for Pa, time had passed in ways we couldn't fathom.

The day he returned, when the gray rolled back to the ocean, we found him naked and shivering at the edge of the woods. Ma ran over, throwing a blanket over his clammy skin. His eyes stared ahead, beholding everything and nothing. His face had been ravaged by an impossible passing of decades. He was stooped and bone-thin, his hair and beard long and white.

After all these years, no one ever leaves this town because everyone's lost someone to the gray. They hope their loved one will come back, even though it's known that if they do, they'll be a shadow of themselves. Some folks reappear years later, looking no different than when they left, but everything inside is gone. Some come back as children, but with lost souls. No one ever speaks about the returned, except in the politest of ways, asking about them only to be told that they're just fine, thank you for asking.

Though Pa hasn't spoken a word since the day he was found, sometimes other sounds emerge from him, like the crackle of static, or an ominous low hum that comes from deep inside his body. Sometimes there's a shriek like the gears of an unknown future machine. Other times Pa levitates and convulses. And my blood goes cold, so cold, I fall to my knees, weeping, begging, praying that the infernal sound will stop.

Still, I tell no one of my suffering. Everyone has suffering of their own.

Some folks say if you dare look outside when the gray's come, the columns of mist look like spirits who've slipped their mortal coils. Some say it's the wandering souls of the returned, stolen from their bodies and replaced with something not of this world.

After Pa came back, Ma got sick with a cancer that blackened her from the inside. That left just me and Joss, though as the oldest, I had to take care of both him and Pa. Soon after, Joss didn't come in fast enough when the clouds streaked the sky with melancholy, and the ocean turned cracked-mirror black. When the gray rolled off the water and crept up the road, I was calling out for him, calling, calling, calling from the window, about to shutter everything. And Pa began to emit a low hum, then his body levitated and convulsed and sounded the abominable shriek.

Then the deafening quiet of the gray descended, enveloping our house in its thick embrace. I slammed the windows shut, and threw my back against the door.

Pa's body lowered to its place on the frayed overstuffed chair. His head lolled on his shoulders, his muscles slack.

I wept bitterly. It might be years before Joss would emerge from the fog, amid the columns of lost souls.

There is a young man in town I've fallen in love with, and he's fallen in love with me. We have agreed never to marry, because we're both taking care of people who've been spat out by the gray, and we're both waiting for others to return. Sometimes, we steal away, and go for walks in the woods, away from prying eyes, holding hands. We don't dare kiss because we fear it will lead to other things, the lovemaking that brings new children into this world. Mrs. James, who runs the village market, teases me, asking me when Jeremiah Clay and I will marry.

"This town could use some joy, Sadie," she says, tucking a curl of silver hair behind her ear while wrapping my things. She stares at me over metal-rimmed glasses. "We could use some new life—something to celebrate. Consider it, won't you, dear?" She smiles and hands me the extra food we can't afford but have been kindly gifted by the people of this village.

I smile reverently in return. Mrs. James means well, but Jeremiah and I can never build a life together. There is already too much loss. We can never bring a new being into this place where they might be claimed by something larger and darker than ourselves.

The next time Jeremiah and I steal some time away in the woods, we hold each other for far too long, and we devolve into kissing, then heavy petting. As quickly as it begins, I pull away, breathless and flushed. I want it so badly, yet I don't want what accompanies it, the loss of control that leads to life, then more loss. As soon as I stand back, the foghorn sounds, signaling the arrival of the gray. We draw our breath in sharply, and we make haste to our homes before we are claimed. Though small safety huts dot the forest, we prefer being with our loved ones. At the edge of the woods, we go our separate ways.

As I approach the cottage I share with my father, the gray advances up the road in swirling columns of mist. I reach my door almost too late—it's already wrapping our home. Wisps of gray grasp toward me as I jiggle the knob, letting myself in. I spot Madeline, the neighbor girl who watches Pa to give me some respite. She cries in hysteria because something black and oily oozes from Pa's mouth. A different sound hums from his body, one that is deeper and rattles the core of my being until my belly grows hot and sick. Madeline throws her small arms around me, crying into my shirt. It reminds me why I can never merge families with Jeremiah or have his children. Because this would be our life: Comforting children against constant horror, or a madhouse full of the returned.

Soon the sound stops, and I pull away from Madeline. I lead her to Joss's old room, and tell her she can rest here until supper if she likes, and if she has to stay with us longer, this room will be hers. She will be trapped in our house until the gray recedes. It could be one night, or a week, or a month. I'm thankful we've been gifted plenty of cured meat, smoked fish, and hard cheese, things that will keep in our cold cellar, along with the preserves, potatoes, beans, and root vegetables from my garden. There is no safe way for Madeline to go home.

After Madeline settles, I bring Pa a basin of warm water and a washcloth to wipe the black that oozed from his mouth. The ooze terrifies me, so I wear gloves to protect my skin, then I clean his face as best as I can. I pull off his shirt, also blackened with the slick emanation, and I feed his emaciated body into a fresh one.

I look out the window. Through the thickening mist, I can barely discern Abigail, Madeline's mother, at her own. I pull on a string that rings a bell outside, signaling that Madeline is safe. Abigail rings her bell in return, signaling her thanks. It is an act of trust to enter another person's home knowing the gray can arrive at any time.

It has been three days. The gray safely receded and Madeline has returned home. I push Pa to town in his wheelchair for a change of scenery and some fresh air. People take to the streets tentatively, attempting to return to their business, or be social, offering each other a plate of cookies, a cup of tea, or a kind word. When we reach the village center, I hear there's been a tragedy—old Mr. Miller lost a son to the gray. But then his wife was returned—she was found shivering naked on the beach, but in a child's form. They say he recognized her birthmark, a dark triangle on her back. He'd known that mark since the first night in their marriage bed. It's hoped he will treat her like a daughter and no longer a wife. I shudder, praying the good people of our village might remain good.

Then I hear that our old town preacher, Reverend Doggett, passed quietly in his sleep the night before. Reverend Doggett kept up the church, though very few folks ever went anymore. Most believe God could not possibly exist so long as our townsfolk go missing in the gray. The reverend worked quietly, visiting the sick when he was welcome in their homes, which wasn't often. He hadn't stepped in our house in ten years.

On our next walk in the woods, Jeremiah seems quiet, stuffing his hands in his pockets instead of holding mine. His mind strays elsewhere, robbing us of the little time we stole away from caring for our ill-returned loved ones.

"A penny for your thoughts," I offer.

He shakes his head. "I'm sorry." He gestures to a log and we sit. He takes my hand, finally. He sighs, then his eyes meet mine in earnest. "I don't know how much longer I can go on this way, being in love without really being together. I thought it was a good idea at first to lead separate lives, but...I want you so much that I feel sick without you. I want you in my home, in my bed. *Our* home, *our* bed."

I hesitate, struggling against my own desires. "I love you," I say, "and always will, but if we merge our lives with my father and your mother both sick from the gray, our home will become a madhouse. What happens if Joss comes back? And your sister? We might have all four at once, mute and ill most of the time, but shrieking when the gray comes. Then what happens if we bear children? That's no life."

"We can make it work, Sadie. The gray only ever comes in summer. That's nine months of relative peace."

I nod slowly, attempting to hide my fear.

"Please think about it. And if you decide to say yes, then please propose marriage to me, on bended knee. Weave a ring from grass. We'll have a simple wedding. Our love will be our guide."

I refrain from sighing, fearing I will alienate my lover. "I will think about it."

He squeezes my hand tighter. The sun lowers toward the horizon. We need to relieve our help and cook supper for our families.

"We should go," I say.

Jeremiah kisses my fingers, then we part.

At the next town meeting, fifty of our few hundred townspeople gather at the small bandstand in the center's green, where folks can sit and listen.

Dabney Pearce, the groundskeeper who tends the center of the village, steps forward at the end and takes the pulpit. He's a former schoolmate, about my age, tall, square-jawed, and handsome, though quiet and reserved. Beads of sweat dot his forehead; his gaze flits from side to side. It's been years since I've heard his voice. He sweeps a shock of hair from his eyes, clears his throat, and begins to speak.

"We all know that Reverend Doggett continued his good works despite our estrangement from his church. And he left no one to succeed him. I have decided that though I have only been a humble groundskeeper, I will take his post as reverend in order to continue his works of service, and I will preach, and pray, and hope to earn back God's love."

Murmurs rise. Some nod, others remain silent, indifferent.

Mrs. James stands. "Respectfully, Dabney—if this is about the gray, your efforts won't matter. It comes for all, sinners and saints alike."

He nods. "I'll take that under advisement, ma'am."

Mr. Townsend, an older gentleman, stands. "Young Mr. Pearce, sir, I know I abandoned the church long ago, and I have remained distant from Reverend Doggett, for better or worse. But it would pain me to see that stately old white building crumble into dust and decay without Doggett to watch over it. So long as you're tending it and making noble use of it, I don't care if you're a reverend, or churchmouse, or bat in the belfry."

Dabney smiles, and takes a small bow. "I shall care for that old building, sir. You have my word."

Mrs. Embry stands with the help of a cane. "I know the reverend was shunned by many, but he helped me greatly while he was alive. He offered words of comfort after my beloved husband Jasper was lost in the gray. Dabney, I welcome you on your new journey. My home is open to you."

"Thank you, Mrs. Embry. I'm honored to follow in his esteemed footsteps."

Dabney scans the crowd, which has gone respectfully silent. Our town has seen too much adversity to fight each other over something so small as a man wanting to take over a dead man's good works.

Dabney nods and thanks us under his breath, then steps away from the pulpit. We make brief eye contact as he forges toward the back row of chairs. He looks elsewhere, embarrassed. There may have been a time, years ago, when Dabney and I had a brief indiscretion.

The meeting adjourns and we all drift away. I push my father toward home.

Mrs. James passes, light on her feet even at her age. "Have you given thought to my suggestion?" she asks.

Clearly, she means our conversation about Jeremiah. "Yes, ma'am, I'm thinking about it very hard."

"Good girl."

I bristle at being called a girl. I'm a woman now, and I make my own choices. I know what's best for my life, yet, there are those who'd have me live their way. That's the burden of living in a small town—everyone knows your business as much as you try to keep it your own.

I bid her goodnight and resume steering my father's chair. My legs and arms ache from the work. When we arrive at our cottage, I'll have to lift him up and into bed, as I've done for shy of a decade. Because of this, I'm strong—stronger than I've ever been.

Sometimes the dreams come. There's one where the gray infiltrates our home and wisps toward our beds, blanketing us in its oblivion. It enters my body through my mouth, my ears, and my nose, gagging me until I convulse, my orifices bleeding black. I bolt upright in bed, gasping and clawing at my face. Thick ooze chokes me until I realize it's not real; it's a trick the gray plays on us from afar.

My nightshirt clings to my back as I slip out of bed, and open my shutters for a quick bit of fresh air. By moonlight, I spot a man strolling with his hands in his pockets. To go out at night is to risk being caught by the gray; its cool mist often appears after dark. The man strolls closer to our cottage, and I can see that it's Dabney Pearce. How long has he been meandering in the evenings, passing by our homes as we sleep? What does he search for? Does he feel that his newfound closeness to God will keep him safe from the gray? I shutter the window softly, praying he hasn't seen me watching.

I strip my sweat-soaked clothes, noticing my body in the mirror, its sinewy solidity and toned muscles, and the way shadows curve around my breasts, hips, and thighs. I'm thinking about Jeremiah, wanting Jeremiah, but knowing I shouldn't have him, not in the way that I crave. Then I think about the cruelty of this—how my body will never know the full weight and heat and thrust of a man's love, what it means to rock together, bodies arced and clasped. I want to touch myself so badly, as I've done many nights in the past, but I wonder if filling my need in this way will worsen it, if it will only lead me back to him for more. I lie back on my sheets, now sufficiently cooled, and spread my bent legs, revealing the flesh that throbs and aches. My hands wander my body, finding their secret place.

At the village market, Mrs. James seems different, not her bright self. As she wraps my things, she doesn't ask if I might marry Jeremiah Clay. Instead, she asks, "Have you seen him recently?"

"It's been a while—I've wanted some time to think."

She nods, hands me my bundle. "Sadie, might I ask you to please drop something off at the schoolhouse for Maisie Stiles?"

School has let out for the summer, but Maisie will be at the schoolhouse a few days, putting things to rest until fall. "Yes," I say, agreeing to help since it's on my way home.

She hands me an extra package, and I leave with a mixture of relief and dismay at Mrs. James' relative silence.

At the schoolhouse door, I hear two voices, Maisie's and Jeremiah's. I stop, poised at the threshold. My breath catches in my throat at the sound of laughter. I enter, and they are standing close together, his chin just over her shoulder as she shows him a page in a book. They are close, so close. Near enough for him to catch the honeyed scent of her hair, or graze her ear with his tongue, or take her body from behind. They freeze at the sight of me, and I place the package quietly on the bench by the door. I retreat without glancing back.

In our town, there aren't enough young men for every young woman who wants one, and I was naive to think Jeremiah would wait forever. Affairs are frowned upon here, as this town is too small for so much heat and anger. I run home as Jeremiah calls out behind me.

Soon, he's on his knees at my door.

My heart is heavy. I wave him in, searching for words.

Like a lost dog, he follows me inside. I nod at Madeline, who's been watching Pa, and she departs, brisk as a soldier. Pa remains in his chair, as ever, a monument to the strange happenings of my life. I lead Jeremiah to the kitchen, and we stare at each other.

"Where do we go from here?" I finally plead.

Jeremiah says nothing, only slides to his knees again and gazes at me with the eyes of a beggar. His lip quivers.

"I don't know."

"Do you want me to set you free?"

"No. Maisie means nothing to me. You mean everything."

I sigh.

He pulls himself up and slips his arms around my body. His breath warms my neck as his lips brush my skin. Tears wet my shoulder. "Please marry me. Please. I love you so much."

A stone of sadness is lodged in my throat.

"Just give me time," I beg. "All I have ever asked for is time."

"I will wait for you, Sadie. I will be better."

We hold each other in silence.

I eventually muster a whisper, thanking him.

We pull apart, and I lead him out, walking past Pa.

At the door, Jeremiah's gaze lingers on me one final time. "I will wait for you as long as you need me to. For years, even."

I nod, closing the door softly as sunset tinges the sky.

Inside, Pa sheds a lone tear. I dab his cheek with my sleeve, then I wheel him into the kitchen so we can keep company while I make supper.

I talk to Pa as I chop and boil carrots, even though he can't reply. I don't know that he hears me, but his lone tear makes me wonder. I try to remind him—and myself—of brighter times, before he was taken by the gray. He was a carpenter and made much of our furniture before I was born, crafting it lovingly with his own hands. I remember his soft laugh, his generous smile, his kind eyes. I remember his warm gaze toward Ma when he came in from the workshop, the quiet way he pecked her cheek. When he angered, he preferred not to speak in a venomous tongue. He'd take a deep breath, and a long walk to clear his head.

On one of those walks he was stolen by the gray.

That day, I deeply violated his trust. I'd taken his father's diary without permission, to learn what our family knew about the gray. When did it start? Where did it come from? Had anyone known? He caught me with the old tattered book, and his face betrayed only a flicker of rage. He'd known in an instant that I had hunted the journal for days and stolen the key that kept it safe. He'd balled his fists and spun on his heels, leaving without a sound, and I knew—or thought I knew—that when he'd return, he'd speak softly, asking me once to never, ever cross him again. Except the gray came, and he was gone.

For ten days, I mourned.

For ten days, self-loathing plagued me.

But then the gray released him, yet his soul was gone forever.

Ma spoke much less in those days. She devoted her time to caring for Pa before the cancer ate her from the inside. Creases webbed her forehead; her eyes seemed not to see. She'd cry faintly at night. Soon after, the pain started, and she grew thin, then emaciated. The sharp bones of her face cut her cheeks. Hollows deepened under her eyes. One morning after sunrise, I knocked softly on her door, telling her I'd bring tea. She didn't respond, and I peeked in. She stared at the ceiling, expression frozen, bleeding black from her eyes, ears, nose, and mouth. Then her body crumpled, her flesh blackening. I wrapped the sheets around her carcass, and kept it hidden from Joss. I told him to hurry to school, and I sent for Mr. Carson, the undertaker.

When Carson came and removed Ma's body, Pa shed a single tear.

After Joss returned from school, I delivered the news. I didn't describe the horror of Ma's end, the way she had bled out the darkness that infected her after Pa returned. He nodded, and said nothing. He'd known that our mother had been sick, and we'd soon lose her.

After that, Joss grew sullen and willful. When I needed him most, he'd make himself scarce, unable to accept his new status as the man of the house, however young.

The day Joss disappeared, we'd fought. I yelled that I wished he'd go away, and he was a burden who refused to grow up. He cared more about running with his playmates than tending to his own Pa or the house we shared, and he'd left me to do all the work, slaving to the bone. I had the garden to tend, the clothing and linens to wash and mend, the firewood to chop, axe to grind, meals to cook, and our father to watch and bathe.

I broke. I took Joss by the shoulders and shook him, said terrible things.

Words I wish I'd never said.

Then he ran.

An hour later, the gray curled up the road, and Joss never made it home.

Every time the gray descends, I'm sick with anticipation, wondering if Joss will return.

A month goes by, and Jeremiah never once asks if I'll marry him. Instead, flowers appear nightly on my doorstep. I hold these bouquets with hands aching and stained from tending to my father and our home.

At the next town meeting, I pass Maisie Stiles, who looks away when she sees me. Jeremiah sits on the opposite side of the aisle, but does not hint that he's desperate for my attention.

That night, a majority decides that all villagers and newborns without birthmarks should be scarred with a small unique symbol, and catalogued, so we'll know who they are if they become lost in the gray and return altered. If Joss returns, though, I'll know him in an instant, he's the only one in our village born with one green eye, and one blue.

Dabney Pearce takes the pulpit as the last speaker. Since he took over for Reverend Doggett, he's grown confident, no longer seems nervous. "Dear residents of our humble township, let me remind you I kindly extend a hand in the name of God. Let me be your servant. I am here to aid against whatever ails you. My doors—God's doors— are always open."

Most everyone murmurs their thanks, and Dabney steps down. He passes me and a twinge of the old nervous Dabney is back, the one I comforted years ago in a tender embrace where our hands wandered for too long.

When the meeting is adjourned, the sky changes. Gray streaks paint the horizon and stretch over us, muting the evening light, bringing with them a chill. The foghorn sounds. Everyone scatters. Jeremiah asks me if I'm alright, and I nod, knowing he must run to attend to his own.

I push my father toward home. Mothers and fathers call in their children. Shutters and doors close.

Dabney appears beside me, keeping pace. "Let me assist you, Sadie."

I grip Pa's wheelchair with white knuckles, and push harder, gaining more ground. "I'm fine, Dabney. Please, go take care of yourself."

There's an intensity in his expression I've only witnessed recently, a passion that lights the darks of his eyes with fire. "God works in mysterious ways, Sadie," he calls as I hurry on without him. "There is a reason for all of this."

Then, from afar, "Will you marry Jeremiah Clay?"

"I don't know!"

"God wants you to make a child for him," Dabney shouts. "Your body sings with God's love."

His words sicken me, and I rush away. Another bouquet lies at my doorstep, which Jeremiah must have dropped off before the meeting. I don't have time to claim it. I struggle to thrust my key in the lock fast enough, then I wheel Pa over the threshold. After, I peer outside once more, deciding there's still time to take the flowers. I put them in water just as Pa's body begins its infernal humming, and the creeping mist chokes the streets.

At summer's end, I enter Pa's room first thing in the morning, and find him dead. His body is disintegrating, growing black as it caves in. My sole purpose for being is gone.

After that, I'm so bereft of feeling that I barely rise from my bed for weeks.

Jeremiah visits daily. He carries me to the bathtub, feeds me soup until I'm strong enough to stand again, never once asking me to marry him. Yet, we marry as soon as September is over because my father, Joss, and my mother are gone, and this home is too empty without them.

Our ceremony is small, a hand-fasting rather than a church marriage. I wear a simple dress, and Jeremiah, a simple suit of linen. We merge houses, then merge bodies in the cool autumn nights, engaged in the giving and taking of seed. His mother lives with us, and we tend our home and family the best we can, with help from Madeline next door. Around the last of June, we'll bring a child into this world.

During a blustery winter the third month after we marry, Jeremiah's mother dies in her sleep, much like Pa did. Jeremiah weeps softly as he rolls her crumpled carcass in white sheets and carries her out to the undertaker's in his arms, never stopping for a coat.

As the days lengthen and spring gives way to summer, the life inside me swells and kicks. I'm heavy and weary—my feet so swollen they barely carry me. I'm to rest often, and only go out when pushed in Pa's old wheelchair. I have one month before I'm due, though I feel the baby demands release before its time, clawing at the tense wall of my womb. At night, I can hardly sleep, but when I do, the dreams are feverish, of an unknown rumbling deep in my belly, and a swirl of choking mist.

The four walls feel close tonight, so Jeremiah pushes me to the village center. In the seat of my being, a pinprick of dread becomes a constant, growing nausea. At the town meeting, a breeze peppers the early summer sky. After everyone speaks their business, Dabney takes the stand.

With new purpose, he declares, "Dear villagers, I wish to engage you in discourse this evening, so let us consider the following: If God created all things, then we must allow for the possibility that God created the gray. If God is omnipotent and great, then He may create things beyond our understanding. We may grasp his intention in due time but only when He allows it. Only when He deems we are worthy. What purpose does the gray serve? Does the gray bring us closer together? Does it teach us to love those around us better before they are gone? And yet the gray returns some in exchange for others. What if the gray were teaching us a lesson by sending us back to live our lives again until we are worthy?" Dabney pauses, scanning the crowd.

"Or, what if it demands sacrifice? What if it only brings back a loved one in exchange for another's soul? What if our God is not kind and benevolent, but angry and vengeful, demanding sacrifice? Did God not sacrifice his only son so that we could be saved? God works in mysterious ways to test our faith. What if He could be appeased?"

The villagers mumble at Dabney's speech.

Mrs. James stands. "What exactly are you suggesting, young man?"

"I'm suggesting that we should feel joy when one of our own is lost—joy that a loss leads to another being found. My own mother was lost in the gray and never returned. Perhaps her life was traded for one of your loved ones. Perhaps one of us—or more—should offer to go into the gray willingly, in exchange for bringing home the others."

"Perhaps you should go, then," someone counters. "If you know what's right for this town."

Shouts uncharacteristic of our people hurl from the seats. A hot sickness sears my insides. I wail, clutching my belly.

The foghorn sounds, slicing my body with a chill. Clouds have gathered, streaking the sky with melancholy. People rush from their seats, and the pain inside me howls.

I hiss to Jeremiah that there is no time—our child emerges here and now. He carries me from my chair, and lays me on the grass of our village green. Dabney stands beside him as I scream with legs parted. Black ooze slicks my inner thighs as my wraith of a child births with the gray behind him, behind all of us. A dark fire roars in Dabney's eyes. He snatches my son, offering him to the sky with a cord of throbbing flesh still strung to my body, and the gray comes, and the gray comes, and all the lost souls.

RED LIGHT/GREEN LIGHT
BY EV KNIGHT

Luna Samson was seven years old the summer she first saw them in the night sky. That wasn't important though, not then. Not when she was finally allowed to play games like Red Rover, Red Light/Green Light, and Mother-May-I with her older cousins. Luna discovered while she might not be strong enough to block a runner from the Red Rover defense line, and her little steps could never outdistance those of nine and ten-year-old's in Mother-May-I, she could sprint and stop on a dime during Red Light/Green Light. When it was her turn to be the light caller, she found the thrill of control almost as good as the race to the finish line. That childhood summer still life, before the storm came, when the wind tousled her baby-fine blonde hair and the smile made her face ache, was the last carefree moment of Luna Samson's life.

Her fun-filled weekend sleepover at Grandma's where she didn't have to sit on the porch watching the rest of the kids have fun because she was "just a baby" or "got in the way" ended with a ruckus of thunder and lightning—a summer storm that sent the kids inside to find something dry to do.

It turned out board games were not equivalent to yard games, and after pointing out the age range, which always started with the seemingly unattainable number eight, Luna had no choice but to give in. This is how, at nine-thirty, on the night of July 11, 1986, Luna Samson saw the impending invasion that would plague her for the next thirty-eight years.

She plopped down beside her grandmother on the glider-rocker and sighed.

"Didn't want to play anymore?" Grandma asked. Thunder rumbled and lightning struck. When the flash lit up the yard and trees across the road, it reminded Luna of a movie she'd sneak-watched called *Living Dead* or something like that. It was in black and white but still really creepy. That's how everything looked, as if the lightning had to draw all the energy from the color of the world just to exist.

"They won't let me. I'm still not old enough." She swung her legs back and forth as her grandmother rocked.

"You're lucky then, because this is gonna be a good one. You can watch it with me."

"Where does the lightning come from?" she asked, wondering if her color-sucking theory was correct. If so, where did it start?

"High up in the clouds, I suppose. I try not to think too much about nature. It's been doing its thing since long before you and me came along, and it'll keep on long after we're gone. No need for me to make sense of it."

"Can I go look for it?"

"Look for what?" Grandma asked

"For the start? The beginning of it." She was already standing up, inching her way to the edge of the porch roof.

"I suppose, just don't stay out so long you get soaked. And be careful. If lightning hits you, that'll be then end of Miss Luna."

Luna only giggled. At seven, she knew nothing like that could ever happen. "Don't worry."

The sky looked so close she could almost touch it. Clouds hanging so low, that for just a split second, Luna wondered if Grandma had a point; could she get hit with lightning? She had an idea.

"Green light!" She called up to the clouds. Thunder rumbled as if the sky heard her call, knew the game, and began to play. Shortly afterward, a bolt of light lit up the night. Only, this time, Luna didn't see the trees or the house. She looked up and she saw them.

In the sky, scattered behind the clouds, the dark shadows of hundreds of spiders appeared. Or maybe jelly fish? There was no time to count their legs. Another burst of light confirmed what she'd seen and the lasting image of the creatures burned into her eyelids, only in negative, so the creatures glowed. The horror of knowing these things were there, possibly moving toward her in the darkness, until the flash of lightning stopped them—just like the game—was too much. She dared not stand outside watching for fear the next flash, or the one after that, might show the invaders ready to drop on her head. The cool summer rain became tangible tendrils that brushed against her, sending shivers and goosebumps up and down her body. She let out a yip and ran back to the porch.

In the safety of her grandmother's arms, it was okay to break down. Grandma let her sob and shake without asking any questions. The old woman simply rocked and soothed. Only after Luna's tears subsided and her shivers died away did her grandma dare ask what frightened her so.

"Sky spiders."

"My goodness! That is a scary thing. Show me," Grandma said.

"They hide in the daytime. You can only see them when the lightning sucks up all the color."

Grandma nodded. "That's very clever of them. Maybe we should go inside?"

Luna thought that was a good idea. Only, what if, while she was inside, not watching, they snuck closer? She wriggled out of her grandmother's arms and ran back into the rain. She looked up at the sky, and held a hand out palm up.

"Red light! I mean it!" There. Now they were frozen. She could rest.

Only, she didn't rest. Not that night or any other night filled with thunder and lightning. She needed to know if they were following the rules of the game or if, in her absence, they were coming closer. But she was too frightened to check, for one thing. For two, how was she supposed to know when it would storm next?

Grandpa bought a game system for the older kids, so the next time they all had a weekend sleepover, no one had time for outdoor games. Luna watched as her twelve-year-old cousin, Tiffany, played as a frog trying to cross a busy road. She grew bored as Trevor, Tiffany's twin, and Dylan, the next-door neighbor boy, fought over whose turn it was to eat pellets in a maze while fleeing ghosts. It wasn't until they put in a different game—a game with aliens that looked like spiders coming down from the sky, getting closer and closer—that she became suddenly interested.

"That's the spiders!" She jumped off the couch and shook Trevor's shoulder. He elbowed her.

"Hey, Jerk-O, you made me lose a guy!"

"But it's them! The spiders I saw in the sky," Luna insisted.

"She's crazy. She sees things," Tiffany assured Dylan. "Grandma! Luna's bugging us."

"Am not!"

"Luna!" Grandma shouted from the kitchen. "Come in here. I have something special for you."

A dark blue backpack covered in sparkly silver stars sat on the table. Inside, a matching journal, purple glitter pen, binoculars, and something called *The Farmer's Almanac 1986*. Grandma explained the kit for her space research. The almanac would help her to know when to expect rain and the notebook was for recording her observations. The rest of the summer, Luna and Grandma marked the days the almanac predicted storms and Luna made important observations. The sky spiders, in her professional estimate, were inching closer—just like players in the game. She always remembered to shout "red light!" before going back in the house.

On Luna's twelfth birthday, her grandmother gave her a telescope and a box of blank journals. Luna's closet was filled with her observations via journal entries, and now that she was older, she no longer used the almanac as she had the weather channel.

"Grandma, what are people who look through telescopes called? That's what I want to be when I grow up," she announced proudly.

"Astronomers, I think."

"Oh, I don't know if our Chipmunk means astronomer, Ma," her dad interrupted. "More like Astrologer—always seeing creatures and things in the night sky." He laughed.

"Don't call me Chipmunk, Dad. I don't like it anymore."

"Well, you look more like a chipmunk now, with those baby fat cheeks and your chubby little bumper!" Grandpa gave her backside a swat.

"Oh, ignore them," her mother added. "They're just picking on you."

"That's right," Grandpa said. "You wanna know a secret, Chipmunk? When boys pick on you, it means they like you!"

Luna didn't like those kinds of boys, and she didn't want them to like her. And she did not want to be called Chipmunk anymore, either.

"Red light," she said.

"What's that?" Grandpa asked.

"It means she wants you to stop," Grandma answered for her. "She asked you both not to call her Chipmunk anymore. And, Luna, I think you'll make a wonderful astronomer. You already know a lot about stars and planets. You can be anything you want!"

Her dad laughed again. "I don't know, Mom. There's a lot of math involved. Have you seen her report card lately?"

"Stop, Michael," her mother touched his arm. "It's not her fault. Math is just harder for girls."

"Ugh," Luna sighed. "Can we have some cake now?"

That night, Luna scanned the sky with her telescope, hoping to catch a glimpse of the creatures, who, in the last six years, steadily kept getting closer. No matter what her mom or dad thought, she did know math and she could understand numbers when it came to space. For instance, she knew the closest galaxy to the Milky Way was 25,000 light years away. She knew that meant if the things she saw in the sky were coming from that galaxy, it would take them 25,000 years to arrive...if they could travel at the speed of light. For people of Earth, using the fastest space ship available, it would take 749,000,000 years to travel to that other galaxy. For the sky spiders to be visibly getting closer every time she saw them, they had to be traveling much, much faster than the speed of light. Now that she had the telescope, she was hoping to be able to estimate how fast the things were going.

The telescope—and all the upgraded versions that came after it, did little to help as the only time the sky spiders revealed themselves was during a lightning strike. When lightning hit, turning the world into a photographic negative, then and only then, could she see the invaders. But she didn't need a telescope to see they were getting closer. The spiders were now the size of octopi.

As she grew, Luna's life became a series of red light/green light moments. Astronomy gave way to an obsession with meteorology. Journals filled with calculations, weather notes, and sketches of eldritch creatures filled her bedroom. The cruelty of puberty coupled with the stress of her self-assigned research added weight to her petite frame. Red light interactions overshadowed the green.

"Weather girls are supposed to be hot; you'll just cover up the whole map!" some stupid jock sneered.

"Red light. Meteorologists are not weather girls."

She tried to explain her frustration to her mother. "Oh, honey, you know how they are. Boys will be boys. You just have to ignore them."

Working the afternoon shifts at the local convenience store in order to save up for college introduced her to an array of humanity that sometimes made her hope her theories were right. A mass of monstrous creatures, if she was correct, headed this way, would reach Earth within her lifetime.

"A pack of smokes and a couple scratch-offs. Hey now, you might be running that register, but you sure ain't running anywhere else, are ya?"

"That's a red light. Eleven dollars and thirty-eight cents, sir."

"Aw, come on; you need to lighten up! Smile once in a while."

"Have a great day, sir."

Luna often wondered if there were other girls in other parts of the world who could see the things she did. When it stormed for them, were they, too, giving the creatures the green light to come on in? Maybe their lives were otherwise filled with red lights. Maybe the only time they found solace was in the colorless world that existed in the split-second blaze that showed them the end of the tunnel. Not a light at the end, but creatures that were, admittedly, terrifying, amorphous things with writhing appendages that must measure miles in length. Unfathomable beings racing onward to bring an end to being told to smile and to just ignore, stop trying, to assimilate to what others expect of you.

"I wish I could see what you see out there," her grandmother told her one late summer night before Luna's senior year of college.

Grandma mostly sat on the rocker watching the world go by. Grandpa was gone, and the kids were all grown and moved away. No one played games in the yard or caught jars of lightning bugs anymore. There was no one asking her for breakfast, no fancy birthday presents to wrap—just money-stuffed cards sent out and unanswered.

"They're getting closer, Gram. I don't think you'd want to see them." Luna stood, hands on hips, watching the dark clouds gather beneath the light of a full moon.

"Can't be nothing worse than what I see on the news every day. We may not look scary like your sky spiders, but we're certainly not any less terrifying. Who knows? By the time your space monsters arrive, there might not be anything left for them to destroy."

Luna shambled over to the rocker and plopped down beside her grandmother. She leaned over and rested her head on the woman's shoulder. A shoulder that used to be fleshy and full—her childhood solace—had been eroded by time to wrinkled tissue-paper skin and bone. Still, she breathed in the familiar scent of her grandmother.

"You know you're my green light, Gram. You always will be."

Grandma lifted her arm and pulled Luna in, so her head rested on her grandmother's withered breast. "You're too good for this world, Luna Samson. I hope when I'm gone, and you look up there, you see a big old green light. Then you'll know that's me watching over you, sending all my love."

"Just promise me I won't have to wait until a storm comes along to see it, Gram."

Grandma hugged her. "That's a green light for sure, Luna."

Living to the age of ninety-eight was a feat in and of itself, and her Gram was getting tired. She'd only hoped her best friend would hold on for one more day. A total solar eclipse was a sight to be seen for sure, but Luna knew that the heat of mid-August coupled with the artificial cool spot from the moon's shadow could create quite an electrical storm. She wanted her grandmother to be there on the day Luna calculated the beings would arrive.

They were close—oh, so very close—and the addition of the eclipse storm would likely be all they needed to touch down. A Lovecraftian apocalypse seemed the proper end for a civilization that strayed so far from humanity, they no longer had the right to call themselves by that name. It was time. No more red lights.

"Gram, can I wheel you out to the porch and help you on the glider?" Luna remembered the time she thought her grandmother couldn't possibly get any thinner, but here she was, a skeleton draped in a sheet of flesh. Worn down by years of living, of sorrows, and joys.

"You gonna look for your spiders today?" the old woman asked, her voice parched not by thirst but years.

"I might."

"You think it might storm? Never heard of that during an eclipse."

"I think there's a pretty good chance of it, yes. You comfortable? Think you can stay awake?" Grandma looked so very frail to Luna. The time ticked away until the eclipse suddenly seemed more like a death-watch counting down the last moments of her grandmother's life. Luna's throat spasmed and her eyes burned with the coming tears.

"Oh, I think I can manage a few more minutes."

"I love you, Gram." It was the last thing she said. Thunder rumbled in the distance as if heralding some celestial phenomenon. The moon's shadow rolled across Luna's world, covering her and her grandmother.

Lightning fought against the darkness by lighting up the strange mid-day night. What little color remained during the eclipse washed away entirely in a crack of electricity. There they were, lower now than the clouds. If their multitude of limbs weren't splayed out, touching each other to form an astrological web beaded with amoebic shaped bodies that undulated and throbbed with an alien lifeforce, then they surely would reach ground.

"Grandma! They're here! They—"

Her grandmother slumped over on the bench. Luna didn't need to look any closer. She knew Grandma was gone, but they weren't. They were here, it was almost as if they'd arrived to take her grandmother away. Luna's chest ached. The moon slid past the midline of the sun and slowly revealed the brightness once again. There wasn't much time left.

There was no reason to fight anymore. In all the time she'd watched this horde of horrors approach, she'd realized that no matter what they wanted, she wouldn't fight it. She'd welcome the change, the possible annihilation of her own species. It didn't matter. It was time. No more red lights.

She reached up to the sky as the final bolt of shadow lightning struck.

"Green light," she said, and touched oblivion.

Golden Hour
By Kathryn E. McGee

The Museum of Manifestations was an explosion of color, the lobby decorated with purple walls, pink chandeliers, and shiny blue floors. Groups posed for photos on a plush green divan, a spangled orange sign above demanding, *Live your most colorful life.*

"Rex would have hated this place," Liv said. She and her friend, Bethany, took in the scene from beneath the rainbow archway that framed the entry.

Bethany nodded. "It would have been way too fun for his lame ass."

Liv winced at Bethany's harsh tone though she silently agreed. Rex had been difficult, always saying he hated bright colors, wanting everything to be black, white, or gray. He'd even insisted on getting married in the dead of winter so the landscape would be smothered in snow.

She adjusted the camera that hung around her neck. Visiting a selfie museum was probably a strange way to spend the one-year anniversary of Rex's death, but she wasn't sure what else she *should* be doing. Having recently launched her own photography business, she felt a rush of excitement thinking about all the photo ops. This location was supposed to be different: A photographer's paradise with professionally lit, color-specific rooms that varied with each visitor, so no two photos turned out the same.

In the lobby, employees handed out waivers, asking everyone to sign. Liv flipped through the lengthy document, which covered so many possibilities. Slip-and-fall accidents. Headaches and seizures. A trauma advisory if the museum amplified any "intense or violent thoughts."

"Yikes. This is a lot," Liv said. "Should we be worried?"

"Just sign it, whatever," Bethany said. "You want to take photos for that contest, right?"

Liv nodded, floating her pen above the signature line. Bethany had always been supportive of her photography. Today the museum was having a contest for the best photos to be reposted to their social media, which had *millions* of followers. If Liv's shots got reposted, her fledgling business could get a lot of engagement.

"Fine." Liv shrugged like it was no big deal and signed the waiver.

When they got to the front of the line, they handed in their forms.

"Great, now we just need a pinprick," the woman at the front desk said. Her nametag read, *Hi, my name is Allison and I love unicorns.* She held up a needle and smiled.

"What?" Liv said, "why do you need blood?"

"To tailor your museum experience using our proprietary Selfie-3000 technology, which enables room customization. It's what makes the manifestation possible."

"I don't know..." Liv eyed the needle. Something tugged at her gut. "Kinda gives me the creeps."

"Don't worry," the woman said, "it'll just be a tiny prick. You'll barely feel a thing."

"Fuck it," Bethany said. "Tickets are non-refundable, right?"

"Right. I just... have a weird feeling. I'm not sure I *want* this."

"I think what you *need* is to take some photos." Bethany extended her hand forward. The woman pricked her finger and collected a drop of blood onto a slide. She then placed a plastic film on top of the blood, sealing it in, and set the specimen on a tray. Bethany looked at Liv, eyebrows raised. *Your move.*

It had always been difficult to argue with Bethany, so Liv held out her finger, too. Soon, her blood had been collected, her slide placed on the tray beside Bethany's, and the tray swept away on a conveyor belt—luggage at the airport, disappearing.

The room was full dark.

"Can you see anything?" Liv whispered.

"Not yet," Bethany said. "Just give it a sec, *relax.*"

"Okay," Liv said though she was breathing hard already. It was a relief when strings of twinkle lights turned on above their heads and the room's black floor, black walls, and black ceiling appeared, the outline of a man at the center.

Liv swallowed hard, unable to avoid thinking of Rex. He had been tall like this guy, with broad shoulders. *Imposing.* The lights grew even brighter, and the man's face swam into view. *He has one of those familiar faces,* Liv thought, *like he could be anyone.* She pictured Rex again but pushed the image from her mind. There was no reason to think about him right now. She didn't *want* to think about him.

"Welcome to the Museum of Manifestations," the man said, "where we use color to reflect your very thoughts and feelings. You will journey through seven rooms decorated in every rainbow hue. The rooms will become increasingly responsive, tailor-made. Once you've left a room, please be aware the door will lock behind. You must continue forward, not backward, but—such is life, right? No takebacks. Should you become separated from your party, please don't be alarmed. You'll come together again or find them after in the lobby. The museum offers many paths, infinite possibilities... and, of course, myriad photo opportunities."

"Let's try not to get separated," Liv whispered.

"Right," Bethany said. "You need me to model for photos."

Liv nodded. "That's the plan."

"Finally, if you plan to enter the photography contest," the man said, "please post your photos by day's end and tag us. Our team will repost the best pictures on our socials." The twinkle lights grew even brighter. Doors lined every wall. The man did a dramatic spin. "You may choose a room."

Bethany selected a door; Liv followed her through.

Yellow covered every surface, lemony shades adorning the walls and floor, as well as the exhibits. Hidden projectors cast changing images, so the space felt as though it was in motion, calibrating and re-calibrating, *feeling* them walk through. The lights brightened in some areas, dimmed in others. The air warmed and cooled.

Photo opportunities were everywhere. Liv and Bethany passed a mountable canary sculpture, a giant martini glass lit with honey-colored lights, a sunken conversation pit with a pool of gold disco balls, and a wagon of fake bananas you could push along a yellow brick road. A sign on the wall commanded, "Smile often!" beside a spray of sunflowers.

There were other people in the room already posing for photos, but the martini glass was available, so Liv suggested they start there. Bethany climbed up, sat on a plush seat within the glass and reclined with her legs over the lip. She had long, black curly hair and wore a flowy white dress, her skirt forming an arc over the curved edge. The lighting was flawless, configured for photography.

"It looks great!" Liv said.

After snapping a few photos, she noticed another installation that seemed to have suddenly appeared in the back of the room—or maybe she'd just missed it before. Walking over, they found a grove of fake lemon trees.

Bethany strode in front of her, under the canopy, standing at the center, yellow all around. The trees were multiplying. *How is this possible?* Liv blinked a few times then raised up her camera, watching through her viewfinder. She didn't want to miss the moment and took several pictures of Bethany, pausing only when she heard a sound like an exhalation.

She looked down. One of the lemons had fallen loose from a tree and rolled across the floor toward her feet. The lemon tapped her shoe. She kicked it away, shocked by sudden and intense déjà vu.

There was no way the museum could know about the day she'd found Rex drowned, but maybe somehow it *did*. She had rushed outside to find his body floating in the pool—it was already too late— and a single lemon had dropped from a tree, rolling toward her through bloody concrete, smeared red when it tapped her shoe.

"You okay?" Bethany said.

Liv tried to snap out of it, refocusing on the yellow room. "Yeah, I was just... It's nothing." She was out of breath.

"You were thinking about him, weren't you?" Bethany walked over, placed one hand on each of Liv's shoulders. "What do we say when the intrusive thoughts come?"

"He isn't here anymore. I am a new person now," Liv said.

"That's good." Bethany nodded.

Liv turned away. "Let's maybe just move on?"

"You're the boss," Bethany said, and chose the next door.

The green room was a field of tall grasses rich in hues of emerald and forest. An island at the center sloped upward toward a park with celery-colored swings. A wall sign shouted, "Live your truth," in lime. There were no other people in sight. Liv and Bethany meandered through the high stalks of grass, which must have been crafted with ultra-thin plastic. The grass felt almost real, brushing their calves and thighs, lighting up, shimmering from contact.

"It's responding to us," Liv said.

Bethany nodded. "And you know what? This really reminds me of that one field."

Liv walked, more slowly now. "I was thinking the same thing. This is... *freaky*." She didn't want to think about Rex, but she couldn't stop the flood of memories.

A few months before he died, the three of them had driven to a party for one of Rex's friends. Liv convinced Bethany to come along since Rex always ditched her at events and she didn't like to be alone. Rex and Bethany were arguing in the car as they often did and Liv ignored them, staring out the window. That's how she spotted the field: overgrown and vividly green, bordered by a broken-down picket fence. *So picturesque.* The lighting and time of day were right: six o'clock, the sun just starting to set. *Golden Hour.*

"Can we stop? I want to take a few shots," she had said.

"Oh my god, yes," Bethany said. "That field is *perfect.*"

Rex shook his head. "We're running late."

"I'll just be a few minutes. The light is great."

"What are you going to do with some random photos of a field?" Rex said. "We should have been there *twenty minutes* ago."

"Your wife is brilliant," Bethany said. "She's going to have her own gallery soon."

"Sounds expensive." Rex kept driving.

"Her dreams matter a lot more than some party," Bethany said.

Rex's face got all screwed up. "Fine." He pulled the car over, tires squealing. "Take your damn photos."

Liv and Bethany walked into the grasses, finding a spot where Bethany was immersed, the setting sun casting a warm glow. Her long skirt caught the wind and when she looked down to steady the fabric, Liv snapped the photo. Everything was in motion, *exquisite.*

After, Bethany looked at Liv's screen. "Incredible photo. You're so talented."

"Come on!" Rex shouted, standing beside the open car door.

"You've got to see Liv's picture," Bethany said to Rex. "Your wife is really—

"Jesus, we're late already," Rex said.

"You're a dick," Bethany said.

Shit. Liv held her breath. She hated it when they fought. Bethany always seemed unphased—like she enjoyed it—but it put Rex on edge. Whenever they went at it, Liv disliked them both, couldn't help imagining them as a creature with two heads and snapping mouths that screamed itself to death.

Liv wished Bethany would chill and she wished Rex would be kind the way he was on morning of their wedding when he'd held her close. *You are my queen.*

Rex drove away from the field in a huff and at the party did his usual thing—ignored her and got lost talking to his friends. Liv and Bethany sat on a bench sipping white wine. When the sun set, their bench fell into shadow in a dark part of the yard with no lights.

There was a swing set on the grass in front of them. A woman in a lime green dress walked over and sat on one of the swings. Rex walked toward her, not realizing Liv and Bethany watched him from the shadows. He stood beside the swing set, leaning against one of the support poles. The woman's hands were raised, gripping the swing chains. One of Rex's fingers grazed her wrist, sliding back and forth. It was not his first time touching her.

"What the fuck," Bethany whispered but Liv couldn't speak. She felt the world shake up inside her and explode. *Hadn't she known?* Rex hadn't paid her much attention—not in a long time. Liv stared at that lime green dress. He'd always told her she looked best when she wore black, that bright colors were obnoxious. He didn't seem to mind color now, did he? Rex looked around, then reached out and helped the woman off the swing, following her behind the slide where it spiraled around into a shadowy grove of trees.

In the green room, Liv gritted her teeth.

"You get the shot?" Bethany said, sitting on one of the swings, sliding her hands down the swing chains. She worked her feet back, kicking off.

Liv's hands trembled. She took a few more photos, telling herself, *I am a new person now, Rex is dead, he doesn't matter.* She steadied the camera and nodded. "I've got what I need."

The purple room bloomed with lilac and iris and lavender; it was vibrant and *alive* with huge vases of flowers surrounding a raised platform with an elaborate, metallic purple chair. *A throne.* Lights centered there cast in shades of fuchsia and walls were hung with thick velvet draperies. A pair of six-foot candelabras with huge tapers burned steadily, dripping purple wax. Something about the room made Liv unsteady, disconnected from reality. Maybe it was the flickering light, the suffocating floral scent, or the looming height of the throne.

"This might be my favorite room so far," Bethany said.

Liv nodded. "It's nice."

Bethany mounted the throne, her white dress sweeping the floor.

She gave a few poses, first sitting tall, hands cupping the ends of the armrests, then turning to the side, legs crossed, heels in frame. Liv heard a humming sound, felt a vibration in the air while she took the photos. She paused, noting the flowers seemed to be in motion, changing, *responding*.

"Do you feel that?"

"Feel what?"

"Nothing."

When they were done, Bethany insisted Liv pose, too, since she was wearing a purple dress to match the room. Liv didn't want to. She didn't like to be in front of the camera. But Bethany insisted, so Liv sat on the throne, reminding herself, she was a queen.

"Alright," Bethany said, "One, two, three..."

A man walked in front of Bethany, blocking the camera. A shadowy figure. At first Liv thought of the man from the black room, but then the figure was gone. Bethany didn't seem to notice. Maybe Liv hadn't seen anything. A trick of the light.

Liv adjusted her skirt, crossed her ankles, the hem grazing the floor.

She'd found the purple dress in the window of a boutique, long and tiered, fitted at the bodice with wide, flowy sleeves. She wore it out to dinner with Rex, pairing it with a gold lace wrap, and felt *amazing*. She hoped Rex would notice. After seeing him with the woman in green, she'd realized there was no point in sticking with black tops and jeans; it had been a miscalculation to dress so drably.

He didn't mention her purple dress, though. Didn't even notice. He'd gotten a promotion at work—that's why he was distracted at the table, telling her all about the job over appetizers. Liv said she was proud of him. She squeezed his hand. She smiled.

"You're amazing, Rex."

He cocked his head to the side. "You say that like you're surprised."

"I'm just so happy for you. For *us*."

He motioned for the waiter to refill his wine glass.

In the purple room, Bethany yelled, "Smile!" and Liv did—she tried.

She climbed down from the throne. Behind it, an oversized bathroom installation materialized. Huge purple floor tiles. A massive plum-colored clawfoot tub. A damask pattern on the walls that looked like real wallpaper though it shifted. Even the floor seemed to be in motion. Liv felt dizzy and steadied herself on a vase of wild indigo. Bethany seemed unfazed.

"You okay?" She sounded distant, faraway.

"Sure." Liv righted herself. She just needed to get used to the strange proportions, the movement, to blink a few times, to *breathe*.

Bethany climbed into the purple tub.

Liv seethed.

That night after the dinner, after being ignored, Liv had filled the bathtub, leaving Rex wine-drunk and passed out on the sofa. *Don't wait up for me.* She turned on the water as hot as she could stand and got in, dress and all, and cried wondering what she'd done wrong.

Now, in the purple room, Bethany posed, heels over the side of the tub, a sultry half-smile on her face. *Like she's mocking me.* Liv shook that idea away. No one was more supportive than Bethany.

"This good?" Bethany rearranged her heels and winked.

I am a new person now, Liv reminded herself. The past was done and over and could not be changed. Would she change it, anyway? Things had been bad with Rex, especially toward the end. Bethany had helped her rise from the ashes, flap her wings, and delve into her creativity. Her photography business was *happening*, it was building up—something she had always wanted. She hated to even think this but... where would she be if Rex had lived?

Bethany sank lower in the tub.

The shadow-figure returned. He was behind Bethany—*in the tub with her.*

"Who is that?" Liv's heart raced out of control. She squeezed her eyes shut and gripped the wall, steadying herself. She heard a voice, a man's voice in the wall, murmuring, but by then Bethany was out of the tub standing beside her, asking if they should do the slides next.

"Sure, I'll be right there," Liv said.

Bethany ran off ahead.

Liv took a moment, waiting for the room to steady.

In the back of the room, a pair of purple slides mirrored each other, spiraling around, and exiting through the floor.

"I'm down here!" Bethany's voice funneled up through one of the slides.

"Coming," Liv said. She didn't like the feeling of being alone.

Following Bethany's voice, she mounted one of the ladders. The inside of the tube was lit with skinny LED lights, turning it into a twisty disco.

She secured her camera strap and pushed off, counting the revolutions while she slid. One time around. Two times. Three. No end in sight. Not yet. Not until the slide turned again and there was light ahead. Warm light.

The warmth melted into orange. Liv landed crouched on the floor and slowly stood, taking in the shades of papaya and tangerine and umber. The colors made her chest heavy; she wanted to crawl out of her body but couldn't.

"Bethany?" Hadn't she heard Bethany's voice in the slide? Her friend wasn't in the room, though. No one else was here. How would she take photos? She'd be stuck with stupid selfies. She really didn't want *those.*

Walking deeper into the orange room, she observed how the space was simple compared to the others, an empty room centered on a big orange pyramid at one end. Projections on the walls formed a pattern of triangles.

The wall projections began to spin. Tiles on the floor tilted side-to-side like a funhouse ride. Liv felt light-headed, as if she might faint. She crouched down. The motion persisted. She wished Bethany was there to tell her what to do.

She crawled toward the pyramid.

"Liv." It was Bethany's voice! Where was she? "Liv." Her voice again. Had it come from the walls? The floor rocked harder. The triangles spun.

"Where are you?" Liv said. "I want to leave!"

She curled into a ball and hoped the motion would end. When it finally did, the walls lit up with the glow of a television monitor. A memory replayed on the wall screen.

She watched herself on the morning of her wedding. Snow fell outside the dressing room, drowning the world in white. Bethany had just helped her get into her gown. Liv took one look at herself in the mirror and began to cry. She turned away from her reflection, staring at the burnt-orange wall of the bridal room, as if it might open a door for her escape. She hadn't slept at all the night before, doubt clawing into her mind. Rex's moods had been so bad lately. Would he be this way their entire lives? Everyone was already dressed and ready at the church. Everyone but her. He was expecting her to marry him. It was too late to say no.

Bethany handed her a tissue and said, "You don't have to get married."

"What?" That was bold, even for Bethany.

"You aren't feeling it, are you?"

"I'm just nervous. Why do I feel this way?"

Bethany sighed. "What you want—what you *think* you want—is not always what you need. It doesn't have to be *him*."

Liv swallowed hard, the words sinking in. "I can't marry him," she said, meeting Bethany's eyes.

Rex burst into the room.

"The fuck?" Bethany said.

"You're not supposed to see me!" Liv shrieked.

"Well..." He cast a glance at Bethany. "I couldn't wait." He held Liv close, looking her in the eye, touching her face. "I know how lucky I am to be with you." He kissed her forehead. "You, Liv, are my *queen*."

When he left the room, Liv looked at Bethany. Her voice shook. "I didn't mean it. I didn't mean I couldn't marry him. He really *is* what I need."

Bethany nodded, managing a smile. "Whatever you want, hon." When Bethany gave her toast at the wedding that night, it was so sincere that Liv wondered if the conversation that morning had ever even happened.

The wall screens in the orange room turned off, and the floor began moving again, *tilting*. Liv screamed and continued crawling. She was nearing the orange pyramid. The door out must be on the other side.

Now that she was closer, she could see the pyramid was not a pyramid. It was a cone, the kind the cops put out to mark evidence at a crime scene. They'd been placed surrounding the pool after Rex died, so someone could remember to photograph the lemon and the brick wall and the blood streaks. A door opened at the front of the massive cone and a man walked through wearing all black, arms outstretched. *Rex.*

"It's not you. It can't be you," Liv said.

"You left me," he said. "You left me to die."

She shook her head. "You were already dead." She ran past him, past the pyramid, until she found a door.

The blue room was filled with a swimming pool, ringed by a narrow walkway and brick planter. The walls were sapphire tile, the water milky cerulean. A sign over the diving board said, *No lifeguard on duty!* in navy lettering.

"Get me out of here!" Liv screamed.

Where was the next door? She stepped onto the walkway, the only way out, but it moved, revolving around the water. She crouched, tried not to fall.

Rex's voice called to her from the ceiling: "You left me to die."

Liv shook her head. "That's not how it happened."

Echoed in the waves of the water, in the slick of the tile, in the rough texture of the brick planter, the memory came.

Bethany had been over that day to grill burgers by the pool. Rex was supposed to be gone on a work trip, but his flight was cancelled, and he came home early while they were setting up the grill. Since the party with the green-dress-woman, Bethany hadn't bothered to hide her dislike for Rex and quickly picked a fight with him about something pertaining to grilling technique.

Tuning out the bad vibes, Liv decided to take pictures. It was the right time of day. She ran upstairs to grab her camera, figuring she'd get a few shots, maybe of the lemon tree, which was engorged with fruit. She found her camera on the shelf below her second-floor bedroom window. She looked outside.

Maybe she sensed it happening. Maybe that's why she'd looked.

Rex lay beside the brick planter, blood around him, his lower half in the pool. He must have slipped and fallen—hit his head. Red stained the concrete. He slid into the water.

Bethany stood nearby, watching him go under, holding a big grilling spatula in front of her like a sword.

Liv screamed and ran downstairs and into the backyard. "We've got to get him out of the water." She started to barrel forward when Bethany reached out, stopping her like a purse in a passenger seat.

"Do we?" Bethany said. "What do you actually want?"

"What?" Liv looked at Rex's body. Time—critical time—was passing.

"He's not a good person. He's been holding you back." Bethany put her arm down.

"No, no we have to *do* something. I'll call 9-1-1." Liv lifted her phone, started dialing.

Bethany swatted the phone to the concrete. "He *sucks,* Liv. Don't you know you're better without him? Can't you feel that much?"

A helicopter flew overhead, the loud humming of the propellers making it impossible to speak. Liv waited. When it passed, a lemon shook loose from a tree and rolled toward her, tapping her foot. *I need to do something.* The lemon was smeared in blood.

There was a splash. Rex spasmed in the water.

"We can still save him," Liv whispered.

"He's already gone, I'm sure." Bethany put a hand on Liv's shoulder. "Look at the colors, at the *light.*"

It was six o'clock. The sun made the backyard glow—spectacularly gold, the composition divine. The way Rex's body floated at an angle with the single lemon on the concrete beside the streak of red, the way the sunlight reflected—it was magically composed, *glittering.*

"Take the photo." Bethany lifted the camera for her.

"I can't," Liv said, but took the camera, held it to her eye.

She lined up the body in the viewfinder, his feet at one end and the bloodied brick wall and lemon at the other, a perfect diagonal, the pool water *so blue.* She took the picture.

Liv snapped out of the memory.

The blue room hummed and hummed. *I shouldn't have done that. I shouldn't have...*

A man's body floated to the surface of the pool, water rippling outward in waves of cerulean and indigo. Liv gasped. *No, no, no.* The body glided toward the lip of the pool, pushing up and out of the water. He turned to face Liv with milky blue liquid oozing off him, dripping onto the concrete while he stood. *Rex.*

"You're dead." Liv shook her head.

"You say that like you're surprised." He walked toward her.

"It was Bethany's fault." Her voice cracked.

"It's like you killed me yourself." His voice erupted from the water and the walls, sounded off in her head. He came at her. "You killed me!"

"You didn't love me." She lifted her camera like a weapon, took a photo to distract him with the flash. The light exploded.

Rex shrieked and collapsed onto the walkway. His neck pulsated, bulging outward. Something grew there, ballooning, breaking the skin. The black, curly hair of a second head emerged, followed by a forehead, cheeks, and a chin. The features were obscured by flimsy tissue but soon white teeth bit through the caul, spitting the film aside. The mouth and nose came into view with full lips and a sharp jawline, erupting with a beastly squeal. *Bethany.* The creature twitched and writhed, bucking on all fours while the two heads snapped into place.

The Bethany head looked at Liv, smiling. "Let's kill him. Bash his head."

"Get that crazy bitch away from me," the Rex head shouted. "She never wanted us to be happy. I loved you, Liv. She's the one who fucked with *your head.*"

"Shut up," Liv said.

"Don't listen to him," Bethany spat. "He's love-bombing you, but his attention will go away. I'm your true *friend.*"

The creature scuttled toward Liv. The humming intensified.

Liv backed away but couldn't find any doors out of the room, just an endless revolving pathway around the pool.

"You left me to die!" Rex screeched.

"You didn't deserve to live." Bethany bit a chunk out of Rex's cheek, spat it away. He squealed while blood oozed down to his chin.

"Stop." Liv cupped her hands over her ears. She crouched down and from the planter picked up a loose brick. She just needed them to stop.

The creature came closer.

She felt dizzy, a sense of unreality, and raised the brick high.

Liv brought the brick down hard on Rex's temple, mashing the center of his skull into a vertical canoe of blood.

"Yes!" Bethany squealed, clapping. "Now take a photo!"

Liv brought the brick down hard again, on Bethany this time. Her brow exploded. Gore matting her curly hair.

The two heads bellowed in one voice, the mashed faces spurting and flopping on loose necks, jaws wagging, eyes bulging.

"We just want to be with you, Liv," the two broken mouths said in unison. The beast shambled toward her. "We're your lover. We're your friend. You're nothing without us!"

The blue room hummed. Liv felt its vibration run through her. She tightened her grip on the brick. She brought it down on the injured heads, one and then the other, harder this time. She brought it down again and again and again.

Brick to flesh. Flesh to meat.

The room turned red. The floor was red and the pool was red and the walls and the ceiling were red, red, red. Liv smiled, feeling elated, feeling *free.* The room was humming so loudly now, vibrations flowing all through her body while her face was covered in tears, happy tears. She felt a euphoric rush of energy. The pulpy, two-headed body slid into the crimson pool of water, a final splash before sinking. Liv hummed and twirled. Maybe there was something in the air.

A door appeared.

Bright with snow, the white room was hung with silvery fluff and dotted with faux ice sculptures rendered in Lucite, lining an aisle flanked by pews. A gazebo stood at the far end. The humming continued, softer now, the vibration a gentle embrace. *You are my queen.*

Liv sashayed down the aisle, blood from her dress rose-petaling the snow. She cradled the brick, imagining a bouquet. When she reached the gazebo, she took out her phone, framing a selfie, the white aisle extending behind.

Look at the colors, at the light.

She took the picture, added a snowflake filter, and uploaded it right away, tagging the Museum of Manifestations in her post.

The lobby greeted her with rainbow colors and a rush of disco music, pink chandeliers twinkling with soft yellow lights. People turned to look, raising eyebrows, but Liv barely noticed. She was buzzing, alive with energy. She felt the pulse of the rooms—even out here, building up to something—and followed it toward the rainbow sculpture where it felt the strongest. A heart pumping the room with energy.

She spotted Bethany—alive and walking toward her across the lobby. *No, no.* Liv turned away, backing up against the fluffy cloud at the base of the rainbow.

She'd already dealt with Bethany.

But her friend was upon her, tapping her shoulder. "Sucks we got separated." She walked around to face Liv. "Shit. Is that blood? Are you—"

"I feel great." Liv said, realizing she still held the brick in her hand. It felt heavy and rough against her smooth fingers.

"Let's get out of here," Bethany said. "I'm driving us home."

"No," Liv said.

"What the fuck?"

Liv felt the thrum of the rainbow. "Look at the colors."

Bethany turned to look.

"Look at the light." Liv lifted the brick, then brought it down hard on Bethany's head.

There was a splash of red. She felt the lobby contract. Then an exhalation.

A final shudder. *Release.*

Liv dropped the brick. Passing under the rainbow and out the doors, she felt all her muscles relax at once. Golden sunlight bathed her face. The air was fresh, the landscape radiant with olive grasses and amethyst flowers that waved in the gentle breeze. Monarch butterflies flew past, and Liv imagined she was one of them, extending her arms outward, flapping colorful wings.

THE DYER AND THE DRESSMAKERS
BY BINDIA PERSAUD

We had begun to despair of a dyer ever again appearing among us. Once there were three, serving twice as many dressmakers. Now, there is only Berta, and she has been old since my girlhood. She is blear-eyed and palsied, and her powers have almost deserted her. Jacquetta is a great talker, and she has cleverly steered the tastes of our patrons in a direction that shrouds Berta's decline. For many seasons now, the ladies of the court have attired themselves in gowns of filmy white, set off with a sash or hat ribbon in some soft vernal shade—primrose, blush, the palest of azures. Things might have gone on like this for some time, were it not for the envoy.

She was a pallid young woman who had come before the Duchess to negotiate a trade agreement. The first goods she displayed were poor and undistinguished, so no one was prepared for what she brought out next. Some audibly gasped when she unfurled the mantilla; the Duchess, schooled in self-mastery, merely pursed her lips and nodded.

I did not witness this, of course. What I know, I gleaned through snatches of gossip overheard at dress fittings. Naturally, I had to see the mantilla for myself. I positioned myself at a high window just as the Duchess was making her way to church. Even from that distance, I could see it was no commonplace thing. It seemed almost alive, a tangle of leaves and roses gracing the Duchess's slender shoulders. The Duchess treated it with no particular reverence; as she walked, it slipped into the crook of her arm and she left it there. Still, I knew our time had come. We would be stripped of the Duchess's favor and thrust out into the world.

I did not tell the others this. What purpose would it have served? I left Jacquetta to her chatter and Berta to her drooling and snuffling. The only one who I considered taking into my confidence was Susanna, but she was preoccupied with her daughter. Theodora was so named because her mother had been getting on in years when she bore her. We had searched her, as dressmakers search all their daughters, when she came squalling into the world, but she had lacked the distinguishing marks. Now, at thirteen, she had that peculiar mix of sullenness and gaiety that characterizes girls awaiting their first blood.

She had been told what to expect when her flowers arrived, and we were on hand with clean rags and cold compresses when the day came. Her mother fussed and made much of her, but she was peevish, almost tearful. "Mama, it hurts," she mewled.

"It's natural. It will pass."

She sat up. "It doesn't hurt there. It hurts here."

She raised her arm. Nestled in the tender hollow of her armpit was a translucent polyp the size of an acorn.

I forgot how to breathe for a moment. I wasn't the only one. Elation, tinged with fear, rendered us immobile. Long minutes passed, and Theodora cried in earnest. Ultimately, Berta had to prod us into action. She bid us fetch a length of unbleached muslin and lay it on the floor. Theodora was directed to stand over it, arm raised. Before she could protest, Berta reached out and pinched the protuberance between her skinny fingers. Theodora gave a whinny as a drop of fluid leaked from the polyp. It was as colorless as water, but when it touched the cloth it spread and bloomed into a rich carnelian red. Theodora was still sniffling, but the sight startled her into laughter. It was contagious, as a child's mirth can be. Berta flashed her gummy smile while the rest of us collapsed into giggles. When we had collected ourselves, I gathered up the material and set to work.

The dress I made was simplicity itself, without frills, without an edging of lace, without so much as an extraneous button. When I had finished, I packed it in a box and slipped our monogrammed card in with it. At first light, we sent it off to the Duchess.

Our fortunes didn't change right away. Theodora's earliest efforts yielded up strong, true colors that were perhaps too much for some. Many were loath to give up their old gowns. Even so, one would behold, in a sea of white, a lady clad in zaffre blue or canary yellow, like an exotic bird among a flock of swans.

We didn't tell Theodora that her work had not found universal favor. We petted and praised her; the first dyer in a generation, how could we not? Still, she discerned the truth. When the girl assigned to clean our rooms stretched upwards to dust the mantelpiece, she revealed a flash of scarlet underskirt. Theodora said nothing, but she looked stricken. Of course, it is established practice for mistresses to pass clothing on to their maids, but Theodora's work was not meant to serve as a drudge's petticoat. Quietly, she asked me for cloth, armfuls of it, as much as I could supply. When she had it, she retreated to her chamber and locked the door.

She stayed sequestered for some time. Susanna was concerned; if we had not held her back, she would have shouted and banged on the door. When Theodora finally emerged, she was limp and exhausted, but a faint smile of triumph played upon her lips. When we entered the room, we saw the heaps of fabric had been transfigured. The new dyes were simultaneously richer and subtler. Harmonious shades blended together, or, conversely, contrasting hues warred with each other. Each new shade was married to a quality that was not color, but somehow served to elevate it— creaminess, or depth, or luminosity.

As Susanna began to roll the lengths of cloth into bolts, Jacquetta, who had a keen instinct for these things, assigned herself the task of naming them. I had the steadier hand, so I affixed labels and took dictation. A lovely rust-red shot through with gold was christened Maharani. Fiamma Rosa was the name given to salmon-pink with an opalescent sheen. Purple edged with green, like a week-old bruise, was dubbed Walpurgisnacht.

We could have held a private meeting, invited our most exclusive clientele, but in the end we decided to set up a stall in the inner courtyard, like the humblest of merchants. In the morning, we attracted mostly curious onlookers, with actual buyers no more than a trickle. By midday, that trickle had swelled to a stream, and by evening, it had become a deluge. I did nothing but sew for a month straight. My hands cramped, I began to see double, and there was a pounding in my head like a great anvil being continuously struck, but it was worth it. We were given grander apartments, and the Duchess sent Theodora a letter in honor of her elevation to the post of official dyer. I still remember her look of shy delight as she broke the seal.

It wasn't long before we began to receive private commissions. One of our first clients asked for a dress the color of snow. It was a cool white, of course, but there was something more to it. Somehow, Theodora had captured the hard glint of the sun against a frost-laden field, the dark hollows where rabbits burrow.

Then there was the masque of dusk and dawn. A lesser dyer would have clothed half the party in rosy hues and half in somber ones, but Theodora could see beyond that. She picked out those colors common to both, but the dyes she created for dawn were pellucid, while those for dusk were wrapped in haze. The astrologer, when she came in for a fitting, said when the revelers danced together it was like a great celestial event, the confluence of the morning and evening skies.

Demand came thick and fast after that, and it wasn't long before we had to start turning people away. Theodora was the arbitrator. At first, we had demurred at this, citing her youth, but she would not be swayed. No matter how many times she was asked, she refused to reproduce the colors of fruits and flowers, perhaps considering them beneath her. She entertained only those requests that struck us as outlandish. We didn't know the cause, whether it was childish arrogance or a wish to discern the limits of her talent.

One such case was that of the alchemist. The woman rarely left her laboratory, so it was a surprise when she presented herself at our studio. Susanna escorted her to a chair where she sat blinking, like a mole that has ventured aboveground. When she spoke, her voice creaked. "I want a dress the color of remains. Do you understand me? It has to be the color of debris, dead things."

For once, Jacquetta was startled into silence. Susanna answered. "Madam, I don't think we can—"

Theodora cut in. "I'll do it."

Susanna looked worried. "Darling, are you sure—"

"I said I'll do it." Her voice was soft, but there was no mistaking the steel behind it.

It took her a whole afternoon. From outside her door, we heard grunting and a cry of pain, but she completed the task as promised. The dye she produced was a dull maroon shade with a thread of brown running through it. It exemplified the notion of decay so perfectly, I was compelled to hold my nose while sewing, even though there was no real odor.

Jacquetta named the new shade Caput Mortuum. The alchemist pronounced herself delighted and paid us twice as much as was agreed. We all crowded around Theodora and congratulated her, but she shrugged us off.

Not long after that, an ancient, doddering lady-in-waiting came to see us. There had been a love affair in her youth, but her paramour had been sent abroad as an ambassador and had never returned. She still wore a cameo at her throat as a token. She wanted a gown in remembrance of their love; love thwarted, love denied. At this, Susanna stepped in and refused; what could Theodora know of such things? Her daughter overruled her, and the gown, ash-violet with a silver luster, was duly produced. That might have been the end of it, but six months later, the lady's lover returned to court. She came back to us, and this time the dress she desired was to be in honor of love ascendant, love triumphant.

I was working on that very same dress when Theodora came and planted herself by my side. She stroked the material as I started on a seam. One might have expected it to be red, but instead it was a rich amber, like cognac swirled in a glass. I stayed quiet so as to invite Theodora's confidence. I was closer in age to her than any of the others, so if she were to unburden herself, it would be to me.

She let her hand fall away. "It isn't right, you know. The color."

"How can you say that? It's perfect."

She didn't reply, and I didn't venture to speak again until the silence pressed in on us. "Why aren't you happy, Theo?"

For it was so; she was unhappy. We had been loaded with high honors, but none of them pleased her. Just the week before, we had been invited to dine with the Duchess herself. True, we were placed at the very foot of the table, but it was a privilege nonetheless. Theodora should have been glad, but she pushed her food around her plate and barely raised her head the entire meal.

She brought her hand to the fabric again. This time she burrowed her fingers into it. "There are colors behind the colors. Colors no one else can see. I can see them, but I can't make them."

With that, she got up and left. Perhaps I should have followed her, but I didn't know what to say. I could have let Susanna counsel her, but there are things beyond even a mother's wisdom. I left well enough alone, trusting that matters would right themselves in time.

Our next assignment came from the Duchess herself. We were to design the uniforms for the new maids of honor, each with a color corresponding to a particular virtue. Red for courage, green for temperance, blue for prudence, white for chastity—what could be simpler? Theodora had got no further than the first two before we could tell something was wrong. The red was a rusty oxblood, and there was something bilious about the green. She looked unwell; her face was pale and slicked with sweat and she was holding her arm at her side in an odd manner. Some maternal intuition prodded Susanna into action. She seized her daughter's wrist and pulled her arm above her head.

The protuberance had swelled into a bubo. It had blackened and was twice its previous size. Theodora swayed on her feet, and Susanna reached out to catch her. We encircled her and ushered her into bed.

She stayed there for the next two weeks. She lay in a fever, weakly clawing at the blanket. When she spoke, we couldn't make out what she said. The words sounded like gibberish, but perhaps they were the names of colors from some realm beyond our own.

We passed her last task on to Berta, but before long, the assignment was forgotten. More pressing matters had overtaken the court, namely, the purported death of the Duchess's consort.

No one had ever seen the consort, but rumors abounded about them. Some said that they had died years ago, after being impounded in a dungeon below the palace. Some said that the consort was not a human being at all, but some manner of beast. The consort's death and the Duchess's grief may have been feigned, but the mourning she imposed on the court was all too real. She came to us personally to apprise us of her will.

We gathered around her in a semicircle, heads bowed. We had never been so close to her before, and it was rather like standing in the full glare of the sun. If she noticed our unease, she had the grace not to remark upon it. Before she spoke, there was a scrabbling behind Theodora's door. She was alone in the room; we would have left Berta to watch over her, but she was our only dyer now, and we needed her. At the sound, the Duchess raised her face, as if scenting the air, before turning to us.

"The rest of the court can make do with black armbands, but I myself will need full mourning; gloves, gown, and veil. You can do this, yes?"

Susanna spoke, her voice tight. "My daughter is ill."

"Is that so? I'll send for the court physician." She turned on her heel. Over her shoulder, almost as if it was an afterthought, she added, "This isn't a request."

As soon as she was gone, Susanna sprinted towards her daughter. We didn't follow until we heard a thin keening emanating from the chamber. When we entered, we saw Theodora face down in a sea of ink. I don't know if the bubo had ripened and burst of its own accord or if she had helped it along, but she had fulfilled the Duchess's command. The sheets were dyed a black so absolute that it was like staring into the void. Theodora herself, by contrast, was a pitiful bone white, as if some vital essence had been leached from her.

There was nothing else for it, so I started on the Duchess's mourning clothes. The sheets glistened, but the dye was fast. One never knows, though; perhaps this dye will insinuate itself under the wearer's skin, thinning her blood, stopping up her breath. I hope it does.

I laid aside a scrap of sheet for Theodora's shroud. She had said she saw colors that no one else could.

Perhaps she can make them now.

THE COPPER LADY
BY JAYE WELLS

Lantern flames burn green when she returns from the hunt. She's always careful to arrive before dawn.

In my small cellar bed, I pull the blankets up to my chin and listen. Her steps on the ceiling are the rhythm of terror: The sharp rap of hoof and the dull metallic scrape of copper.

Rule Number One: Always keep a shiny penny in your pocket.

When I rise after dawn to begin my chores, the house is still and quiet, but the stink of copper remains.

I use the mop to scrub the hall until the bucket's water turns red. After that, my day is free. She never eats food, of course, and I'm not allowed in her private rooms. Mama says I should never go near them, especially alone.

Most afternoons, I sit outside in the sun and read. I daydream that one day I will go on great adventures. Maybe I'll have a life worth writing about instead of this daydream-and-nightmare existence.

Sometimes I wonder how I came to live here. The one I call "Mama" is not my real mother. I know this deep in my bones, but I have no idea how I know it or why she insists on pretending. If I think about it too hard I get migraines, so I don't think about it at all.

I'm not totally alone. Sometimes, a black dog visits me. She only has three legs—two in front and one in back—but she manages to hop around pretty well. She must belong to someone because she wears a collar with a tag engraved "Fidelity". It's a serious name for such a sweet girl, so I just call her "Honey".

We've spent many afternoons together sitting under the willow tree on the edge of the stream. She never stays past sundown and I'm never sure when she'll show up or where she goes when she leaves. I assume she lives nearby, but, just in case, I leave out food and water for her. It's never been touched.

Something wakes me from sleep in the middle of the night, a bad dream perhaps or a strange noise, I think, but an ache deep in my tummy explains the disturbance. Even though Mama told me to never leave my room at night, I am confused in the liminal space between nightmare and consciousness. I stumble up the cellar stairs in search of water.

Isn't it curious how much we thirst in the night?

On my way to the kitchen, I find myself in the library. Tall bookcases dominate three of the walls. The fourth wall is all windows. The candles are out, but a full moon's glow creates a halo of safety on the stone floor. I stare out at the pale lunar visage and imagine it is the smiling face of my real mother.

The snick of a door opening shatters my peaceful moon gazing. Every sconce in the room flares to life with green flame.

I wake fully as reality rushes back, bringing with it the terrible knowledge that I am trapped.

Rule Number Two: Curiosity is dangerous.

Down the long hall, the dreaded *clomp-thunk* as the butcher returns to the abattoir.

My heart, my tiny heart, clings to my ribs and pants like an animal. Icy blood pools in my feet. Hiding is futile, but the body never listens to reason when fear is in charge.

I run for the ladder and climb to the tallest shelf, about halfway up, where I hide behind the painting of Narcissus nailed to the front of the bookcase. I place a hand over my mouth and wait. Hot cramps scream in my belly.

Copper flashes from behind black skirts. Skin pink as raw pork glistens wetly in the green light.

Behind her, a large shadow. A human unlike Mama or the Copper Lady—hairier, harder, horrific. This monster has a deep voice and dares put his hands all over her.

The Copper Lady snaps her fingers and the visitor falls to kneel before her. The broad back and shoulders seem impossibly wide.

She smiles with a flash of verdigris fang. Her shark's eyes glint cold and black.

"You're so beautiful," the monster with the deep voice says.

Is the creature blind?

The Copper Lady parts her black skirts. The monster's head disappears inside them.

The feral noises haunt me, and the salty musk forces bile to the back of my tongue. I close my eyes and pray for it to be over.

A muffled scream shatters the night.

The Copper Lady's head tilts back and a hiss escapes her blood-red lips.

There is a brief, futile struggle. The large body crumples to the floor. She giggles.

In the sickly light, a black stain crawls over the stones and seeps into the edge of the nearby rug.

The visitor is dead.

I gasp.

"Do you have my price, child?" The wretched voice skitters across the floor and up the ladder to climb into my ears.

I crawl from behind the painting. The twin black holes trap me, frozen like prey.

My mouth opens but no sound comes out. The first rule has been broken. When I finally manage to speak, fear makes my voice flinty. "I—I forgot my penny, ma'am."

Sparks dance off the stone floor where her copper foot strikes. She is fast, too fast.

With strength borne of adrenaline, I climb. The ceiling expands upward with each new shelf I grasp.

Noises that are not human chase me—predatory screams and metallic screeching.

She's on me fast. My hand scrambles for the edge of the next shelf. Her metallic nails claw into my right calf. A bright current of pain stabs through flesh and down into marrow. My hand slips and I fall. The wet wound smacks against cold stone.

"Penny for your sin," the Copper Lady screeches. "Penny for your sin!"

I roll into a ball. Her fingers are daggers on my skin. Fright-blind and hoarse, I slide down the black throat of terror.

When I wake, all is silent. Memories of the library explode behind my eyes, and yet, there is no pain.

I open my eyes on a whimper. Surely I'm dead.

But I am in my own small bed in the cellar. Mama is nearby in a straight-backed chair. She wears a black dress that covers her ankles.

Her pale face, though not kind, is at least familiar. I begin to cry.

"Hush, child." She comes to the bed and places a cool rag on my forehead.

"My leg."

She says nothing, but her gaze travels down. I finally notice the thick bandage encasing my leg from hip to toes.

"The dog attacked you."

I frown. "Honey would never hurt me. It was *her*." I pause and swallow thickly. "I-I angered her."

"Who?"

"The Copper Lady."

She laughs. "Who?"

I tell her everything I can recall. My chest is so tight and hot but cold sweat coats my chest. My leg, the one wrapped heavily, is numb.

When I finish admitting my sins, a chuckle shakes the bed. "You just had a bad dream."

"But she hurt the man! And she attacked me. I felt it. There was so much blood."

She tilts her head and brushes my hair back from my cheek. "Sometimes dreams are there to teach us lessons, is all." She scowls at me. "Never leave your room at night."

Rule Number Three.

"I'm scared, Mama."

"Of who?"

"The Copper Lady," I point up.

"Don't be silly." She places a hand on my forehead. "Are you feverish?"

I am cold. "My stomach hurts."

"That's normal. I'll get some cotton for you to use."

"Cotton?"

"For the blood, dear. The pain you'll have to get used to."

"But the blood is from my leg—"

"You and your imagination. The blood is punishment for breaking the rules." She sighs. "As long as you follow the rules, you'll be fine. Now, what are they again?"

I swallow to dislodge the knot in my throat. "Always keep a penny in my pocket. But—"

Mama sighs. "But what?"

"Why a penny?"

She's quiet for a moment. Then, finally, she whispers, "There's always a price for safety, love."

Rule Number Four: Mama knows best.

We do not speak of the dream again.

Eventually, I get used to the bandages.

When I ask about them, Mama says I hurt myself when I fell from a tree—didn't I remember?

"You said it was the dog," I say.

"What dog?"

I never see Honey again.

When I finally work up my nerve to go to the library, I discover a new rug on the floor—a soft, white sheepskin hide.

When I asked Mama about it, she says, "What are you talking about? You were here when that was delivered weeks ago. Remember?"

I don't, but she gets angry when I ask too many questions.

Weeks after the bad dream, Mama enters with a basin and a pair of scissors. She lights the oil lamp next to the bed. "Time to remove your bandages."

She eases the scissors underneath the thick layers of gauze. She tells me to lay back and close my eyes.

I am relieved to have the burden gone. Maybe now I will be able to take a proper bath. Although, I realize, the skin underneath has not been itchy or uncomfortable. A blessing, I decide.

"Look now," she says, her voice different.

I open my eyes.

The lamplight is no longer warm gold—every surface glows green.

Mama's eyes shine like two black marbles shot through with emerald.

Something cold and heavy sinks to the bottom of my stomach. I want to cry, but tears anger her.

She taps my leg. I feel nothing, but the sound is odd, metallic. "Isn't it beautiful?"

My leg is gone. In its place, a bright copper limb.

I paste a wide smile on my lips. "It's so shiny."

"Just like mine." She lifts the hem of her black skirt to show her oxidized prosthesis. She tries to hide her other limb, the hoof, but I see its outline in the shadows. She sniffs as if moved, but the emotion doesn't reach her eyes. "You're a woman now, too."

Rule Number Five: We all become our mothers.

GRAY ROCK METHOD
BY LAUREN C. TEFFEAU

We sit, you and I, as we always do every week in my drab little office in a respectable part of town. We're past the initial pleasantries and my baseline assessment, ready to start the session proper. And yet, I find myself hesitating.

You notice, offense and hurt all wrapped together, and I hold up my hands like a penitent.

"I'm finding it difficult to maintain the necessary distance during our sessions. Your tragic history..."

I shake my head at my inadequate words. When I think of the push-pull of our wide-ranging discussions, it feels like we're only treading water sometimes, instead of the deep dive into the psyche we both need. Me to do my job, you to plumb the depths of all that still haunts you. But our lack of progress is my own fault. I'm not strong enough to share in the full extent of your burdens. I've never turned my back on my professional obligations, but I'm already bracing myself for what's to come out of your mouth, as if I can make myself smaller, unnoticeable, overwhelmed before we even begin.

"I feel it would be best if you found someone else, someone who'll—"

Your eyes widen with heartbreaking alarm. "How can you say that? You're the first person who's made me believe I'm not hysterical for having all these impossible feelings."

At some cost to myself, though.

I've always believed we must be the cliff face, exposed to the elements, all the ravages nature can throw at us, yet remain untouched by what we hear in each session. That's the best way my colleagues and I can help our patients, by being neutral in our judgment, keeping sympathy from teetering into the ethical morass of empathy. We absorb your words but give you nothing of ourselves to latch onto. For your own good. And ours. And yet with you in my office every week, I cannot be the gray rock, devoid of any facet you can pry into, exploiting the fissures that lead to my very soul.

But when you look at me, your wounded soul pooling there in your gaze, I'm swamped at my selfishness for placing my own comfort above the possibility of true healing.

You reach for me—a short, abortive gesture—your hand coming to rest on the seat cushion between us, the smooth, tapered fingers twitching in uncertainty. "I assure you our conversations have helped me dramatically. To start over again, with someone else..." Your other hand goes to your heart, still beating steadily despite everything you've faced. "This time together means so much. I couldn't bear it if we—"

You cut such foul words off, tears glistening in the corners of your eyes, and I curse inwardly for causing you any more undue pain. I already determined any interruption of your treatment would have an adverse reaction on your progress, and now my own doubts are aggravating the situation.

"You're certain you wish to continue?"

Your swift nod absolves me of any more misgivings. I'll find some way to be worthy of the trust you've placed in me.

"Very well, then," I reply. How can I say otherwise? "Same time next week?"

Your smile, brittle with relief, is a promise.

I made a promise, too, once. To do no harm. That's what brings me to this shop of curios in a seedy neighborhood when I have nowhere else to turn. But I'm doing this for you, I tell myself as I enter. A bell chimes overhead. Camphor and incense and dusty, cluttered shelves filling my nose, making my eyes water. Better than the smoky damp of the streets. Girding myself, I press forward into the cramped space.

The clerk, a smartly groomed man of middle age, eyes me as I make my way past rows of oddities I try not to examine too closely. "How may I help you?" His voice has a surprisingly well-heeled polish to it.

"I hoped to find..." It sounds so ridiculous out loud. I'm a professional with a decade's worth of experience sorting through people's problems. But you... Nothing prepared me for *you*. "I was told you carry something that would help me manage my emotions."

His gaze skates over me with a light, curious touch. "Occupation?"

"Doctor."

"Something to steady the hands during surgery, eh?"

"No, no." I laugh nervously. "Not that kind of doctoring. Psychiatry."

I brace myself for the sneering condescension my young field garners—assumed to be full of quacks who bilk desperate fools and sell poisonous tonics as curatives—but it doesn't come.

"To settle the mind, then. Hmm." He turns his back on the register and unlocks the cabinet behind him. "Let's see..."

A trill of anticipation rolls through me as the clerk finally brings forth the object that will help me—help *us*—continue on. You need so much of me, and I cannot say no, not when I'm so certain I can help you. I want to. I want to desperately. You deserve so much more than what you've been given in life.

But instead of forcing you to start over with someone new— some stranger—I hope I've found a way to keep you like you requested.

Holding my breath, I watch as the clerk opens the small box with a flourish.

"It's just a rock," I say, my confusion plain. Lumpy and gray. Featureless and seemingly undeserving of its silk-lined box and exorbitant price tag.

"Carry it on your person, and it will aid you in your sessions."

"Like an overlarge worry stone?" A recent study praised their efficacy for treating high-strung, nervous individuals, a technique dating back to the Greeks. But after all my discreet inquiries to find a shop such as this, I confess I was hoping for something *more*.

"If it helps to think of it that way," he says in an aloof voice.

If I hold it in my fist, my fingers barely close around it. Not really practical for anything. "More like a paperweight."

The clerk fusses with the hand-lettered *All Sales Final* sign in front of the register. "If it's bad enough you're here, do the details really matter?"

You tell me everything, it seems. A flood of words and impressions and emotions—always those—that tears through me like a riptide until I'm fouled by the same murk you seek to rid yourself of. The gray rock's my anchor in those moments as I wade through the miasma of your personal journey into healing. I vow not to stand in your way. With each clench of the rock in my hand, I imagine myself smaller, slighter, hardly daring to breathe lest I interrupt your transformation. I hunch my shoulders, keep my legs tightly crossed, my arms wrapped around myself so nothing escapes. I'd curl into the settee, sink into the floor, and disappear if I could.

Some sessions, it feels like we can't both possibly fit in here together, with all your secrets spilling forth and displacing the air in the room. I tell myself I don't need air. I am the rock I hold in my hand, gray and featureless, and no matter how much pressure I exert, it remains untouched, undeniably itself.

And it's working. Even when it started out tucked away in my pocket. I'm better able to muster up sensitive responses to your painful disclosures. Offer suggestions for recasting the trauma into something lighter, more manageable, as you go about the rest of your week.

My fingers may be numb at the end of each session, but my palm's warm against the rock that's my salvation, and yours. I'm jealous it can remain unaffected by the goings-on around it.

Until one day, it isn't any longer.

I can't remember a time I didn't want to help people.

After the war, seeing our boys come home broken men and knowing they left something of themselves back at the front besides their sweat and blood and screams, even the hardest heart would be spurred to action. The stubborn suffering they had sublimated down into the deepest parts of themselves was challenging to unpack, but I like to think I did my part to help them return to civilian life.

Private practice followed, and I gained a reputation for my results. By the time you walked into my office with your fragile poise and fraught history, I was already an accomplished listener. An expert at identifying the roots of any issue thanks to my studies in psychoanalysis and the topography of the human mind.

But you were different. I realized I couldn't feign professional indifference if your treatment didn't take. That was the moment you looked at me for the first time, instead of gazing over my shoulder at something behind me or contemplating the Turkish rugs that cushioned the hard words said in that room.

Our souls touched that day, despite the as-yet unspoken horrors in your eyes or your off-putting manner, the only reliable armor you had access to at the time. I could see *you* in there fighting. And I told myself I would fight just as hard to see this through.

Because you'd been shuffled from doctor to doctor, I knew you couldn't afford another change even though we had so much distrust to work through. But I think I've proven myself worthy of the deepest, darkest parts of you.

I never expected to drown.

Like a pill bug unfurling, the rock stops being rocklike and scuttles up my forearm and burrows there like some sort of exotic beetle. The kind I saw every time I visited my professor's office, pinned and placed under glass and hung on the wall. I should be disgusted. I remember what that feels like, but it's distant, like looking at something through fogged-up windows on a rainy day. I try to pry it off, but it's rooted against me. So strange and unexpected, I dare not pick at it like some newly formed scab I'm half-appalled, half-impressed my body made.

But you'll be here soon, and I pull my sleeve down to hide it from view. Thankfully, I'm wearing black these days, one of the better colors for blending into the background. No distractions, not for you.

As soon as you start talking, the familiar anxiety your words always conjure takes over. A dead feeling in my stomach followed by a queasy fluttering in my chest. My hand reflexively clenches around air. But then warmth spreads up my forearm like sunlight. My not-rock anchoring me to this room, despite the horrors you share as casually as what you ate for dinner last night. And so we go on, you and I, exploring such dangerous territory to rid you of the burdens you carry, always.

When I wake one day, weeks later, my rock's simply gone. There's a pale, slightly depressed mark on my forearm where it once rested against me. Revulsion at the loss and what it means for us rises up on wings of panic. But the stress and fear are replaced by a new warmth radiating from my neck. Some time in the night, the rock crept up my arm to nestle at the juncture of my neck and left shoulder, like an off-center goiter. I select a shirt with a high collar so no one will see, not even you.

The rock's larger, warm like my skin, like the sunlight it pumps through my veins whenever you're nearby. It absorbs all the darkness you bring into our sessions. Surely you feel it. It's why you keep coming back. Not for me, not exactly, nor the healing course we're charting together, but for the rock that absorbs what I cannot.

And you have so much inside you, no wonder it grows fat taking it all in. My head bows at the weight of everything, but we're making this journey together. What's a little discomfort?

"You look different," you say halfway through our next session.

I prickle all over at the thought of *me* disrupting our progress. No distractions, isn't that what I promised? No insertions of myself into your narrative. I am the rock in the background, lending you my strength and resiliency, but nothing more of myself.

"I'm certain of it. Whatever's wrong?" you ask.

Another time, I would be thrilled you're capable of acknowledging someone else. Progress that you can look past your own immediate concerns to the world around you no matter how many times it's turned its back on you. But I can only manage a pained gasp.

The rock's moved again, lodged into my skin like a second spine, trailing down from my neck to my sacrum now with gray-black appendages that embrace my ribs. They squeeze like an ancient back brace, support that can cut if I move the wrong way. But I'm careful, so very careful, to stay still and small and unworthy of attention.

"Nothing," I say, inwardly cursing the catch in my voice. My outsized jacket covers everything, I made sure of it.

But you insist, pointing out my drab clothes of late, mussed hair, the bags under my eyes that distract from all the good work we're doing in this room. That I didn't notice, that I accidentally upset the delicate dance we do each week, is nearly unforgivable.

"I'm terribly sorry," I tell you. "I'll endeavor to do better next time."

You nod, doubtful, then I feel the moment you dismiss it and move on to more important things, along with the corresponding quickening of the rock in its eagerness for your pain. But that's scaffolding enough for me to endure the rest of the session and see you on your way, confident of the progress we're making. Because we are, yes? You would tell me if we weren't. You need this outlet as surely as I do.

We live for these meetings, the rock and I. And you do, too. I know it. You cannot hold all those evils you carry inside by yourself.

I take extra care with myself this time. No matter the rock's impatience to see you, the pinchers squeezing around my ribs, spines digging into flesh. I'm not enough for it, no matter how much time I spend reviewing our sessions and planning the next, as if by dredging up all that old feeling could ever keep it satisfied. I've cut out other patients to give our sessions greater priority, did you know that? But it's not enough. It's never enough, and I no longer know how to be myself.

I'm a shadow in my own life, and still there's too much of me in this arrangement we've created, you and I.

But today, I vow, there's only you. When you walk through the door, I know I've done well as your eyes pass over me unseeing, nothing to distract your focus on our work today even with the slight hunch to my back. We take our customary seats on the settee and start with the usual pleasantries. Even now, knowing you're here, the rock's impatient with me as I keep to the pattern, the baseline questions that help me evaluate your mental state each visit. Then it's your turn, and you never disappoint as you share the darkness inside you, rich and malignant and seemingly bottomless. Instead of horror and shame, I feel lit from within, sunlight—no, *fire*—ready to burn me up from the inside. And it will one day. The rock told me so. But you're here, still so full of tragedy, and it's hungry, so hungry.

With a snap and a hiss, the rock dislodges from my spine vertebrae by vertebrae. You take my arms. "What's wrong?" you ask, scared now for someone other than yourself.

Once, my heart would've warmed at that, but it's too late. Too late. For all of us.

You came to me, raw with distrust, desperate for anyone who'd listen without judgment to the terrors you'd endured. I thought I was ready to help you sort through all the evil bits, and set the truly awful ones aside, so you could move on and be *more*. I so wanted to be that person for you. You understand that, don't you?

I did everything I could. And when I no longer couldn't, I took the steps necessary to make things right. And things are finally right now. Can you feel it?

If not, you will.

"Good God, what *is* that?"

The fear in your voice is intoxicating. A siren's call to the gray rock, but it already knows you so well. How you always freeze in the moment when something horrible is about to happen. Despite all our sessions, I never could cure you of that. So as the rock detaches itself from me, you sit there as though made out of stone, an offering far more attractive to it than a used-up vessel like me. Past the pain bright as sunlight and the warm wetness trickling down my spine, I can feel its exultation, its hunger, as it drapes itself over your shoulders and sends its appendages scuttling down the back of your shirt, before settling against you more intimately than any of your lovers. I know how desperately you've craved such closeness that doesn't come with a cost. But this is one I think you can bear, yes? One you're made for. The tears in your eyes tell me so before they roll back in a pleasure that teeters deliriously on the edge of pain.

Oh, I know about that too. You told me, remember? We charted so much territory in our sessions.

Gasping, you lurch to your feet like a marionette, arms outspread to welcome the relief that comes from knowing you are no longer alone in the darkness. Don't you see? This is the best gift I could give you to commemorate our success together. The gray rock that made it all possible.

But wait. Where are you going? I thought—

Fine. Go in your terrible heartbreaking suffering, and let the rock be your support in all the future holds for you.

And you do, with only the barest hint of a backwards glance at my drab little office in a respectable part of town. No word of thanks or whispered concern. You don't even say goodbye.

I tell myself you mean no offense. You simply don't need me anymore. Not when you can fly. You've been searching for respite from the awfulness inside you so long, nothing else can compete with what you're feeling now. I know. I *know*, even if I only felt a fraction of it.

But as my lifeblood soaks into the settee, I know how little that matters now, too. Cast aside, adrift, unmoored from the cliff face I've clung to for so long, I'm but an ashen husk with nothing left to give, not even for myself.

"DOUBLE HAPPINESS"
BY GENEVE FLYNN

Double Happiness:
Chinese calligraphy character which symbolizes enduring love, loyalty, and luck.

Popular decoration on hung pao—red packets which contain money and are often given as gifts at weddings. The color red represents good luck and is thought to ward off evil.

"Master Jin! Master Jin!"

Wong Jin pushed himself up to a sitting position with a groan. His head felt like an overripe gourd and his mouth tasted like a pig had shat on his tongue. His coin purse, which he must have been clutching in his sleep, slid off his stomach and onto the bed. It made a meagre clink. Jin sighed. Damn his friends at the college. They had invited him to a game of pai gow, knowing he couldn't resist, and now their wallets were fat while his was much reduced.

His fingers itched to turn the tiles. He grinned. He would go again tonight. His father was rich beyond compare, so his losses were a fleeting inconvenience. Besides, he knew his fortune would always rise in the end. He just had to hold his nerve.

Cheung, his father's servant, banged the door open. Jin cursed and the little man bobbed a swift apology. "Master Jin! Your father has taken a turn for the worse. You must come at once."

Jin was instantly alert. He pawed the ground for the clothing he had shucked last night and shuffled his feet into his shoes. "Lead the way, Cheung."

It was about time the old cockerel crowed his last call.

Wong Enlai, Jin's father, lay beneath thick blankets in the airless heat. The room was heavy with the aroma of herbs and incense. They were not enough to hide the sour, greasy smell of unwashed sickness.

"Your father has refused to see the doctor," Cheung said quietly. "He will take no more medicine."

His father was pale and still. Jin leaned over his body and peered into his face. Enlai crabbed his fingers over Jin's wrist. He yelped and jerked back.

"Ahhh, my faithful son," Enlai whispered.

Always, that mocking tone. Even at death's door.

"Have you come to weep at my bedside?"

Jin bowed to hide his anger. "I am here, Father."

"Yes, but where will you be once I pass into the afterlife?" Enlai broke into a viscous bout of coughing.

Jin waited until he had recovered. A vein pulsed in his father's forehead.

Let it burst. "I will honor the family name."

Enlai snorted. "A likely story. You will drink the wine and burn the family tablet."

"Do you think so little of me?"

"No. I believe you think so little of yourself."

Jin snapped his head up. Instead of the usual disdain, his father's expression was one of pity and deep sadness.

"I have failed you," Enlai said. "After your mother's death, I have allowed you to run wild, and have not taught you the value of family. I will correct this."

Jin's heart was a stone in his chest: cold and heavy. He licked his lips. "What do you mean?"

Enlai waved an emaciated hand at his servant. Cheung shuffled forward, holding out an official looking envelope. Jin took it and broke the seal. He read quickly. The stone in his chest hardened until his throat ached. "What is this?"

His father's eyes drooped. "My final wish..." His mouth fell slack.

Jin leaned closer.

Was he—?

A snore. Curdled breath washed over him.

With a grunt of disgust, Jin straightened and looked at Cheung.

The little servant stepped back and blinked rapidly. "Your father has had a copy of this will sent to his solicitor. Your father wishes for you to marry so a daughter will honor his memory; so there will be someone to look after the ancestral altar. His words were, 'If my son does not find a bride before my death, he shall not inherit a single yuan.'"

Jin drew furiously on his cigarette and paced the matchmaker's office. The harsh smoke burned the back of his throat but he hardly noticed. "So, can you help me?"

The matchmaker probed his teeth with a toothpick and shook his head. His jowls wobbled. "You know how it is. Not enough girls. Too many heading off to the city for work." He left it unspoken that baby girls were often abandoned or aborted in favor of boys. "The earliest I could organize a meeting is in three months' time."

"Three months!" Jin paced and ran a hand through his hair. He picked up a tea cup then put it back down. "I really can't wait that long." Jin tapped his fingers against his leg. He drew on his cigarette again.

He had heard rumors. "What if I paid extra?"

The matchmaker's toothpick stilled. "Paid extra for what?" He began packing his tattered folder containing photos of successful matches.

"A ghost bride."

The matchmaker looked at Jin for a long moment. Jin held his gaze, even though his skin prickled.

Eventually, the matchmaker sighed. "It is very difficult. Do you know how much families will pay for a newly deceased girl? The latest auction at the hospital fetched over two hundred thousand yuan. And the girl wasn't even dead yet. Do you have that kind of money?"

Two hundred thousand? Fuck!

"Are there other options?"

"Options?" The matchmaker's expression fell blank as a piece of slate.

"You know." Jin swallowed. "Other ways to find a ghost bride. The news story about the cemetery—"

The matchmaker suddenly stood and grabbed Jin by the elbow, steering him out of the shop. Jin struggled to stop himself from tripping on the boxes and camphor chests in the maze to the door.

"I'm sorry! Please, I need your help!" He threw his arm out and caught his momentum on a filing cabinet. Jin fished into his pocket for his wallet. He yanked out a thick handful of money, everything he had, and held it up. The matchmaker paused, a sweaty mass against his back.

The wad of cash was plucked from Jin's fingers and he was shoved outside. "Come back tomorrow. At midnight." The matchmaker clicked the door shut.

The bones weighed far less than Jin expected. When the matchmaker handed him the plain, unlacquered box, they shifted slightly.

A muted rattle.

The box was heavier on one side; Jin assumed this was the skull. His stomach roiled, but he told himself that the girl was already long dead. He was providing her spirit a place on his family altar. She would be lost, otherwise: an aimless ghost. What was the harm? Besides, his father was really to blame.

His hands were damp but he did not want to wipe them and risk dropping everything that the matchmaker was piling into his arms.

"Once you perform the wedding ritual, you'll need to burn these." The matchmaker laid paper effigies of a house, clothing, furniture, and servants onto Jin's bundle. "This should satisfy her in the underworld."

"Where did you get them?" Jin blurted.

They locked eyes. "I buy the effigies from the city." They both knew this wasn't the question he had asked. "I go once a month. Lady Chang has the best quality."

Jin had no choice but to nod.

The matchmaker drew out a life-sized dummy of a young woman in a traditional wedding dress. Her face had been crudely painted a heavy, inhuman pink. He grinned. "Congratulations. Here is your bride."

The effigy's mismatched eyes seemed to stare at Jin. He gathered his courage. It was only bamboo and paper.

Nothing more.

He accepted the final burden, then tottered out into the night. Dawn was several hours away and the streets were deserted. Still, he hurried home as fast as he could go.

When everything was ready, Jin told Cheung to open the door to his father's room. He had set up the effigy of the bride in the central courtyard, along with the paper accoutrements that would accompany her after she passed from this world. A table was draped in a festive red cloth and laden with food and wine. The bones, in their plain box, were set at the feet of the paper bride. Jin was dressed in his finest suit.

As the door was drawn open, Jin saw that Cheung had propped the old man up with cushions. A weak smile broke across his father's face and it was as if Jin was basking in the warmth of a spring sun. Even though the ceremony was a farce, finally, he had won Enlai's approval. Jin tugged his jacket straight and approached.

"Father, I have done as you asked."

"A ghost bride." Enlai chuckled. "Always cutting corners."

Jin's nostrils flared and the stone that had lifted from his heart pressed down.

"Still," his father continued, "I will have someone who will care for my shrine when I am gone."

Jin gave a curt nod and returned to the courtyard.

We'll see.

As Enlai watched, Jin went through the mummery of the marriage. When it came time to intone the final rites, Jin saw that his father had fallen into a doze. With a sneer, he rushed through the last formalities, leaving the ceremony incomplete. Cheung opened his mouth but Jin silenced him with a hard shake of his head. He took up the matches and set the bride and her possessions alight.

Jin's father snorted and jerked awake at the sudden rush of heat and noise. He nodded with satisfaction and beckoned Cheung over. Cheung reluctantly drew out the new will from an envelope by the bed and handed his master a pen. Enlai signed the paper with a shaky hand then collapsed back. His eyes drifted shut and he seemed to deflate.

Enlai took another four days to die. When the coffin was prepared, Jin tucked the box of bones at his father's feet, then returned the lid to its place. If the old man wanted a daughter to care for him in the spirit world, he might as well share his burial with her.

After the funeral, Jin took the keys to his father's safe room. Enlai had made his fortune in mining, and while he trusted the land to give up its wealth, he had not trusted the government. He had eschewed all banks and stored his money in an underground vault excavated beneath his bedroom. A single metal door in the floor was the only way in and out. Jin allowed himself a smile as he took in all the treasures that were now his. His face ached from feigning grief.

He was finally free.

Jin stirred, rising to within an inch of wakefulness. He had replaced his father's bed with a queen-sized monstrosity, and had ordered Cheung to throw out everything that once belonged to Enlai. The room still smelled faintly of illness, so the windows were thrown open to the night.

He rolled on to his side and tried to settle. As he drifted deeper into unconsciousness, the mattress behind him sank. The sweet smell of lilies wafted around him. The sensation of an arm fell across his side, as careful and gentle as snow falling. Jin frowned in his sleep but the darkness pulled him down.

The next morning Jin woke with a start. He lay frozen in position. The slight weight of the arm was no longer draped across his ribs, but something floral tickled the back of his throat. Slowly, Jin rolled off his side of the bed. He planted his feet and scrambled back.

The other side of the bed was empty except for a single red packet.

Jin licked his lips and leaned on the bed to get a better look. The packet was a hung pao with the symbol of double happiness marked in gold. What did it mean? Who had put it there? He reached out to take it then remembered the sensation of someone embracing him in his dream. With a shiver, he withdrew his hand.

"Ah, don't worry," the matchmaker said as he shuffled paper replicas of violently pink grooms around on his shelves. "It's an old trick to nab eligible bachelors. Now that you're a rich man, you'll be an irresistible target." He tucked a stray paper-and-bamboo arm away, then sat with a satisfied groan. He shook his finger at Jin. "More of this ghost marriage nonsense. Whatever you do, don't pick up the red packet. Otherwise, you'll be obliged to pay the family a bride price, and marry their dead daughter." He chuckled. "Then you'll have two wives, and still no one to warm your bed."

When Jin arrived home, Cheung was sweeping the central courtyard. Jin peeked into his bedroom. The red packet still lay upon the rumpled sheets. A breeze lifted the gauze curtains at the open window; it was entirely possible for an intruder to have climbed in under the cover of darkness. Jin ground his teeth. How dare someone enter his house and try to cheat him! He stared at the packet and clenched and unclenched his hands. He was tempted to snatch it up and just take the money. The person who thought they could trick him could go to hell. There was nothing to say that he had to abide by this ridiculous custom.

Yet why take the risk? Jin was a gambler: He knew when to fold and when to hold his nerve.

"Cheung! I have something for you."

The little servant set his broom aside and entered, bowing low. "Master Jin?"

"I want to give you something for all your years of loyal service to my father, to the Wong family."

Cheung's eyes disappeared into the folds of his smile. "That's too kind. It's not necessary. Master Enlai always looked after me. It was an honor to care for such a good man."

The stone in Jin's chest grew cool. Such loyalty. He wondered who would have inherited his father's wealth if he had failed in securing a bride. He returned Cheung's smile warmly and pointed to the red packet. "Please, take it. Whatever is inside is yours."

Cheung looked from Jin to the bed, a slight frown on his face. Hung pao were usually handed from giver to recipient. This was most irregular.

"I prepared it last night and was so weary I fell asleep before I remembered to put it on the bedside table," Jin said. "Please, I will be offended if you refuse."

Cheung bowed even lower. "Forgive me, Master Jin. I am overwhelmed by your generosity." He hurried forward and took up the red packet. "Thank you. Bless you."

Jin puffed up his chest. "Not at all. It's the least I could do."

A nightingale's song drifted in through the windows. Jin's eyes opened and he stared at the wall. What had woken him? The bird's call had lulled him to sleep throughout his childhood; something else had disturbed his sleep. He strained all his senses. A faint floral scent lingered in the air. Had the trickster stolen into his quarters again? Anger boiling up inside him, Jin leapt up and snatched the guttering lamp from his bedside. He swung it over his mattress.

Nothing.

He held the lamp up to the windows. The gauze curtains hung straight and still. He shook his head and returned the lamp to the table, then climbed back under the sheets and closed his eyes. The trickster must have seen that a lowly servant had received the red packet and given up.

His fortune was secure.

The sun streamed in. Jin stretched and smiled. He had slept exceptionally well and was ready for whatever the day would bring. He turned over.

A body-shaped depression lifted from the mattress across from him and disappeared. A single red packet came into view. Jin sprang up as if he had been doused in ice water. Gasping, he stared at the bed.

The hung pao lay half buried in the sheets. Its sides bulged, as if it strained to contain its contents. Double happiness.

"Cheung!"

The little servant was twice as delighted to receive his reward. He plucked it off the bed and bowed until he was almost folded over.

Jin slept in his old room. He demanded that every window in the house be locked, despite the heat and humidity. The Ghost Month was approaching, and he would take no chances.

Even though his circle of friends had grown since his inheritance, Jin refused every invitation. What if a cashier or betting agent handed him his winnings in a red packet? How would he know if it was genuine, or if it was something sinister? He couldn't be too careful.

Every day, he watched Cheung like a cat, shadowing him as he went about his duties, trailing him to his home, huddling around the corner as the man ate dumplings in a coffee house. So far, his father's servant seemed to have suffered no ill effects.

By the seventh day, Jin could barely stand upright. Each night was a slow and heady torment as he swooned and bobbed between wakefulness and drowning sleep. The days were spent following the tedium of Cheung's life. Honestly, all the man did was work, eat dumplings, and go home to sleep.

On the eighth day, Jin got lucky.

He trailed Cheung to a tailor. After half an hour, his father's servant emerged, resplendent in a suit. It was made of rich material, and on his feet were new shoes.

The red packets.

Cheung would never have been able to afford such a fine outfit, not on the wages Jin paid him. A flush crept up Jin's neck. Who had been by his father's side, all these years? Who had been whispering in the old man's ears while the sickness set in and addled his mind? Who else could have gotten into Jin's room so easily? Who was loyal, beyond doubt, to Wong Enlai's memory?

Tonight, Jin would lay a trap.

Jin ordered Cheung to make up his bed in his father's room and ordered the windows to be thrown open. Cheung kept his eyes downcast as he worked; his face was gray and sweat trickled from his temples. Jin noticed that he had changed back into his servant's tunic.

"Master Jin, I am not feeling well," Cheung said faintly. "Please, may I retire for the night?"

"Of course. You should get some rest."

Cheung bowed himself out of the room and shuffled off, stumbling slightly. Jin smirked. Such a performance. The man should audition for the Shanxi opera.

Jin listened to the sounds of the city settling for the night. His father's house—his house now—was situated in a quieter part of the prefecture and above the cries of hawkers offering the last call for buns and cakes, he could hear a nightingale singing.

Finally, darkness descended fully and a somnolent cloak fell over the buildings. Gooseflesh chased across Jin's body, but he reminded himself that the visitations were only Cheung: a snake who had been posing as a faithful vassal all these years. He pictured the look on the traitor's face when he was caught out.

As the minutes and hours wore on, Jin's head became unbearably heavy. His eyelids drooped. His breathing slowed. He got up and paced, smoking cigarette after cigarette. Halfway through the eleventh cigarette, he broke into a barking fit that would not stop. Lunging at the ashtray, clumsily stubbing out the ember, he sucked in desperate breaths between propulsive coughing. Tiny points of light filled his vision. When the sparkles worsened, he lay down. The coughing spluttered to a stop.

Better.

He closed his eyes, just for a moment.

The scent of lilies. A soft body molded against his back. A feminine sigh. Still drifting in a deep, warm, and silent sea, Jin turned towards the embrace. His bride had skin as fair as the moon, a delicate chin, and large, dark eyes. Her lips were the color of fresh peonies. Her hair fanned around her head like a silken veil. She lifted the sheet and, in that instant, he saw the curve of her hip and the tips of her perfect breasts outlined by her nightgown.

He positioned himself on top of her. Her sweet perfume filled his nostrils and he pressed his mouth to hers. She moaned and he stiffened. Urgently, he tugged at the ties that secured her gown closed at the neck. Beneath his fingers, she felt thinner than she looked—almost skin and bones. He would send Cheung to buy nourishing meals from the market.

Cheung.

Jin pulled back and blinked. Was he awake?

His bride smiled, her pale pink lips slightly parted. With infinite slowness, she unlaced the ties that had confounded him. He could not look away as the thin material slipped from her alabaster skin. Instead of two softly rounded breasts, a cage of nut-brown ribs rose and fell in her chest. Where her heart should have been, rested a red packet. It throbbed with hideous life.

With a shriek, Jin woke.

He scrambled from the bed and fumbled for the lamp. It had extinguished some time ago. He had been slumbering with the unbroken night crowding against him.

With small, frantic gasps, he patted the table, searching for the matches, certain that, at any moment, he would feel the light caress of petite finger bones spidering across his hand.

The match flared, almost blinding him with its brightness. The flame sent juddering shadows across the room as he lit the lamp. He swung it over the bed. It was empty. With a trembling pinch, he drew the sheets off. There was no flash of red and gold as they fell to the floor.

He crept around the room, checking each shadowed corner. He was completely alone. He hurried out to the courtyard, spinning in the moonlight, searching. There was something just before the door to the outer courtyard. A shoe, tipped over as if its owner had left in a hurry. Fury burned away the terror. Jin raced to the outer doors and slammed them open.

That snake.

Jin slowed as he neared Cheung's modest house. He controlled his breathing and wiped the sweat from his brow. The door was slightly ajar. The man must have gotten in just ahead of him. Good. He would catch him red-handed.

The door swung open soundlessly. Jin tip-toed in then straightened from his crouch. He was no burglar. He would confront this trickster as a master. He swept through the rooms. When he got to the second bedroom, he saw a line of dim light beneath the door. He twisted the handle and pushed.

Cheung was hunched in the corner, over the scant, guttering source of light. Perhaps a single candle. Did the man soon hope to have a hall filled with golden lanterns? Did he envision himself stepping into Jin's father's safe room, sweeping the shelves empty while Jin was locked up, babbling about ghosts and haunted hung pao?

With a roar, Jin rushed forward and knocked the little man aside. Cheung toppled and money exploded from the red packets in his hands. Some caught alight and were consumed in a flash. Jin faltered. *Paper* money? He turned to where Cheung lay. A swift current of fear ran through him.

His father's servant remained crouched, like a dead centipede curled in upon itself. His hands were claws and his face was a desiccated gray mask pulled taut over his skull.

Stumbling back, Jin exited the room and slammed the door behind him. *Goddess of Mercy!*

What had happened to Cheung? What would happen to him? He hadn't touched the red packets. Cheung, the fool, had spent the money.

Surely, he was safe.

The scent of lilies. Soft lips and a yielding body beneath his. He retched and wiped the front of his body over and over. There had to be something he could do.

This all began with the matchmaker.

"Open up!" Jin hammered on the door to the shop. A light glowed from the back. Heavy footsteps approached from inside and he exhaled and sagged when the matchmaker's round face appeared between the door and the jamb. "Please, you have to help me!"

The matchmaker nodded solemnly and stepped aside to allow Jin to enter. As the door closed behind him, Jin grimaced. The air was stale, as if the shop had been unopened for many days, and the matchmaker had hunkered inside, alone and bathed in his own perspiration. He turned and saw that the man remained standing at the entrance, like a giant, silent statue of buddha. Jin's skin tightened all over his body. He looked back towards the office.

Every surface was plastered with red packets, marked with gold double happiness. The walls were pinned with hundreds of hung pao. The once-tidy desk was littered with bright envelopes. He heard a shift behind him and spun. The hulking body at the door was gone.

"She has visited me." A disembodied voice spoke from the darkness of the shop to Jin's right. How had the man moved so noiselessly? Jin twisted, beginning to edge towards the door.

"The ceremony is incomplete." The voice was closer. "You must perform the rites."

Jin took an agonizing step towards the entrance.

"She comes every night." A sob. Right beside him.

Jin spun.

The matchmaker's bulging eyes loomed from the darkness. His hands were behind his back. "She will not leave me alone until she has what was promised." He tittered and licked his lips, leaving a wet sheen across them.

Jin took another step. The matchmaker lunged, thrusting something at him.

A red packet, fat with notes.

Jin yelped and jumped back, his hands held high. Like a fish slipping from a net, he wrenched free and bolted for the door.

There was no way the matchmaker would catch him, not with his big belly and swollen, splayed feet; still, Jin ran all the way back to his house. It seemed that his shoes barely touched the ground.

He rushed inside and clunked the lock in place. He whirled, trying to see each dark corner of his house at once. Nowhere was safe.

No. There was one place.

Jin fumbled for the key as he hurried to his father's room. He grabbed the lantern and the matches. He unlocked the door and yanked it open. His back gave a brief scream of pain. He scurried down the steps and pulled the door shut behind him, locking it tight. He tugged on the bolt. When he sure that it was secure, he sagged against the wall.

He would wait out the night here, safe. There were no windows. He had the only key.

A scuff to his right.

"Who's there?"

He fumbled for the matches. The first snapped in his hands. He tried again. The second flared then extinguished with a sad puff. Jin's breath sobbed in and out. The stone in his chest was crushing him. Something tugged at his coat and he squealed, shuffling sideways blindly. His ankle struck the bottom step and he fell. Something snapped with bright agony.

He felt for the matchbook. One match remained. He tore it free and struck. It flared to life.

A gliding hiss in the far corner. With trembling lips, Jin forced himself to look.

Cloaked in shadows, as if she absorbed the paltry light from his flame, was the bride's effigy. Something brushed his chest, as delicate and gentle as the shy caress of a new lover.

Jin looked down at his coat. Jutting from his pocket was a single red envelope.

TANGERINE SKY
BY RED LAGOE

The memory of a tangerine sky lived rent-free in Sylvia Ramsey's head. She needed to let it go. Her therapist had suggested releasing the image by painting it, so now a blank canvas stood between Sylvia and her mental health. Painting as a hobby vanished into the past because she feared her reds and yellows would accidentally mix on the palette, dredging up the color orange and the haunting image from sixteen years ago.

Arms hanging limp by her sides, Sylvia stared into the stretched canvas, attempting to imagine that sky, but her stomach churned as if she'd ingested a bucketful of cadmium orange acrylics.

"I want it back," she whispered to herself. For too many years, this color tormented her. It was time to reclaim it.

Sylvia closed her eyes. The 20 by 16-inch canvas burned into her retinas, displayed on the back of her eyelids. A rectangle of possibilities.

Could she paint those tangerine skies, dappled with fiery clouds as the sun dipped into the horizon? The black pier had cut across the water, speckled with tiny people. A little girl, twelve years old, spinning in the foreground as a silhouette, forever trapped against that hideous orange prison.

Sylvia opened her eyes. The memory of her little sister came to life as a phantom upon canvas. She should paint it. She *needed* to paint it. To reclaim the color. To memorialize her sister in the last moment she was ever seen.

It was the moment that forced her to grow up. Sylvia had only been fifteen, but if she were watching her sister more closely, Hanna would still be with her.

Another silhouette crept into the depiction in her mind. He took Hanna in his grip and stole her. A pony tail whipped to the side, but she left without a fight. She was so far away. Sylvia couldn't run fast enough against the tide of boardwalk strollers and bicyclists. The tangerine sky devoured Hanna's small silhouette forever.

After Hanna was taken, that hideous, monstrosity of a color appeared everywhere. During questioning, an officer peeled a mandarin at his desk nearby. Her eyes gravitated to the color of the fruit against the white cinderblock wall as his nubby fingers dug into the peel. That day, she'd hated the officer who casually thought of food during her tragedy. His wet, sticky fingers—she envisioned as blood-orange injustice clinging to idle hands.

Sylvia gave up oranges. And carrots. She rejected every orange thing. The pumpkin-toned walls of her family kitchen suffocated her so many times, her parents had to repaint them blue. She avoided orange like it was a monster that could swallow up everything she loved.

Not that she allowed herself to love anything anymore.

Her job came first. The rage which fueled her was all there was to live for. After school, she'd studied criminal justice and then became a police officer, doing grunt work for years until finally, she made detective. That's all she'd ever wanted since August 18, sixteen years ago—to do what the sticky, mandarin-eating man never accomplished. Sylvia would bring down child trafficking rings. She'd hunt them and scour those stains from humanity. In some small way, she'd always hoped to find her sister, but she'd come to terms with the reality years ago.

Painting could aid with processing those imprisoned emotions. Spew the bottled anger.

A knock at her door broke her focus from the canvas.

Her chest tightened, breath trapped beneath the weight of revelation.

Go away.

Another series of knocks thundered through her veins.

"Yo! Ramsey!" Martinez called through the door.

The pulse between her ears beat in sync with her footsteps as she approached. She unlocked the dead bolt and opened a crack. "What?"

He scowled. "What do you mean 'what?' Why aren't you at the bar celebrating? We've been calling you all night."

"I know…"

"Damn!" He covered his nose as the stench from her apartment hit him. "What the hell died in there?"

"It's best to breathe through your mouth." She stepped into the hallway and closed the door, feigning a smile. "The rat poison my super put down—they're dying in the walls. Add to that, I haven't been home much lately so everything in the fridge is…well, there's some Chinese in there that—hooboy!"

"Alright, alright... but are you good? You need to talk or whatever?"

She cringed. "I don't need to talk."

"I know this is a big one for you. You got the fuckers!" Martinez held up a fist and bit his lower lip. "This one meant a lot—your life's work, or whatever. I thought you'd be celebrating with us all. But after the raid, you were gone. I figured I'd stop in to make sure—"

"I'm fine!" Sylvia rolled her eyes. "Look..." She held up her hand, fingers still wrapped around the handle of a paintbrush. "I thought I'd be celebrating this moment too. But I just need some quiet for a minute. I need to process." She waved the brush. "Therapist's orders. You feel me?"

Martinez nodded and placed a hand on her shoulder. "Yeah, okay, but—"

"But what? You wanna talk feelings? Come in and help me bust open some walls looking for dead rats? Have some Chinese? I think there's some hairy lo mein in one of those boxes..."

"You're nasty." He pointed a finger at her face. "But we love you anyway. Okay, Ramsey. You do what you gotta do tonight— tomorrow, though—you, me, and Burke are getting drinks!"

"Okay."

"Promise?"

"Get the fuck out, Martinez." She smiled.

After Martinez left through the elevator, Sylvia reentered the apartment. The odor assaulted her senses on reentry.

Standing in the dining area, converted to an art studio, Sylvia faced the small kitchenette. On the floor, where she'd left him wrapped in a blue tarp, lay the body of Victor Cambridge. She pulled back the corner to expose his face—pale, eyes open, slack jaw. The acrid odor of death plumed. She turned away, holding her breath.

He was a young guy, maybe in his late twenties. Peeling back the tarp further revealed thin shoulders and the rest of his shirtless torso. Congealed blood had pooled in his gaping abdominal cavity.

Immediately after the raid, Sylvia didn't feel the much-anticipated relief she'd been expecting after all these years. Her team took down an entire syndicate of child traffickers in one sweep. They got the head of the organization in hand cuffs, but as he was carefully guided into the backseat of a cruiser, a sorrow filled Sylvia's heart. Sorrow that it wasn't the man who took her sister. There were others, like this dead guy on her kitchen floor, who acted as lures. Every foul piece of shit who ever stole a child was still out there. The tangerine sunset bled out of her brain and into her heart, filling it with rage. It pumped into her veins, pulsing through her entire body, feeding every organ and every muscle until she was so full of fury she wanted to cut it out of herself.

The orange rage propelled her to the last known residence of one of the men. Victor wasn't in the building during the raid, and he was too low on the totem pole to go after without risking the big-picture win. All guns needed to be on the main location, but as soon as it was complete, she needed to get Victor too.

She needed all of them. Every last one wiped away, blank like the canvas.

The moment was a blur—a splotchy nightmare. Without telling anyone where she was heading, she apprehended him at home. The scrawny guy was in his underwear, scratching his head as he opened the door. After tackling him to the cement floor of his apartment, the memory went hazy. He pulled a knife from somewhere and she fought it from him. During the tussle, she must have slashed into his belly. Glimpses of a memory flashed in her mind—the knife repeatedly sank into his gut. Gouging, carving until her arms tired. Desperate eyes pleaded with her to stop, but she couldn't.

Tangerine skies were blotted out completely by the fiery clouds in her head. As she spewed the madness from her body, the clouds rained red. So much red, until she couldn't see the traces of orange any longer.

In a daze, she stuffed him in an oversized rolling duffle and lugged him to her vehicle.

Now, he lay covered by a tarp in the kitchen, decomposing until she could process how she'd gotten here. Dreams of violence and righteous vengeance had come to her in the past, but she never thought they'd ever manifest as more than wishful thinking.

She stared at the canvas, desperately seeking guidance.

Sylvia grabbed a large tube of acrylic lemon yellow and pressed it directly to the canvas, squeezing a small splotch onto the surface where a sun would soon be painted.

"A sunset..." she whispered. "Release it."

She smeared the streak of paint with a brush, pressing it into the white backdrop.

Her peripheral vision couldn't ignore the blue tarp in her kitchen. Toes poking out of the end. Eyes brimming with tears, she turned to face him. He'd taken so much from her... from others.

She launched toward him, swinging her foot into his ribs. Bones snapped under the assault. She kicked again and again until his ribs collapsed. In her fury, she'd squeezed her tube of paint so hard that the lemon yellow seeped out and landed onto his body. A ropey yellow glob atop his bloody insides. Mangled intestines and clotted blood beneath.

The fiery red insides bled through the yellow. Sylvia's fist remained clenched, squeezing out long ropes of paint which fell into his body cavity. Tears dripped into his open abdomen, mixing with paint and bile and organ and blood.

She admired the colors, yellow and red...how she loved them on their own. Knees buckled and she dropped, arms held high above her head with the paintbrush in hand, she plunged it into his gut, stabbing, screaming, hoping the anger might take away the pain. But all she got was a mixture of yellow and the blood of a monster, swirling into the perfect shade of orange. She stirred, hypnotized by the dance of colors, the fluidity of movement, and the catharsis of justice.

With her palette restored, she smeared the paint-blood mix onto the canvas. Varying shades from blood-red orange to bright yellow. A fading skyscape of color recreated a replica of the backdrop which devoured her sister.

The hours ticked by and Sylvia Ramsey finished her painting. She sat in the corner, body smeared with yellows, black, red, and orange. It clung to her clothes, her fingers. The image lived outside of her mind. On the canvas, a silhouette of a spinning girl, forever joyful in that moment before the terrible thing. Forever dancing against a tangerine sky.

THE COLOR OF FRIENDSHIP
BY KC GRIFANT

The cabin, an edifice of glass panels and wood, pressed in by billows of clouds, emerged as the jeep jolted up the last of the switchbacks.

"Ladies' getaway weekend, here we come!" Brianna squealed and strained in the passenger seat to glimpse the lake. She started when she saw it; murky and dark green beneath the clouds, it made her think of sewage water. Certainly not the pristine blue in the rental pictures.

Just the lighting, she thought.

"Made it in time before the rain," Monique said, maneuvering the car up the muddy path.

"Thank God we have Wi-Fi." Ginger tapped at her phone.

Brianna resisted rolling her eyes. Of all the friends in their group, Ginger was the one she had hoped wouldn't be able to make their weekend getaway. She threatened to spoil everything with her snappy attitude. *Gingersnappy,* she thought, her private nickname for Ginger.

"It's so nice to take a break." Amita pressed her tablet off. "Remember the time, oh so long ago, before we had kids and jobs and responsibilities?"

"I can't believe it's been literally years since we've done a lake house cabin. Almost half a decade." Brianna smiled at memories of their high school New England weekend trips. She wiggled in her seat as they pulled to a stop in front of the door.

"So much glass, really?" Ginger's berry-glossed lips pushed into a frown. "Ugh, no privacy."

Brianna bristled, tugging on one of her curls. She was the one who had pored over dozens and dozens of Airbnbs, looking for the perfect listing. "I'm pretty sure I highlighted in the email thread the note about the glass. Sunlight reflects against the windows during the day and at night you just keep the lights dim."

"Not like there's anyone around to see us for miles," Monique said, turning off the car and stretching her perfectly manicured hands.

Brianna ignored a pang of jealousy and hid her own bitten, teal-colored nails in her fists. Monique was always polished but not overdone, and her French and South African accent and world-traveler vibe gave her a coolness Brianna couldn't even come close to.

They climbed out and unloaded their bags—Monique a slim duffel, Ginger a suitcase that looked more fitting for a week than a weekend, and Amita and Brianna with luggage somewhere in between.

Brianna grabbed two of the grocery bags with her free hand. "Steaks for tomorrow. Got Monique's favorite chips, gluten-free pastries for Amita, and tea for Ginger," she said and beamed at Amita's squeal of delight.

"You're like our personal assistant," Monique laughed. She said things like that sometimes and Brianna made sure to laugh too, even though the comment evoked pricks of irritation.

"The air is...weird. Is that the lake?" Ginger said. "Gag me."

"Smells like sewage." Amita wrinkled her nose and turned to Brianna. "Did anyone mention this in the reviews, Bri?"

Like she was supposed to read all of the hundreds of reviews. Even though she was the only one of them who was without a job—*between* jobs—it's not like she had all the time in the world.

"Hundreds of five stars." Brianna sniffed, trying to squash out any notes of defensiveness.

"Maybe something kicked up from the last few storms," Monique said. "Reminds me of being in NOLA."

Brianna punched in the number keypad and they fanned out into the living room. Inside the smell was gone, she noticed in relief, and everyone but Ginger oohed and aahed over the chic, modern rustic décor and the expansive fireplace. Brianna took on the role of hostess and pointed out the different amenities she had read about: Nespresso machine, hot tub, game room, and of course, lakeside access from the back. She demurred on the best room overlooking the lake, but the others politely insisted. Ginger's loud Facetime call with her supposed prodigy toddler floated through the house along with the hum of the TV as everyone settled in. Brianna lingered in her room, taking longer than needed to unpack as she admired the view.

Even though the color of the lake was still muted—gray-green rather than azure—the water stretched larger and more majestic than the photos she had stared at for weeks in anticipation of this trip. A single bird's silhouette cut through the rolling fog over the water in the last of the twilight.

"I really needed this trip," Brianna declared aloud, but the others didn't chime in with their usual affirmations, probably unable to hear her over the TV and Ginger's blathering toddler. She half-listened for a mention of her name—someone admiring her work in finding this place or commenting on how much more together she looked than the last time they met at Amita's twins' baptism last year, when Brianna had arrived a smidge too tipsy.

"Heading to bed, night y'all!" Amita called, breaking Brianna's train of thought.

"See you in the morning for the hike," Brianna called back. "Rain should stop around 4am so hopefully it works out. Good night!" The others mimicked some version of the same.

Brianna dozed for a few hours before the sound of rain woke her up. Drops beat against the sliding glass door in her room so loud she thought someone was throwing rocks. She turned on the balcony light and cracked the door to see, beyond the stairs leading down to the lake, rain chopping the water, turning it into a black froth. Clouds ran like liquid illuminated by flashes of lightning. The entire room was glass, she reminded herself, but the idea of someone watching her, unlikely a possibility as that was, didn't scare her. Instead, curiosity—and a bit of excitement—nipped at her.

Until the stench of something rotten hit her nose, stronger than before, bordering on putrid. Her stomach twisted and she tried not to gag. Something the rain had kicked up, undoubtedly, and she wished it away.

"You aren't going to mess up this vacation," Brianna said to the smell and flipped off the light switch. The darkness pooled back onto the balcony.

The morning greeted them, clear and cool, as they hiked the five miles around the lake. It was like old times, Brianna thought triumphantly, brushing past the thick leaves and wiping the sweat from her forehead. Everything went just as she pictured, the rain holding off and the peacefulness ushered in a quiet, seeming to still the birds and insects into silence. Even Ginger seemed awed into being less annoying.

Brianna turned to Amita. "This is fun, isn't it?"

"It's so nice to get away." Amita brushed her short bob back and though her words were kind, Brianna felt a stab of some old pain leftover from when they were in high school, and Amita hadn't been as nice as she was now.

"I really needed this too. You know, I've been trying to figure out the next step in life." Brianna sidestepped a mud puddle surrounded by moss. "I kind of forgot how much I like to organize and lead. Maybe I need to find some way to channel that, you know, like an event planner business."

"What is *that*?" Monique's voice rang out.

At the edge of the lake, under long stalks the color of bile, sat a bundle of something on a patch of clovers. It looked like an army jacket, but as they neared the object, the septic-tank stench almost knocked Brianna over.

It wasn't a jacket, but leaves, tangled in clumps of mud. Flies swarmed above it.

"Is that seaweed?" Brianna gasped.

"Ratched." Ginger placed two fingertips on her nose. "I'm going to hurl."

Monique used a twig to poke at it. A nearly translucent paper-like chunk twisted up in the mud and leaves.

"It looks like snakeskin. Are there anacondas here?" Amita said.

"*Anacondas?*" Ginger said. Brianna took a discrete step back from the edge of the lake, so that Ginger was closest, just in case.

"Not this far north. That would be cool though." Monique chuckled. "It's probably just overflooded systems, backing everything up."

"Sick," Ginger shuddered.

By the time they got back, the others decided to head in for a nap despite Brianna gently pressing them to try out the canoe, a banged-up thing the color of an olive left out too long.

No problem. She'd go out on her own. She untied the rope from the house's dock, determined to make the most of every minute of this trip. She glanced back to see the three of them in the kitchen, cutting limes for margaritas and laughing at something. A whisper of old pain hummed through her.

Not that she wasn't happy for her friends, of course she was. She was just catching up to them, on the brink of having it all together, like they did. She had, after all, been the one with the best grades, all of the extracurricular activities, and Bobby as her boyfriend their junior year. But it fell apart when they were seniors. When Bobby broke up with her to go out with Amita, she had taken it in stride. And when Monique made valedictorian over her, *obviously*, Brianna was happy for her friend. And Ginger had gotten the fashion internship they had both tried for their first year of college. Monique was the smart one, Ginger ambitious, Amita prettiest. And where did Brianna fit in, aside from organizing their occasional get-together? Spinning her wheels, constantly waiting for the next big thing.

She stopped paddling to open a pistachio nut bar, forcing herself to—what did her therapist call it—*take a positive reframe.* Maybe this trip would be just what she needed to get her out of her rut, inspire her to find the precise course of actions to get her life back on track.

A gulp of water bubbled up next to her. Brianna screeched, dropping her bar into the lake.

A mound the size of a soccer ball and the color of overcooked peas broke the surface. A flipper—no, a hand. A cross between the two, with three dark green, finger-like webbed digits grasping the bobbing bar.

The flipper hand and bar disappeared.

A scream choked in Brianna's throat.

Don't call attention to yourself.

She forced herself to pick up the paddle but froze. *Alligator.* Brianna's thoughts struggled to name it. *Shark, fish.*

None of those.

Of course, it hadn't been a hand.

Some sort of lizard, obviously. She had dated someone with a pet iguana once. They could make good companions. Curiosity got the better of her and her breath came easier as the lake stayed still, peaceful. She lowered the paddle and rummaged in her backpack. She pulled out another bar, unwrapped it and threw a piece in the water, farther away from the boat.

After a second, bubbles appeared again, and the hand-flipper grabbed the bar. She waited, hoping to see more of the animal, but the water grew still again.

Brianna laughed to herself. "I made a friend."

Slowly she paddled back, scanning the water for a sign, but the lake had closed up again. Her reflection moved along the glass of the cabin as she neared the dock, the boat cutting a symmetrical scar through the swampy water. She tied up the canoe and hurried up the porch stairs to tell the others.

"She can't even get her life together after what, decades." Ginger's voice was low through the screen door. "Laid off, drinking *so* much. That girl needs to look in the mirror, but she's allergic to the truth."

Brianna froze. *Just go in*, she told herself. Surely, they weren't talking about her.

"She does seem to be struggling," Amita admitted.

"You can't say anything." Monique paused for a second. "But before the drive, she told me she's probably getting a divorce. So if she's kinda off, I bet that's why."

The air disappeared from Brianna's chest while the ground reeled. *Stop*, she wanted to yell but couldn't move.

"Maybe that's why she's so desperate. So *passive aggressive*. How many times did I try to bail and she changed the reservation to make it work?" A jangle of Ginger's charm bracelet before she continued. "And she's like, literally green with envy when we talk about *anything*. Someone should do her a favor, tell her straight up to move on. This is my last pity trip. I wouldn't have come at all if it weren't for you guys."

"It's kind of nice having her around," Monique said. "And we're her friends."

"Are we though?" Amita said, hesitant. "I mean, we hardly talk..."

Brianna bit her lip to keep from sobbing as she backed away from the door. She grabbed a bag of chips that had been left in the car and headed to the lake loop by herself.

Passive-aggressive.

Brianna had run the accusation over in her mind a thousand times by the time she was a mile out. How could Ginger say that about her? And the rest agree?

Memories drifted to her as she rubbed tears away. They couldn't have known how, when she found out about Bobby, she had snuck into Amita's house to let her cat out, never to be found again. Or how, when Ginger got valediction, she had keyed her car. She had been careful, meticulous. She had needed to do those things to forgive them, ultimately. Childish, she knew. She wasn't perfect, but she was trying.

She threw some chips on the water and held her breath hoping—she didn't know what for. It was stupid, but her breath seemed to come easier when she saw the bubbles appear on the surface. It wasn't a hand this time, but a set of protruding eyes, ringed with emerald bands.

Watching.

The head rose from the water and paused. Almost adult-human sized, but gray, with a ridge along its top that rippled in the breeze. An oblong, lipless mouth puckered between rows of gills.

In the back of her mind, thoughts sprang up simultaneously, running in a loop of their own accord, while the rest of her body crashed and short-circuited, torn between screaming and running.

This must be a new species of creature, she should call someone, maybe it was dangerous, maybe she'd get her picture in the paper, mutated, genes, undiscovered—

She took a step back, sucking in a breath to scream. The creature cocked its head, reminding her of a Labrador she once had. She noticed its mouth again—opening and closing.

"Are you...hungry?" she asked.

It opened its mouth again.

She tossed the full bag of chips. Its finned hand scooped up the snack into its mouth. At least she could do something right. Its round shoulders rose from the water, covered in barnacles. A smell, like a public toilet had exploded, hit her. Her stomach lurched but she ignored it, too fascinated by how the creature ate. Rows and rows of tiny fangs flashed in the receding light like a rusty zipper. Its tongue, the color of smoked salmon, flicked out to catch crumbs.

"Where did you come from? You look as lonely as I feel," she told it, dabbing at her wet eyelashes. It felt good to talk to something, someone, even if it was a lizard creature. "Real friends help each other, you know? They don't stab you in the back."

It slowly blinked its jewel-like eyes and slipped under the water. She stayed for a while, waiting to see if it would come back up.

When the sun had set, she finished the loop, but her thoughts kept churning like broken glass in a blender. By the time she came back in, Amita was standing alone, scrutinizing the inside of the fridge, empty solo cups, dirty plates, and a chip bowl on the counter behind her.

Amita turned. "We thought you fell in."

"You're supposed to be my best friends," Brianna managed, hating how she sounded like she was in high school all over again. Desperate. Lonely. And worst of all, whiny. "I heard you. Earlier."

Amita's forehead creased into the lines it did before she laughed or cried. "Listen, we are your friends. But we're not in high school anymore."

"What does that mean?" Brianna wouldn't let her look away. "Just tell me."

Amita sighed. "You wanted to be liked to the point of obsession. You still do, and it's hurting you. Look, I'm only telling you because I'm your friend."

"Friend." Brianna repeated. *Practice radical honesty,* her therapist had urged her and Brianna squeezed the words out now. "Sometimes I feel like you guys don't appreciate me."

"That's exactly what I mean! Your obsession with validation seems...pathological. I know you're getting help, that's really good."

"Maybe if you hadn't betrayed me." It came out harsher than Brianna meant and Amita gaped at her in surprise.

"Are you still sore about Bobby? Wow. Um, that was decades ago, Bri."

"I know that. I'm just saying it threw me off." Her voice wavered. "Made me out of step with my life."

Amita shook her head, eyebrows raised. "Are you serious right now?"

"Never mind, that's not what I meant. I'm tired." Brianna pushed past her to take out her leftover grilled steak. "Whatever. See you in the morning."

Brianna went to her balcony and watched the moonlight rim the lake, sharper than a mirror shard. The inside of her eyes felt raw and scrapped, everything in her empty. If only she could will herself to disappear.

Once the house was silent, she tossed the steak as far as she could toward the water.

"Hey friend," she said when the stench of sewage floated up. "At least we look out for each other."

The lake creature stood a few feet from the base of the balcony stairs, its jade-like eyes glowing. The ridge along its head stretched like a fan and Brianna caught her breath. The creature looked so strong, so *different*, it was almost beautiful under the moonlight. Beads of lake water rolled down the knotted muscles of its finned limbs. It stretched taller than her, with a short torso and long rubbery legs. Its teeth flashed as it tore into the steak. Half a layer of discarded scales clung to it, a smaller skin it had shed.

It swallowed the last bite and gnashed its teeth, watching her.

She left the sliding door open and stepped down from the balcony, keeping her distance. The lake creature opened its mouth again. Pleading, she realized, for her to help.

"You're still hungry, huh? Poor thing."

It cocked its head and the thought of someone that strong, that unusual, needing her help, made her brighten. It all clicked into place. She wasn't the one who needed to change, to disappear.

They were.

"Not friends." Brianna pointed toward the open door. She felt lighter than she had in a long time. Like she was finally on the right path. This is what her therapist might have meant by *standing up for herself*, by *cutting out toxic friendships*.

"Food. Go ahead."

The lake creature rushed forward and up the stairs into her bedroom, fast as an ape. She untied the boat and let it go silently out on the water by itself while shouts rose up behind her.

"Oh my God! Oh my God!" Ginger screamed.

Brianna looked back.

Through the glass walls of the cabin lit by a soft hallway nightlight, the lake creature clamped onto the back of Ginger's neck until the kitchen knife slid from her hand. Red bloomed down her shoulders. The creature charged down the hallway to lift the thrashing form of Amita over its head and twisted her like a rag doll until she was limp. It shot forward to grab Monique, who was trying to barricade herself into the bathroom, and slammed her against the wall. Catching all its food, Brianna realized, so it could eat slowly, in peace. It would feast well tonight.

At least Brianna had been a good friend to someone.

She'd clean up in a bit, take Monique's car, let authorities know they had taken a late-night drunken boat trip.

It was a boating accident. They disappeared in the water.

Resolution flowed into her as she gazed across the dark green water, still as a mirror under the moon. She'd find new friends. And if they took advantage of her too, well, she could always suggest a trip to the lake house.

THE OASIS
BY CHRISTA WOJCIECHOWSKI

"What do I do with it?"

"Just flush it down," the doctor says, peering at me through the webcam.

"Okay. I will." I stare at it, the gelatinous scarlet blob. Frothy bubbles line its edges against the encroaching toilet water, an island in a colorless sea.

"It's just like a heavy period." She blinks repeatedly, waiting for me to respond.

I remind myself it isn't really a baby yet. I'd researched online before my decision. The embryo would be the size of a pea at this point and resemble the offspring of a frog. Then I wonder, would I even do this to a tadpole? I felt a baffling sense of power when I swallowed the pills—a sacrifice for the good of all. For myself, Bill, and the individual who would be spared a future with us. Still, remote abortion seemed too easy. I should suffer more. I should feel shame. Is that what I feel but am too stunned to access it?

"Take ibuprofen and get some rest. If you experience anything unusual, please call us right away."

"Uh huh."

"And our mental wellness team is here for you, too."

I tap the red circle on my phone to end the call. I tell myself I didn't have a choice. I couldn't even entertain the thought of becoming a mother. It would mean never getting out of our neighborhood, of always driving around in our old Toyota, of only seeing and tasting the world through daytime dramas and trashy Netflix series. The book I'm reading about victim syndrome said I was the only one holding myself back. It was up to me to take responsibility for my happiness. I was planning to leave Bill unless something drastic happened. Having his baby would eliminate any possibility of ever getting out.

But this is my creation—the gleaming clots. They float in a stillness that disturbs me. Only the color is loud, a scarlet so deep and vibrant and vital. I'm fearful that I might see it twitch, but also hoping for a sign of life—curious to meet this alternate reality diverted. This possibility snubbed. I imagine he is the little boy Bill always wanted. I think of all the first moments—the birthday cakes, Bill teaching him to ride a bike, me helping him with his homework, him growing into a man, bringing home a girl. Getting married. Grandkids and Christmas dinners and someone to care of us when we're old, like we did for our parents as they defragmented into foggy impressions of the people they used to be. And I wonder if I sift through the blood that I would find the tiny creature with its bulbous head and curled tail, nestled in the gore.

I can't bear the thought of him sliding down slimy pipes and intermingling with the fecal matter of Ludwig County. I scoop out the clots with a stainless skimmer spoon and slip them into a Ziploc bag, vowing that one day I'll dispose of it with some sort of ceremony. For now, I save it in the freezer, nestled between the tater tots and the frozen Italian vegetable medley.

I name him Bubbles.

I love you. You are enough.

That's my affirmation. The book says I have to repeat it whenever I notice a negative thought, like when I catch my reflection in my black phone screen and I hate my face. I feel the scorn of Vera Vander who pummeled me in the 5th grade, a cruelty and rage that I can't understand. I've been annoyed at myself for existing, hating myself from the outside. Who is this third person, the snarky narrator, who hates me?

So, it was always Bill's fault I never pursued my degree because "I wasn't smart enough." And in the 9th grade I let Ricky Jones cheat on his girlfriend with me over and over again, content to be the side chick because "I wasn't pretty enough." And when my half-hearted attempts at getting a job failed because I let my social anxiety take over and make me so small that I wanted to vanish entirely. Bill was supposed to make up for all of that, and when he didn't, I would passive aggressively unman him. And when I made snide remarks about his waistline or his income or his mother, he brushed it off with a sad smile. When he wanted to get intimate and I scrunched up my face, he said, okay hon. What a vicious idiot I was, living inside my head, expecting Bill to make me happy. It wasn't his job.

Bill is a good man, but he is not the ambitious type at all, happy doing taxes for lowlifes. I really can't stand the way he smells anymore. Something he's eating. Like liverwurst. Maybe I never liked his smell? Maybe I told myself I liked his smell because I wasn't worthy of a man who smelled good. I latched on to the first person who noticed me. "You're a bombshell," he would always tell me. "Out of my league!" And I was grateful to him like a shelter dog who's picked out of its piss-filled cage.

There was a fleeting urge to tell him about the pregnancy. To ask him what we should do, but when I pictured his smiling eyes, the joyful tears that would flood them, how he would rub my belly, it made me want to vomit. I locked myself inside my room searching the internet for a way out. Home-based medical abortion. I could receive the abortion pills in the mail after a video evaluation, as long as I wasn't beyond eleven weeks.

That night, we went to the supermarket to get a ham for dinner. As we waited at the red light where eight lanes of traffic converged, Bill patted my knee. "You're quiet, hon."

"I'm fine," I said in a way that would discourage any more questions. As I pressed my forehead to the cool glass of the window, I noticed they'd changed the billboard on the corner. It used to say, *This is the sign you've been looking for.* Now it said, *Ludwig County's first towers.* The sun set behind it, and it floated against the backdrop of fiery orange skies and cobblestoned clouds. Beneath the words, four spires pierced the ether. A couple leaned on a balcony, sipping coffee and staring at the sunrise, its warm rays giving their serene, post-coital faces a peachy glow. The terry cloth robes that loosely covered their evenly tanned bodies glowed with white purity. It wasn't too hot. It wasn't too cold. They weren't too skinny, nor too fat. Their hair was beautifully styled but mussed just enough to suggest a breeze. I knew they smelled good, like hotel soap. They had great sex and never argued. The rich tang of espresso rose from the steaming demitasse cups, which they held with smooth manicured fingers. Another day of happily ever after. Would they lounge by the pool? Or would they take a walk around the lake together, hand in hand, smiling and gazing into each other's eyes with a look that said, "We've finally made it."

After dinner, while Bill was snoring, I scheduled my online consultation. He would never have to know.

Three days later, a hollow fatigue sets in. I am not sure if I'm tired or depressed. Bill comes home with a bottle of Merlot and a tray of

Ferrero Rochers, like he does whenever I seem sad. He never asks why I'm down, as if he's afraid I might actually tell him. Today, he has good reason to be concerned, but I don't say, "No, you shouldn't have." I say, "Thank you." The book about victim syndrome says to accept gifts. Then I see that sappy look in his eyes when he moves in to kiss me and I think about flinging his hands off my waist and that I deserve to go to dinner with someone who looks like Cash Thomas on the detective series.

The Old Me got me here, with this husband, in our little house, with a faded, brown Toyota. The New Me should never settle for less than she wanted and deserved.

"You are so beautiful," he says, with a tender look in his eye that makes me cringe. Before, I'd tell him he was crazy, but the books say to accept compliments. So now I say thank you again, even though I want him to call me a cunt.

I love you. You are enough.

Loving yourself doesn't happen abracadabra. It is harder than loving anybody else. I have been living according to anyone and everyone's desires except my own.

But I am in a good place now.

I tell Bill over crab cakes at Red Lobster, our date night spot for Saturday nights, that I've been reading, doing a lot of inner work, and that I'm not happy. He looks so wounded with all that mush in his gaping mouth. I feel like I'm him for a moment and the pain makes the food in my stomach turn sour. All those nights he tried to cheer me up when I was in one of my moods, and all the times he loved me when I couldn't love myself. But the book says to be direct. Say what you mean. *You deserve better.*

I never saw Bill cry like this before, like a splintered, hollow boy. If he knew about Bubbles, he would not be crying. If he realized that I made the decision to deny him the chance to be a father. I want to get up before I change my mind, leave him there with his stuffed cheeks, round and wet in the glow of the miniature Tiffany lamp, and the basket of dinner rolls tucked in linen, and the crab cakes and the memories that he shared with a shadow. But I don't. I can't.

"We need a change," I said. "I was thinking about those towers."

"Here is the Victoria model." The saleswoman slides the floorplan toward us. Her smile is framed by glistening pink lipstick that matches her acrylic nails. "Huge master closets. A sunken bathtub. His and hers sinks. You've got a lake view balcony and vaulted ceilings."

I squeeze Bill's hand. He is worried we won't be able to afford it. But he doesn't know what we've sacrificed.

"You will have access to the gym, the pool, the spa. We have a community cocktail hour every Friday in the gazebo."

Bill's face is tight, like he's trying to hold his breath. "Do you know anything about the resale value?"

"I don't see why we have to worry about that right now," I say. "And you're supposed to get that promotion in a few months."

"Their value should steadily increase," Cassie says in a clipped tone. "It's an exclusive community."

I think of the billboard, *This is the sign you are looking for.* And then how the towers appeared there. I try to imagine a new Bill as he slouches so that his little pot belly protrudes, revoltingly feminine. He isn't fat at all, just drooping, like wax melting off a candle. But I have no room to judge. The daily economy bottle of chardonnay has accumulated around my middle. It's not him. I've learned not to blame my circumstances on others. I'm tired of *us.* Bill and I operate in a superficial dance. Pandering. Tight-lipped. Conversations about anything other than anything that matters. I remember us in our twenties, constantly intertwined. Bill naturally trim and full of energy. I was in love with his large, wise, strigine eyes when our happily-ever-after was in front of us.

"Sign here," says Cassie, sliding over the contract and tapping her glossy nail on the page. She passes me more pamphlets, displaying couples and families enjoying amenities, wearing linen pants, and sweaters tied around their shoulders. One with a woman poolside, an elegant sun hat in the foreground that dips pretentiously on one side. The model faces away from the camera so I can imagine myself under that hat. Bill slides his glasses up his nose and squints at the paper. His mouth twitches when he grabs the stack of legal forms.

I know he is leagues away from his comfort zone. We are from the same ilk. Our depression-era grandparents brainwashed neurotic frugality into our parents who passed it on to us like some genetic mental illness. There was never enough money, or food. We could never afford anything, even if we really could. That was for Those

People. Our family's Shangri-la was the all-you-can-eat buffet and a TV show at night. That was what they told themselves, as they glanced at each other from recliners at opposite sides of the chipped coffee table, "We've finally made it." My grandfather had been half-starved in a Nazi prison camp for 14 months. My grandmother lived through the Dust Bowl. For them, being safe, being comfortable, being able to eat at Golden Corral was heaven's pearly gates. But we Gen Xers had it all. The couch, the endless TV, the buffet. All you can eat, all you can watch, all you can recline. But we wanted more. At least I did. The Oasis at The Dunes. If Bill and I lived here, we would finally become Those People.

I squeeze his hand again, harder. He's the type who will usually read every word, but I told him there was no reason not to go for it. There was only yes. "You will get the promotion," I tell him. "You just have to believe you deserve it." Turnkey new selves. Insert Bill and I and watch us transform. There's a gym. We'll finally get in shape. Look at the pool. We can have romantic swims together. Cocktails in lounge chairs. We will live the good life, the one we see movie stars and soap characters living. We will be the first in our families to break out of our neighborhood and re-program our working-class genome.

Bill scrawls his signature out. The hollow grind of the ballpoint pen against the desk turns me on. I grip the keys and feel them press into my palms, stamping my skin to prove the reality. I squeal as we step into the elevator. I haven't squealed at anything since I was fourteen. It proves to me that I am already changing. That my decision about Bubbles was the right path. It wasn't an end, but a new beginning.

Bill stands with his hands in the pockets of his khakis, watching the buttons light up as we vault skyward. I slip my arms around him and give him a kiss, a kiss from a twenty-five-year-old me. He is stiff at first, but something in him awakens, and he begins to kiss me back, attempting to return my enthusiasm. A chime breaks us apart. Our reflections in the brushed stainless steel are two oblong blurs. The doors slide open and wait as if invisible footmen welcome us. The halls smell of wet minerals from the recently poured concrete and pungent plaster and fresh paint. Brand new walls, untainted, a blank canvas to paint our dreams on.

After a few weeks, it still feels like someone else's place, as if we're on vacation and it's going to end. I hope it always feels this way. We're making love every day. We smile at each other whenever our eyes meet. Bill looks younger, more put together here, and I feel strange if I walk around without having combed my hair or washed my face. It's like we live on a movie set and must get into costume before breakfast.

"That's a sexy thing you're wearing," Bill says.

"It's from the Red Vixen catalogue. I found it in our mailbox."

"How much did it cost?"

"Sixty bucks."

"Pricey."

I expect him to go into a lecture about the credit card balance. But instead, he stands up and wraps his lanky, hairy arms around me. "Pricey for something that you won't be wearing for long."

There it is again. Proof that I did the right thing. We may not be able to afford the fancy espresso machine yet, but the old drip smells better here. I know we will become the people who lived in places like this. Everything is different here. Cleaner. Crisper. Even after settling in, it still has that new smell. I washed all our linens and clothing so no residue from the old house would permeate the virgin sanctuary around us.

I look up a few new recipes online. The kitchen is compact but modern and merits gourmet cooking. Salmon with dill. Shrimp with prosciutto and saffron sauce. My dinners don't come out well, but they are a step in the right direction, and I can see me getting good at them with a little more practice. I know Bill didn't care for the Wahoo with capers, but he smiled and rubbed my thigh like when we first moved in together, when I was even worse at cooking than now. I routinely set off the fire alarm, but he still doesn't gripe at me even for that. A few more weeks immersed in our new world, and we'll become the couple on the billboard. Maybe I'll book a massage together. Or we can learn how to use the tennis courts that are always quietly baking in the sun. I think I remember Cassie saying there is a sauna on the premises.

The best part is that whenever we pull in at the gate, we have to check in at the security kiosk. "Resident," Bill says with authority. It's sexy. The guard steps to the back, sways into the red haze of the brake lights to get our plate number and scribble it on the clipboard. Then he raises the barrier and we slide through while the traffic continues its cacophony behind the wall of manicured hedges. The

Oasis, our own little world. Even though we struggle to manage the mortgage, we save elsewhere. Repairs are on them. No yard to worry about. It's not like we have a family to feed. We're not meant to. There were no children in the billboard. Just me and Bill. And Bubbles fits so nicely into our lives, an ice nymph trapped in a spell of ruby shards, dreaming this fairy tale around us.

We shop at the fancy boutique organic market, but we can't afford it for long and end up going back down the eight-lane highway to the supercenter near our old neighborhood. The billboard for The Oasis is fading. The couple is blanched of color and the whole scene has taken on a garish pink hue. When we return to the complex, the sputtering of Toyota echoes in the dark garage where we park it, a bruised and rotten apple among the BMWs and Mercedes and Teslas. But the sacrifice for this place will be worth it. Bill will not be able to help but become the man who earns the kind of money our neighbors do. We will soon be the kind of sensible, connected couple where I can tell Bill about what I did, and he will be the kind of man who will understand. I will show him Bubbles and Bill can even hold him.

I resist the urge to complain when Bill hunches over the coffee table in front of the TV to watch sitcoms. He wants to eat there. This is not what our new selves do.

"What is this red stuff?" He stares at a plate as I slide it in front of him.

"Meat-free burger."

"Are we going vegetarian?"

"Not officially. It was all I had in the freezer from that trendy market."

"Oh," he slumps. "I thought we planned ahead for meals."

"We did."

"This is not dinner food. It's not really like food at all. Why is it this color?"

"It's made from beets," I say. "We have veal patties too. You want a veal patty?"

"Baby cows?" he snorts. "Why bother with meat free, then?" He lifts the edge of the bun with his forefinger and thumb and drops it. "It's okay, hon. Thanks." His mouth twists and clearly it is not okay.

"We should keep to the budget until you get the promotion," I say. He was sure he would get it. But he hasn't said anything yet, and judging by the way he goes to work, wrinkled shirts and a crooked tie, one cockeyed hair sprouting from the back of his cowlick, he doesn't seem to be anticipating a management role. I won't bring it up, though, in case it isn't going well. I know we can make it if we just believe that we are good enough. That we deserve it.

Sometimes, I take Bubbles out. I sigh as I rub the frost off the smooth frozen surface of the Ziploc, the color of a black cherry crushed to the palate.

We drink our coffee on the balcony every morning. I insist on it, even though it's not quite like the picture. We squint at the sun and get sticky with sweat. The sound of the highway resonates between the grouping of towers, creating an unsettling vibration.

"You notice that there is no birdsong," Bill says.

"What?"

"Remember at the old house, the morning was filled with chirping."

"Now that you mention it, I don't hear any birds."

"There are no trees here. That's why. They totally levelled this property. You think they could've left a few trees. Guess the local pines weren't stylish enough."

"Maybe we can hang a feeder somewhere?"

"I don't think the association will allow things like that."

I thought we'd have a million things to talk about, like the couple in the picture, with their heads thrown back, Colgate teeth gleaming. Everything they said would be clever or romantic. Their jokes were always funny. But we mumble the obvious to circumnavigate that conversation we never have. The one about the abortion. I feel he senses it, but I tell myself that it's my imagination. There is no way he could know.

I flip through clothing catalogues, which keep coming, though I never ordered them and no one has lived here before. Neiman Marcus, Macy's, and Bloomingdales. I don't have enough money to buy a new wardrobe to match our new home yet. But I keep the magazines to make notes on what the new me will wear. Maybe the new me could go out and work. The new me could even start her own business. She is not afraid of the world like the old me. I bet other female entrepreneurs live here at The Oasis.

I wear my chemise every Sunday, a litmus test I repeat obsessively. If Bill is receptive, he still doesn't know, and everything is okay. After he goes to sleep, I tip toe to the kitchen. I stand in the dark and sing lullabies to Bubbles until I finish my bottle of wine.

It creeps up on us. Only a few months inside our new habitat, and Bill has lapsed back into his habits, neural pathways stronger than any change of scenery can alter, generations of settling for the easiest, most comfortable path in the same way water inevitably winds its way to the sea. It's easier to fall into a worn groove than to keep fighting to excavate a new one.

I did my best to become the cook I think the woman in the billboard would be. I was discouraged about the gourmet recipes. They never tasted as good as they sounded. Maybe I was doing something wrong. Maybe it's just me. I default more and more to my old repertoire—pasta, casseroles, meatloaf, and chicken in the oven. Bill doesn't object, but he barely looks at me through dinner as he reads from his phone.

The flashing light of the TV makes the walls look stark and cheap. There is a wet, gray spot where something is leaking into the ceiling. In the middle of the stain, the paint is bubbling and flaking off like dandruff from a scalp. The air conditioner is too loud, too cold, a cold that makes my head ache. I notice the condo echoes when we talk, our shuffling a rasp against the walls. The TV blares so that the news, the shows, the movies tumble into garbled nonsense.

In the morning, white sun blasts into the living room, blinding us. We have to shut the curtains if we don't want to be cooked. For half the day, we are forced to live in a dreary cave. We never use the pool. It's too much trouble to get dressed and take the elevator, and the chlorine is so strong it burns the eyes and saturates the skin. Same with the gym. Empty machines, pistons motionless, like an abandoned factory. The equipment seems sad, inanimate. A combination of parts never utilized for their purposes. Apparently, none of the residents use it either. Maybe they are like me and Bill. This was a dream that they weren't up to living.

We've given up on the balcony too. Mosquitos congregate and whine in the corners. We've stopped pretending we're enjoying the heavy, diesel air and the roar of semis hurtling down the highway behind "the lake," which is really a retention pond that's injected with greasy runoff every time it rains. Iridescent rainbows whorl on its surface, ripples getting caught on the edges of rotting water lilies. The midday sun cooks it like a kale soup, a rank vapor rising on the updraft. Neither of us say anything about it. We've been staying indoors in the air conditioning, sitcoms filling the tension between us with manic cackling. Bill has stopped responding to my chemise, so I've returned to my faded and pilled kitten pajamas. He slumps in his holey t-shirt and faded boxers.

Bill doesn't say it outright that he regrets the move, but his hints increase the longer he goes without the raise. The building is made cheaply, he says. I can't negate it when the faucet came off in my hand the other day, stinging me with spraying water. When the damp walls are breeding patches of black mold. When the fridge is leaking some weird, brownish fluid. As if absorbing and regurgitating my unease, he says, "Still doesn't feel like home..." Whenever he farts, whatever's left of the mirage evaporates.

It's Friday night. I'm determined to steer us back out of our rut. After telling myself I'm enjoying a half bottle of cheap Chardonnay, I decide it's time for me to pamper myself like the woman in the billboard. Surely, she doesn't take hasty showers so that she can get back to her glass of wine. I run the bath, but the hot water runs out before I can fill it all the way. I steep in the lukewarm water until it cools completely, until I shiver and my skin prickles. I imagine this is how Bubbles felt when he was ejected from the feverish, pulsing womb into a toilet filled with cold county water. I wrap myself in the white, terry cloth robe. I throw back the wine that was left to warm on the 'hers' sink and let it slide down my throat like piss down a urinal. I walk into the living room. "Bill?"

"Huh?" Bill grunts over the solitaire game he is playing on his phone, the electronic sound of the flipping cards are auditory paper cuts. *Ffflit. Ffflit.*

"Why do you love me?" I ask.

"What do you mean?" *Ffflit. Ffflit.*

"Why do you love me?"

Bill looks up from his game with a mix of bafflement and anxiousness. I am past the point of tipsy and feeling needy. I hate when I get like this. Normally, it would mean my time of the month coming, but I haven't started getting my periods and I am beginning to fear that they will never come back.

"I love you for lots of reasons, honey."

"Like what?" I lift his arm, sit in his lap, and wrap my arms around his neck.

"You're beautiful."

"Used to be."

"You're a bombshell!"

His owlish eyes dart around, looking for answers. And I don't know the answer I'm looking for, the one that would satisfy me, but there must be one.

"What else?"

"You're efficient..."

"Efficient?" I cock my head back.

"Yeah, look how you moved us in. Even the stuff from the old fridge and freezer. Everything methodically packed up and reorganized..."

"I'm putting you on the spot."

"No, I mean, there are just too many reasons..." He stammers.

I wait. There has to be more. "I just wondered, you know, after all these years, why do you still put up with me?"

"Okay," he says, his expression becomes grave. "I have a confession." He squeezes me and whispers in my ear. "I only married you for your cooking."

I throw back my head and laugh, throaty and true. Finally, that billboard perfect moment.

The next morning, I wake up alone. I hear the sizzle of Bill cooking in the kitchen, the clang of pots and pans, the smell of fried liver. I know we made love because something cold and sticky is gluing my thighs together, but the night is smothered in a hazy, yellow Chardonnay fog. I slip out of bed and wash up, pick up the robe on the floor and tie it around me.

"Hello, my love," Bill says. "I thought I'd let you sleep in."

The blood rushes from my head when I stretch and yawn. I lean on the counter and wait for the black in the periphery of my vision to clear. "What are you cooking?"

"I figured you'd be hungry after last night." He winks at me. "We need something more substantial than Cheerios. Like steak and eggs. I found a piece of meat in the freezer, but it just seems to be melting into nothing."

It takes a second to process what he's saying. Then I fumble for the pan, flick off the heat, hiding my face in the crook of my arm. I shove the skillet into the sink, run the hot water, and turn on the garbage disposal. A plume of noxious steam hisses from the pan, filling the room with the smell of my cooked blood. I cry into my elbow and nearly throw up on the mess in the sink.

"My god! What's wrong?" Bill asks.

I dash to the freezer and slide my hand between the bags of frozen food. Bubbles is gone. I look in the garbage can. Sure enough, there is the Ziploc, bloody residue in the seams.

"Why are you crying?"

I make hollow, choking sounds.

"Baby, what the hell is it?"

"That is not food."

"What do you mean?"

The odor clears, and I recover enough to blurt out a few words. "It was a bag of scraps. I forgot to throw it out on garbage day."

He laughs it off. He's used to my meltdowns.

I tell him I'm too hungover to eat breakfast.

Every time I walk past the kitchen, I catch myself talking to Bubbles. When I remember he's gone, I feel his absence, a black open sore infecting my heart.

I languish in bed all day watching cooking shows. After the sun goes down, I lock myself in the bathroom. Curled up in the frigid tub, I bite into the meaty flesh between my thumb and forefinger to muffle my crying. I want to tell Bill what I did, but now the situation has gone past the point of reason. Too sadistic to let him know that there could been an alternative future for us, one back in the old house with an infant on a blanket on the carpet, kicking his legs and filling the house with his soft gurgling and velvety scent.

When I can't cry anymore, I squirt Visine in my bloodshot eyes and lay a cold cloth over my eyelids until the swelling goes down.

I come out to the living room where Bill mindlessly sips on a root beer in front of the TV—grumpy, human, fading. I notice how vulnerable he is. The crinkles around the bags under his eyes, the thinning hair on the top. His voice breaking at awkward times, that sad stooping posture from all the hours spent over a desk, working for us. A body sitting there. Breathing. Just like all the bodies before and all the ones that will come after. Dying already. Every minute wilting. And I feel an unexpected rush of tenderness so penetrating, my chest constricts. We are all just bodies, sprung from virtually nothing, animated by a mystery.

No *body*.

Any *body*.

Some *body*.

Every *body*.

I have to take a moment to swallow and breathe, to let my heart unclench. Bubbles is gone, swept through the plumbing, to the sea, intermingling with the plankton and krill who float in the saltwater like cheerful motes in the breeze. Bill is happy with me, just me as I've always been, and I think of what my life would be without him and all the memories we created. Mediocre, bland—on most days— but ours. Forget the life that could've been, the life of *those people*. What about the moments that really happened, that seem so fragile and dreamlike that they evaporate with every passing second? It's only because we shared them that we can remember at all, to know that we exist, at least in someone else's dream.

I love you, Bill. You are enough.

As if he hears my thoughts, he turns to me. His smile is warm and good-natured. "Hey. You want to go to the buffet tonight, hon? Take the night off of cooking."

"The buffet sounds heavenly," I say.

Maybe I only wanted more because I thought I was supposed to want it. And Bill would try to give me whatever I asked for. Even the mirage he didn't see.

GREETINGS FROM SUNNY DAYTONA BEACH!
BY CHRISTINE MAKEPEACE

It was half-buried in the sand. One tip protruded proudly, funneling the sunlight to throw dizzying refractions across the low dunes. The object twinkled merrily from its place by a large formation of rocks. The waves dashed against them, slowly whittling away their mass. Slowly chewing at their bones.

Felicia saw the uncovered corner from very far away. She sat on her blanket, brushing away errant grains of sand, staring at it. Prisms of light crawled across the dust. The sea grass. Her towel.

When she stood, her long legs unfolding like a spider's, she wasn't sure exactly where she headed. But she couldn't stop herself from chasing down the strange patterns of color and light.

Felicia padded down the beach, the sand almost too hot against the soft skin of her bare feet. The prisms dissipated, dissolved like a rainbow, and she stood, confused, watching the hulking mass of rocks in the near distance.

It caught her eye then, the corner and not the lights it exuded, and she shuffled over to it. With her toe, the nail painted a fresh, bright peachy-pink, she kicked it loose.

She thought it might be a bottle. Maybe metal. Something faceted and bright enough to steal the sun. But it was just a small piece of wood. *No,* she thought. *Something else.* She picked it up and balanced it in her palm.

Not a plain piece of wood, but a statue or figurine. "An idol," she said to no one at all. Only the rushing waves and frothy sea could hear her.

Felicia carried the small figure—about as big as a soda can—back to her blanket. She settled in and threw an absent-minded glance over her shoulder to see if any light still danced across the sand. It didn't and she rolled the strange, smoothly carved piece of wood between her hands. It was cool to the touch, almost like a tumbled stone—but it was wood, she was sure of it. It had the weight and quality of driftwood—the salty finish. But the ocean hadn't carved the curves and slashes into its face. No, that had been done by a human hand. She studied it and decided it must've been a lost or discarded souvenir. A crude approximation of some tiki mask or doll. Except it looked nothing like the rictus-grinned, hollow-eyed things she'd seen in bars and on goofy, tropical t-shirts. The figure held an approximation of a face, and an impression of eyes and teeth and expression. But when she held it aloft, away from her face and toward the sun, all she could see was the image that she'd first seen: a tiki mask, just like the one hung behind the register of the bar in her hotel.

She slipped it into her bag before checking the time. She was late.

Felicia threw a billowy blouse over her head before climbing the small, sandy incline back up to the boardwalk. She checked her phone again and saw she had no messages. She hurried across the slatted boards that covered the ground, racing to the hotel lobby.

Grace wasn't there.

She checked her phone again. Sat down in a creaky rattan chair. Stood up. Checked her phone. Then Felicia leaned, as casually as possible, against the check-in desk.

"Can I help you?" the man there asked.

"Um..." Felicia hesitated.

He raised a dark eyebrow at her.

"Have you seen a woman waiting here? Blonde? Petite? Probably carrying a stack of suitcases?"

He paused, seemed to think for a moment, then asked, "Are you Ms. Lockland?"

"Yes, I am." She narrowed her eyes suspiciously. "Why?"

"A Ms. Collingwood left this for you."

He pushed a piece of paper at her, folded over once, down the middle, and she swallowed thickly as she opened it.

Had to leave. You didn't show. I can't believe you're this selfish. My mother was right about you. – Grace

With a lump in her throat, Felicia asked, "When was this left?"

"About five minutes ago, ma'am."

"And she left?"

"Yes, ma'am. She left right before you walked in."

"Oh..." she trailed off miserably. "Is the bar open yet?"

Felicia drank her sorrow away. Or at least, she attempted to. She couldn't believe Grace would just leave—leave her all alone in a strange place with no one to help or watch over her.

She threw back another shot before wrapping a stiff hand around her beer bottle. It was almost enough to block out the truth.

After her third shot, she texted Grace. With self-righteous fingers she typed out, *I never meant to hurt you, but what you did was intentional.* She deleted it and replaced it with, *We could've talked it through.* Finally, she sent a semi-genuine, yet fully pitiful, *She meant nothing.*

Grace was looking through Felicia's phone for instructions on how to log onto the hotel's Wi-Fi. Instead, she'd found a dating app and multiple, explicit interactions.

Felicia didn't have a leg to stand on. And she left when Grace asked her to.

She said she'd needed time to think. Felicia hoped with some time to cool off, Grace would be more willing to talk calmly later. So, she'd grabbed her beach bag and went to sit in the sand. And wait.

She was supposed to meet Grace in the lobby at 3:00 p.m.

She'd arrived to the lobby at 3:30 p.m.

She had no idea where the time had gone. But that loss had caused another one. Grace had taken her things and left. She'd likely switched her flight and headed back to Connecticut early. It wasn't like Grace to do anything halfway, and while Felicia hoped she'd just checked-in at a new hotel, she knew she hadn't.

She sat at the bar for a long time, and found she was staring at the mask behind the register. She must've been at it for a while, because the bartender—a short, stout woman covered in tattoos—cleared her throat to ask if she liked it.

"Like what?" Felicia asked.

"The mask." The bartender laughed. "You've been drilling holes in it with your eyes for hours."

Hours? she thought, but didn't say. "Have I?"

"Yep. Everything all right?"

"Yeah, just dandy. What do those things mean?" she asked, gesturing sloppily toward the mask.

"I'm not sure."

"Why's it up then?" Felicia slurred.

"Cultural appropriation?" the bartender offered.

Felicia snorted, low and bitter. She reached into her bag and pulled out the stone-like piece of wood. "Is this cultural approp—appropro—appropriation?" She lowered it—with a bang—to the bar top.

"What is that?" the bartender asked.

"It's one of them tiki guys. Those cultural ones. It's one of those guys, like the masks." Felicia barely noticed, in her drunken rambling, that the bartender had picked the figurine up off the bar.

She studied it, weighed it in her hands and held it up to the dull overhead lights. "Where did you get this?"

"Found it," Felicia mumbled before realizing the object in question was no longer in her possession. "Give that back," she demanded in a tone that sober-Felicia wouldn't have dared use in public.

"Yeah, it's all yours," the bartender pacified. "But for the record, that thing looks nothing like my mask over there. It looks Egyptian maybe? Like Anubis."

"Who?"

"The Egyptian dog-god guy?"

"I like cats. Grace and I were going to get a cat. I wanted to name her Sadie. We were— What?" Felicia asked suddenly.

"I didn't say anything," the bartender replied, hands raised.

"All right I'm done. Bill it to my room. 237." Felicia picked up the idol and cradled it against her chest. "Me and my new friend are going to take a nap," she muttered as she slipped out of the bar.

When Felicia woke up it was dark out. The ancient digital clock on the nightstand read 9:26 p.m. She felt hungry, and her head hurt, but most noticeable of all was the sharp pain shooting through her left arm.

She'd passed out on it, the idol clutched in her hand. Or at least she must've, because when she peeled her eyes open, the first thing she saw was her soft, peach-fuzz fingernails curled around the grinning figure.

The bartender was right, she supposed. It didn't look like the mask. In the dim, single room of the hotel, it looked like a ghost. Big eyes, twisted mouth, eerily white. But when she finally clicked a table lamp on, she found she couldn't quite see what she had before.

She set it down, ate a banana, took some aspirin, and checked her phone. There was nothing from Grace, but she found she'd been blocked on Instagram and Facebook. Her left hand ached as she used it to press a cold bottle of water against her forehead.

She picked the idol back up, appraised it solemnly. She thought about the rainbow of shattered light that had caught her attention. It was a strange detail that didn't seem to fit anywhere, but she couldn't stop chewing on it.

She texted Grace again, but assumed she'd been blocked. Felicia considered her options, or at least tried to as her head and arm continued to throb. When Grace had found the messages, asked her to leave the hotel, she thought this might happen: Being trapped in Florida without her girlfriend. She hoped it wouldn't, but she knew she deserved it. She'd played too fast and too loose with Grace's heart. And with nothing waiting for her, she was in no real hurry to get back home, because what then? She wanted to hide in the sunny state as long as possible.

She Googled Anubis, and only spelled it sort of wrong. The bartender must've been mistaken because her idol looked nothing like the Egyptian god. In fact, from the angle she was at, it looked more like the carving of a helmeted man's face. She grabbed it and squeezed it. The piece of wood had no give but it soothed her, like she was pumping life back into a quiet heart. Felicia's left hand was still too sore, so she used her right.

She fell asleep again, and only woke when the light from the open window slapped her across the face.

To her horror, her left arm was totally numb.

She'd been careful not to lay on it, but even so, it didn't feel like it was asleep. There were no pins and needles. There was nothing. Just a dead heaviness that pulled on her shoulder.

Her right arm was also stiff, and she cursed her drinking, assuming it was the most obvious—and only—cause.

Felicia shuffled to the shower, washing as well as she could with her weak and/or unusable arms. As the cool water cascaded over her chest and stomach, she noticed a small web of veins just above her bellybutton.

She rubbed at it. The area was sore, but nothing like her arms, and she was too distracted by the constant hope that her left one would suddenly spring back to usefulness.

As she dried, leaning toward the fluorescent ringed mirror like a light-starved fern, she saw the same web-like pattern developing over her cheeks. She groaned, vowing to curb her drinking before turning out the light and dressing in darkness.

Felicia texted Grace again. She then ate a subpar brunch during which she convinced herself her arm felt better. She wore over-sized sunglasses, to hide her splotchy cheeks, but in the restaurant's bathroom, she found they looked almost normal. With slightly less dread in her gut, she retuned to the hotel to decide the best way to wallow.

Her thumb hovered over the dating app before she tossed the phone down and picked up the idol. She'd left it on the night table. Its eyes looked almost red, and she thought again about the colors that had led her to it. A rainbow of light had called to her from her blanket. And all she'd found was a weird piece of wood that almost looked like stone. It was cool; even though she clutched it in her sweating palm, it remained cool. It was an unyielding stress ball and she squeezed it absently as she stared at the wall.

When her arm became too sore, she balanced it atop her stomach and stared at it—looked right in its eyes. And when her own eyes become heavy and dry, she closed them and pictured its shifting gray-brown-green exterior—its red but not red eyes.

She woke with a start, still in the chair she'd settled into, still with the idol atop her belly. Her arms ached and standing was a challenge. She fumbled into the stark bathroom and flipped on the light. She screamed.

Her eyes burned as if they'd been set on fire. Hot and sharp and unforgiving, they filled her head to bursting. She rushed to the mirror and screamed again. The chocolate brown irises she'd expected were instead milky white and muted. The whites looked yellow and everything else was pale and filmy. It was difficult to see and the light sent searing pain through her. With the hazy vision of the milky eyes, she next saw the webs on her cheeks. They were a hot, wet red, like licorice whips or bloody worms trailing across her flesh. They were hideous and wildly painful. Fiery and swollen.

A stabbing pain lanced her abdomen and she doubled over. Dread and bile rose up the back of her throat as she gripped the hem of her shirt. She *knew* what was underneath. She *knew* what she was going to find, and as much as she wanted no part in the discovery, she had to look.

Skittering across the smooth skin of her stomach were more sinewy, worm-like red veins. They looked foreign, something that shouldn't be allowed on her body let alone a part of it. But they were, she saw. It was clear that the ropey protrusions were coming from under her skin. She dared to run a finger over one, then she passed out.

Felicia woke up on the bathroom floor. She had the lingering thought that the last couple days had become nothing more than her waking to new and terrible horrors. She managed to get upright, her arms feeling less heavy, but more painful. Her flesh felt like burning ice. Like what she imagined frostbite would feel like, and her skin turned vaguely purple.

With her big sunglasses, a sun hat Grace had left behind, and her room key, she made her way down to the bar.

She didn't know where else to go. She felt disoriented and weak.

"Hey!" the same stout, tattooed bartender greeted before cringing and recoiling involuntarily. "You okay?" she added.

"Yeah, why?" Felicia asked, but it came out in a rasp, like she'd been in a fire. Like she'd nearly suffocated.

The bartender attempted to compose herself. "You don't look great."

"Thanks." Felicia smiled indignantly. The bartender recoiled again and the act enraged her. "What's your problem?" she barked.

"Uh, nothing. Nothing." The bartender shook her head as if she meant to erase what had just happened. "What can I get you?"

"Beer."

"You got it."

Felicia sipped her drink, the thick rim of the pint glass knocking against her teeth. She pulled the glass back, set it down, then picked it up again. She did this again and again, as if in a trance, until the short, sharp, shrill squeal from the bartender roused her from her stupor.

Felicia placed the glass down and peered up at the other woman. Her face was a pale and terrified mask. "Lady..." she started with no planned finish.

"What?" Felicia asked, but it sounded slimy and wet. She smacked her lips, suddenly aware of the beer's bitterness. She stuck out her tongue in distaste, running from the acrid flavor. A thick strand of spittle fell from her mouth and slapped against the bar.

It was crimson and coagulated. Blood.

Without thinking, Felicia dragged her arm across her mouth, trying to wipe it clean. When she pulled her sleeve back to look, it was streaked with more blood. Red stained her hands. The front of her shirt. She looked down at the glass and saw delicate wisps of red swirled throughout the golden Pilsner.

She looked to the bartender, opened her mouth to speak, but all that came out were her teeth. Two of them. They plopped, without preamble, onto the filmy bar top.

With jerky, frenzied movements, Felicia swept her front teeth up and clutched them in her purple fingers as she ran toward the elevator. The double doors shimmied open and she stepped inside, the harsh florescent lights biting at her eyes. She could see herself in the metal doors, hunched over, dark stains covering her once white blouse. The webs were more subtle, but they extended further down her face, crept over her neck.

She patted the idol absently. She'd stuffed it into the loose pocket of her linen pants.

Finally in her room, Felicia tore off the goofy sun hat. With it, she ripped out fingerfuls of her wavy brown hair. She dropped hat and hair unceremoniously to the floor. Next came the glasses; the nose pads and ear pieces were stained a sticky brownish substance, but she didn't care. The excruciating ache from her eye sockets was too much of a distraction.

In the bathroom, with the lights off, she did her best to examine her cramping, oozing visage.

It was worse than she'd thought. Worse than she could even see in the shadowy room. But she could feel it. With every swipe of her tongue, more teeth rattled in her gums. She spit, and two molars flew into the sink basin along with the splatter of dark fluid. She attempted to pull her rapidly thinning hair into a high ponytail, but the tension hurt. Her arms hurt. And she gave up when she pulled the scrunchie out, only to find the elastic had taken the majority of her once luminous mane.

Patchy, wormy skin covered her entire head.

Felicia's hands shook with a mix of terror and agony as she tried to wash them clean. The water ran red with no signs of stopping or slowing. Rust-colored liquid swirled down the drain. She held her swollen, raw, violet fingers close to her face. The skin was broken and peeling away in long, clean sheets. Blood crept out from under her peach-painted nailbed. It stained the polish and pooled in the creases. It wouldn't stop oozing. And when she reached down to apply pressure—to will it to stop—she felt the nail slide. Slightly. Enough to tell her to stop. She gagged as she thought about pulling the nail off.

She didn't have to pull.

The nails slid off. Quickly and quietly, like the delicate pelting of a springtime rain shower, they fell.

They sat in the sink, a piece of her that was suddenly apart from her, as she wept.

The tears tasted sharp and muddy as they trailed down her face and into her mouth. Felicia vomited, and even in the ever-darkening room, she could see things floating in her juices. Things that shouldn't have been there. Things no one should see on the outside of themselves.

The idol dug into her thigh and she could see more liquid seeping through her thin pants.

When she fumbled up to standing, she left a puddle on the tile where she'd been sat. She was leaking.

She picked up her phone but couldn't unlock it—her fingers were too slippery. Too slimy. Not enough like fingers.

With a scream that cost her three more teeth, she threw the phone and grabbed for the idol. She squeezed it, pumping it like a heart, as she ran down the two flights of stairs to the lobby.

With greasy steps, she slid past the check-in desk and the bar and hurled herself out into the sun.

The sudden brilliance hurt her eyes, which had become less eye-like and more like open sores. Her sandal caught in the wooden boardwalk and she tripped. Felicia lost her shoe, and when she turned toward it, purely by reflex, she found she'd lost more than her flip flop. Bruise-purple meat hung from the strap. Another part of her was apart. She was dizzy and holding in something between a burp and a shout as she stumbled onto the sand. It stuck to the gore that was once her foot. It stuck to every inch of her. She was like glue.

And she vomited again. This time on someone's towel. In the sunshine, it looked darker than she'd expected. Deeper. She was throwing up her deepest possessions. Pieces of herself, all over some kid's dinosaur towel.

Every step brought a fresh wave of agony. But with every step her body became less her own. She was a pinpoint of pain in a huge world that she no longer felt a part of. The idol was still in her fingers, but they were just bones. Bone on wood. She left a trail of fluids as she went, racing and flailing down the beach.

Screams echoed alongside the juicy sounds her body emitted, and she knew they all belonged to her.

With the water in sight, she ran faster, her clothes the only thing holding her together. Legs pumping, she could feel the muscle melting, stealing her speed, but she knew she just had to make it to the water, to run into its embrace.

She had no idea why.

The brackish ocean may have stung inside her open wounds under different circumstances, but Felicia felt nothing. She'd lost her nerves. Her muscles. Her skin was a distant memory. She sank into the water, unseeing and unfeeling. She was bone and connective tissue; she was a collection of pieces. Until she wasn't.

Then she was sea foam.

The waves crashed and mixed with the chorus of screams back on the beach.

The ocean lapped at the rocks. It kissed the land and the sky, and as the sun began to set on Daytona Beach, the idol made its way back to shore.

It lodged itself in the sand, a whirlwind of color painting the air around it, and waited.

FROM THESE COLD MURKY DEPTHS
BY K.P. KULSKI

When she dragged him from the ocean, it was under a blanket of darkness. Threatening storms blotted out the moon and stars, while coughing slow rumbles beyond the mountaintops. His home, just over the beach, jutted from the ridge, sketching a house-shaped void upon the sky.

She had already spent many days on this beach and despite the absence of light, knew how the sand glinted obsidian under the sun, belying its volcanic origin. From here she had spent long hours studying the once proud structure, imagining the lives of its occupants.

The man she caught in mid fall to sea bottom, lay still and perfect in her arms, beauty incarnate. She had glimpsed him on the ridge long before he threw himself off the edge, plunging into the liquid blackness. She had been a sinuous thing, cutting through the darkness, tail and fins parting the water, pushing back at the heaviness of the sea. He, an animal of the land and air, seeking to fly to his end. Why he would wish to end his life, she did not know and did not care. But she did know that she must have him. Possess him. Make him part of her.

Coveting, she coiled herself around his form, need coursing through her veins. She wished to consume him, to gnash at his soul with her pointed teeth, flicking blood with her tongue, sucking at the essence of his humanity.

Some might call it love.

Others obsession.

For Areum, this was hunger.

She cut a path with her serpentine body, cradling him against her scales until she reached the shore. Still as a golden statue he lay, but soon his chest rose in slow steady breaths. Areum circled him, forming a nest against the chill air. Translucent appendages unfurled from her mouth, over pointed teeth, imbedding in the man's ears until finally she found her way into his mind. Pulling at his soul, she began to sing.

She sang about how she nursed him back to health, brought him back from the dead in both body and spirit.

"My savior from the sea," he called her, looking on lovingly. Each morning she painted his face with crushed pearls flecked with gold dust, lining and smudging his eyes with mica powder. He kissed her, letting her raven hair mingle with his. They were one soul. When Areum finally came back to herself, her lips stained with his blood, she grew even more feverish, intoxicated with him and had to force herself to slow down so she did not consume all of him too quickly.

When he walked the jutting black cliff over the sea, Areum followed. She still saw the impulse in his expression, the very impulse that led him to her in the first place. Together they stood on the precipice and watched the churn and twist of the shadow ocean below.

"I've often wondered what secrets the ocean holds," he said.

"Dark ones, my love," Areum answered.

"Really?" His gaze did not rise, entranced by the movement of the murky waves. The ocean does that to people, like a woman rolling her hips. No matter how much a person loves flowers, trees, and the land, they peer at the depths and wonder, and imagine.

"Deep below is perpetual night. A silent pitch-black that can even suffocate creatures of the water. Those who dwell there dream magnificence into the rocky towers they build." Areum paused, her own gaze drawn to what churned below. "They dream of warmth and breath." She wrapped her body around him, resting her head on the flatness of his chest.

"What stories you tell," he laughed and held her close.

"Do I?" she asked.

He shifted on the sand and Areum sunk herself deeper into his mind, keeping him stunned and in her thrall. There was more to give, to share together. "Hush," she hissed. He stilled. And so the song went on.

They wed, right there on that rock, with only the sea as a witness. Her hair flowed like oil down her back, until the salt air tousled it along with the gossamer veil. Areum's face was the moon on the twilight, lighting his way to her.

"Who are you?" he asked.

The question surprised her a little. How she loved him, as he should be loved. She would give him all the happiness he desired and lacked for so very long. So long in sadness and gloom. Now he could have everything that she wanted to give him.

"I am yours. Your little mermaid," she answered, opening her arms. He fell into her like a stunned thing and Areum gorged herself on his sweet warmth.

The house expanded with Areum's presence. "An ancestral home, a remnant of history from the time of the great imperial dynasties," he explained. "My family were *yangban*-nobles from long ago when such things were still important. We are no longer important and this place knows it."

The house seemed to suck in the sea air, in a wordless agreement. He led her up the stairs chiseled from volcanic rock, though now crumbling in many places. Black tiles overlapped the roof, taking on a perpetual look of wetness. Long beamed eaves constructed from driftwood jutted well over the edges of the stone wall. Two heavy doors adorned with rusting iron rings guarded the entrance. These he pulled and they swung open with low complaints, like old men grumbling.

Taking Areum's pale hand in his alabaster one, he pulled her through the ancient doorframe into a courtyard lain with marble paving stones. In the large gaps, a moss-like plant sprouted in sparse patches, cutting forth tiny crimson leaves. These fascinated Areum, she who knew so little about the land and its growing things. Red like the insides of a man, like the heart within the chest of her beloved.

"I love you," she announced and his smile warmed her, ivory teeth flashing.

"And I love you," he answered simply. "Yet..." He paused as soot-colored clouds rolled overhead. He whirled to face her, holding out his arms as if to present the estate as a gift. "All of this," he said, pearl painted face suddenly downcast and moody. "Is for nothing."

"Surely, it is not for nothing, my love," Areum soothed, bringing her body to him, the thing she used to keep him calm, distracted, and to keep him... hers.

He pushed gently away. "It is. This place crumbles because I am the last. The only one left of my family."

"What sorrow, what tragedy," Areum murmured, placing a hand on a driftwood beam.

His hair fell over an eye, giving the impression of a growing crack in a marble statue.

"What if," Areum let her eyes dance with excitement, "you weren't the last? What if you were to have children?"

Raising his head, face filled with wonder, smudged eyes heavy with the idea. "I never thought..." He let out a long sigh filled with longing.

Areum pressed her mouth to his, swallowing first his words, then his hopes and desires. Pulling these into the pit of herself, to her shimmering center where the seedlings began to grow.

So, she gave him children, a single boy and a single girl. It didn't matter that they had been tickled and brought forth like seaweed pods, from things not unlike spores. Areum constructed them with the golden threads of his sanity, pulling at the seams in the gray matter of his mind.

She pushed them out with great gasps, letting them fall into the world of twilight. His joy at the sight of them, she lapped up like crimson syrup.

Each blank-eyed child never cried or insisted on anything at all. They emerged raven-haired and bloodless, with eyes of darkness, lacking pupils. The full black shine of their sight spoke of something more, of their soullessness. How their offspring were by nature, empty.

Enchanted, he never took note, taking the children's lack of complaint and noise as contentedness and by extension, he grew content as well. No more did he go to the cliff and stare at the sea. No more did he wonder what lay below those cold waves. He lit candles and held the soft swaddled bundles and didn't ask how these beautiful creatures never ate or dirtied themselves.

He danced with the children in his arms.

As they grew, Areum dressed them in silk and lace, bows on the girl's dresses and bows at the neck of the boy's collared shirts. The four of them moved only by candlelight like the secret things they were, soundless across the driftwood floors. Four shadows flickering in the soft darkness. The children listened as he read them stories and Areum showed them the wonders of spiders in their webs.

"My love," he said. "I am truly happy. I have all that I could have ever hoped."

Sweet nectar, his words showered over her and she beamed at him. "As am I. So very happy." Her giddiness made her pull too hard, golden strands unraveling much too quickly. Areum drank too deep.

Something within his eyes changed, focused. Then the world crumbled and began to slip through her fingers.

The ocean made no noise, suddenly as mute as the children, the house melted like a sooty candle. His eyes widened in surprise and then confusion, looking around as if suddenly seeing with new eyes. Then his face darkened when he looked at Areum, no longer the joyful visage of a man in love. "Who are you?" he asked.

Still, Areum remained calm. She had him in her thrall, this bond they shared could not be so easily pushed aside for such cold realities. *Remind him of what you give.* "Why my love, I am your savior from the sea, your little mermaid."

Slowly his eyes mellowed. Warmed. "My little mermaid." He nodded to himself. "My sweet one. Sing to me again."

Bittersweet, she knew that the time had come to finish this, but even that, the finality, didn't need to go quickly.

The sand shifted under his form and he stirred, the sun only a distant promise on the horizon. Areum's serpentine body cracked open from jaw to tail, the midnight of her scales pulling back so that the great jelly-like pouch slipped out, blanketing him with its digestive juices. He shook, just a little, as her translucent appendages probed deeper into his mind.

She wanted more. Everything he was and could be.

His beauty made Areum weak, made her slow down the process, to make this life with him last longer. After all, it was her gift to him. The lovely thing she could give. She continued to sing into his mind even as it melted to her touch. Give him a song ending worth her devotion.

The children crowded him. "Shall we take a walk together, my love?" Areum asked, letting the soft black curls fall about her face. He stared at her for a moment, a smile growing on his lips. "How did I find someone so beautiful to share my life?"

Areum laughed in the candlelight. "How lucky I am to have found you in the sea, to make you all mine, for always."

She extended an alabaster arm, lithe and poreless. "You are a goddess," he said taking it and kissing her hand.

"I've been called many things, none so sweet as your words."

Together, with their mute children trailing, they stepped through the heavy doors. The ocean greeted them, rushing toward the black rocks of the black cliff, lifting its churning ink tentacles as if it could reach them so far above.

"How angry the sea seems today," he remarked.

The children stared morosely over the edge, little ruby lips pursed tightly.

"Our time is coming to an end, my love," Areum said, stepping closer to him. "Can you feel it?"

He put his arms around her, resting his chin on her head. "Yes, I've known for some time."

Areum looked up in surprise. "Known?"

"When you wouldn't answer my question," he said slowly. "Then I thought, well perhaps, it doesn't matter."

She nodded, tears gathering in her eyes. "You chose to stay here with me?"

"What else did I have? I only have this imaginary world that gave my meaningless life, some...meaning."

Areum touched his sweet lips with her fingertips. "This way, you will always be with me."

"Eternity as part of you is a lovely fate."

Falling into one another, their lips met. Hungry deep kisses in the darkness. His breath echoing in the cavern of her mind. The mute children dropped unnoticed into the ocean, transforming into sleek silver fish in the liquid dark.

The translucent pouch had folded over what was left of his body, still vaguely identifiable if anyone looked closely. Her gastric juices had done their job, rendering his flesh runny, his bones soft. The great scaled hide pulled the pouch back, closing itself, reknitting the crack until her serpentine form became whole once again. Areum sighed; he lived within her now. She had consumed him all, every bit and particle of his being. In the end, all of his memories that mattered, were of her. His very essence infused into her bloodstream, until her heart pumped on the memories of him. In the middle of her, everything he had been, melted into yolk.

Areum slid back into the sea.

I've often wondered what secrets the ocean holds. She could still hear his words.

"I shall show you the perpetual night of the deep," she said, diving far from where she had caught him in his ocean fall. Deeper until she reached the realm where the silent pitch-black absorbed her back into its fold. In these cold murky depths she rested, dreaming of the many lives she had lived with all her loves.

Of course, there had been others. All of them part of her now.

But him, she loved best.

Soon she would awake again, stirring in the heaviness of the dark. Then she would swim back to the world of men and find the next one that she would love best.

And it would be—magnificent.

BLUETTES
BY JACQUELINE WEST

It's been four years since I was home.

Long enough for my memories to swell and shift, taking on those stained-glass tints that emotion casts over everything. Long enough for the house in my mind to turn vast, rambling, every room a cavern of mood-dyed moments. So when I pull up to the white wooden house at the end of the gravel road, I have to check the porch numbers twice. This house is so worn. So small. It couldn't possibly hold so many words, so many minutes, so many silences.

If the woods behind the house didn't look as deep as I remember, I'd wonder if I imagined it all. But green-blue shadows still swim in the hollows where Mina and I used to hide all day, every day, out of reach of that house and everything in it. At least that memory is real.

Mom doesn't answer my knock at the front door.

I've never knocked before. I'm sure the key in my bag still works, but it doesn't seem right to use it on a door that isn't mine.

I knock again. This time a voice from inside calls, "Come in."

The door isn't even locked.

When I step across the threshold, the first thing I notice is the smell. The house doesn't smell like him anymore. His sweat, his weekend cigarettes, that too-sweet citrus soap he used. What's left is my mother's scent. It's faint, delicate. Lavender. Like dust. I couldn't have described it before, when it was buried beneath layers of stronger things, but I know it now. I'd know it anywhere. It's woven into me from my very start, before I knew anything else at all.

I glance around the living room. Everything is smaller, dimmer, softer than I remember. And everything is covered with clutter. Leaning stacks of books. Bundles of plants. Clusters of fallen petals, tiny white stones. The skeleton of last year's Christmas tree—or maybe from the year before—still stands in the front window, its brittle branches strung with fairy lights.

Without my stepfather here, my mother has been free to fill this place until there's only room enough in it for her.

And maybe for me.

"Is that you?" her voice calls from the kitchen.

My mother is the kind of person who invites someone in without knowing who they are.

Too much trust. Even now.

"It's me," I call back.

I step through the kitchen doorway.

My mother looks up from a pile of potatoes on the counter. Her hair is still pale and long, her eyes still soft. She throws out her arms.

"There's my girl," she says.

And I am.

We sit at the tiny round table with a pot of tea. There's so much to talk about that we forget lunch, and the vegetables waiting on the counter turn into dinner instead.

After we've covered everything else—my job, my friends, the town where I live now; her health, her garden, the birds she feeds—we move closer to what we've both been circling. I feel us taking careful steps, holding hands, the way we once danced to "Ring Around the Rosie," back when I was so small that she towered over me, her face shade and sunshine all at once.

"So," I say, setting down my cup. "There's still no sign of him?"

"No," says Mom softly. "No sign."

"And no word, right? No messages, no calls, all year?"

"Nothing." She turns toward the kitchen windows. A knot of finches swing from the feeders outside.

"You reported it to the police, right?"

"Oh, eventually." Mom lifts one narrow shoulder. "For a long time, I just expected him to come back. I didn't think anything bad had happened. I wasn't worried. No one else was worried either." She gives me a tiny smile. "It's not like he had a job. Or anyplace he had to be. But finally, after a month or two..." She trails off again, turning back toward the finches.

"Did they ever declare him a missing person?"

Mom shakes her head. "People can disappear and not be missing."

"I suppose so."

"They don't suspect foul play. He just took some money—my money—and left. He's a grown man. Grown men can do that."

"Yeah, but—" I let out a breath. "I can't believe he would actually get up and leave." Not that I hadn't wished for it. Not that I hadn't prayed, made promises, left gifts for the fairies, begging them to take him away. To leave my mother and me alone again.

But he stayed. Dug in like a tick.

"Things had gotten..." Mom doesn't finish. She stares at the flittering birds. "I kept waiting for him to show up. Maybe in the middle of the night. Looming over me. But he hasn't."

She shrugs once more. Then she turns away from the windows, placing a hand over mine, her bright eyes focusing on my face.

"It's so good to have you home," she says.

My memories of the first eight years of my life are green-gold. June sunshine. Grass-stained knees. Mom and I alone in the little white house, with the rustling woods all around.

When he showed up, everything turned dim.

He was nice to me at first, smiling, bringing me a doll, a tiny plastic tea set. Soon he moved in, with his heavy footsteps, his smoky smell, gray trimmings of his beard in our bathroom sink. And the niceness stopped.

He told my mother I was spoiled. Disobedient. That I'd been raised wrong, too demanding, too odd, too wild.

And I went about proving him right.

I spent each day in the woods with my friend Mina, who lived nearby. Neither of us ever stepped into the other's home. We both had reasons to choose the woods instead.

We built castles of woven branches, dug pits to trap beasts, ate raspberries and stolen apples and the wild blue berries that grew in the shade, down the slope, out of view of my house. We called them "bluettes" for some reason. Maybe one of us had seen the French word *bleuets* on a package of blueberries somewhere, or maybe the flowery sound of it just seemed like the perfect fit for those berries, like drops of indigo ink dusted with powdered sugar. We would lie on our backs in the blue forest shadows, fingers stained with blue juice, under the distant ice-blue sky.

Then I got too old for pretend castles and fairy spells. I traded them for stolen money from my mother's purse and nights in friends' cars. Anywhere but home, where my stepfather stood between me and Mom like a wall.

As soon as I turned eighteen, I moved out.

I came back just once, at Christmastime, because my mother had called me, pleading. We only made it halfway through the meal before I was stalking out of the house again, yelling *go to hell* at him over my shoulder.

I had wanted to say that for so long.

My childhood bedroom is unchanged.

The smoke blue walls, the quilt on the single bed.

Mom has kept it this way. It must have been a battle: Her against him, to preserve this bit of space even after I'd stormed out.

Somehow, she won.

I lay down in the bed, and twenty years close around me like curtains, fine and inky blue, telling me that they've been waiting, too.

"You remember my friend Mina?" I say to Mom, late that evening. We're washing plants in the kitchen, the nettle and wild mushrooms she gathers in the woods, stalks of dill from the garden.

"Mina?" Mom echoes.

"Yeah. She lived nearby. We spent practically every day together when I was eight, nine, ten years old."

"Mina," Mom says again.

"She was dark-haired, smaller than me. Usually in an old sundress." It's possible my mother never even met her, I realize. That Mina and I stayed hidden from everyone during those green-blue days. "I'm sure you remember me talking about her, at least."

Mom tucks a strand of cobweb-colored hair back into her thick braid. "I'm not sure I do." She rinses a handful of leaves in the sink. "What made you think of her right now?"

"I've been wondering what happened to her. Whether she moved away, where she is now. We lost touch when I was eleven or so."

"Hmm," says Mom.

"I'd try to find her online, but I can't remember her last name." I pinch a feather of dill between my fingers. Its scent fills the air. "I'm not sure I ever knew it."

"Hmm," says Mom again.

And that's where we leave things. We go on with our tasks, circling each other in the kitchen that's just big enough for the two of us.

I sit up in the middle of the night.

Blue-purple light fills my bedroom. I know where I am but not when I am. Whether I will hear voices arguing or my mother crying from beyond my closed door. Whether I'm a grownup now with somewhere else to go, or a child with nothing but the woods.

I look out the window. The forest is blue-black, rippling in the moonlight. A memory I haven't touched in ages comes drifting back to me, a memory of escaping out this window in my nightgown, running deep into the trees and finding Mina there too, even though it was the middle of the night.

I wonder now if that memory was a dream. Or if Mina was so much like me that we would flee on the same nights, to the same place.

I kick the quilt aside and step out of bed. I need to make sure I'm awake. That I'm myself. I open the door and pad down the hall. I still know which boards will creak. Where not to step.

My mother sits on one corner of the worn living room couch. There are no lights, only the moonbeams tinting her with blue, like something at the bottom of a swimming pool.

She glances up at me.

"I thought I heard him," she murmurs.

I sit down on the couch beside her. A blanket is wrapped around her like a cocoon.

"Something woke me too," I tell her. "I don't know what."

We sit quietly, side by side, for a while. After a few minutes, I lay my head in her lap. Mom strokes my hair.

We fall asleep. I don't know which of us falls first.

The next morning, after toast with honey, my mother leaves to run an errand. I pull on a pair of her boots and head through the backyard, down into the woods.

I've been waiting for the chance to wander here alone. I'm almost afraid to visit the place now, to find it has shrunk, faded, changed after all. To see the meagerness love can hide.

But that fear dies when I step into the shade.

The woods are just as huge as I remember. There are still endless secrets to discover, still infinite spots to hide. I climb through the trees, through the whispering dimness, down the slope of what Mina and I called the Valley, a cup made of tilting land with a rim of box elder, ash, elm. And like they were waiting for me, there are the bluettes. Thousands of them. Tiny deep blue drops hiding under their green leaves.

I put one in my mouth.

It's sour at first, then sweeter, with a dark tang. The taste is a wire pulling me straight backward, and suddenly I'm eight years old again, barefoot, thorn-scratched, dandelion-stained. From the corner of my eye, I can see Mina picking berries in the shade beside me. The fluttering edge of her worn sundress.

When I turn to face her, she's gone, of course.

I wish she were here. Not her child self, but the Mina of now. I wish I knew that she had made it through, too.

Finally, I stroll back uphill toward the house. My mother's garden has burgeoned over the years. I suppose she needed her own excuses to stay outside. Behind the rosebushes, there's a new flowerbed, rampant with blooming daisies and phlox and cosmos and poppies—leggy, quick-growing, soft-stemmed things. For a second, I want to lie down in it. That's exactly what Mina and I would have done, pretended it was a fairy bower, its flowers the ingredients for our magic spells. It's the perfect size. The same dimensions as a twin bed.

I run my hand through the nodding flower tops. Sleep, some imagined magic whispers. Lie down. Be still.

But I'm a grownup now. Too old to believe in what I can't see. Too old to want to believe it.

My stepfather visits me that night.

I feel his weight on the side of my mattress, too heavy to be my mother. Too heavy to be anyone but him.

When I open my eyes, his back is to me, broad but slumped. In the moonlight that comes through the curtains, he glows blue: hair, skin, and clothes. He sits like a sack of wet cement.

When he stands up, I slip my legs out of bed too. The floor seems suddenly far away. I am a small child and a grownup at once, held in the quiet of this dream, pinned to this house by memory. I follow his huge form down the hall.

The living room has changed again. His armchair is back in its spot, his table pulled close to it, glass ashtray glistening. The dead Christmas tree has grown larger. It brushes the ceiling now, its brittle branches reaching out around us.

My mother sits on the couch, just where I found her last night. So small. Almost as small as me.

"I thought I heard him," she whispers again.

I point across the floor to the spot where my stepfather stands, still as a stone slab.

"He's right here, Mom."

My mother blinks. She shakes her head.

She can't see him.

Even though he's close enough to touch.

I study his body again. His skin, blue-gray, the color of nothing alive. The way he stands, his back to both of us. The dirt that clings to his clothes.

Slowly, slowly, he begins to turn.

I don't want to see his face.

Oh god. I don't want to see his face.

I don't want to hear what he's going to say.

If I hear it, something will happen. Something wrong. Something that will rip the floor out from under me, turn the walls inside out, swallow up this home that my mother has started to make ours again.

I catch the first glimpse of his eye—a damp black pit—before I jerk awake, back in my little bed, with the moonlight cutting itself into shards on the curtain's lace.

We make breakfast the way we did fifteen years ago. Mixing pancake batter, dropping it into moons and hearts in the hot black skillet, sprinkling raspberries and snowy sugar over them all.

Maybe we'll make wild berry muffins tomorrow. I'll still be here in the morning. There's no rush to get away anymore. I can stay, safe and welcome, as long as I like.

My mother flits around the kitchen, giving me a tiny smile each time she brushes past. I notice a fragile jerkiness to her motions that didn't used to be there. A tremor. A readiness to dart away. Maybe this happened gradually, over the years spent with him hulking around the house, that huge, gray body filling every space. Maybe it's gotten worse since he disappeared.

"I love your new flowerbed," I say, forcing my thoughts in another direction, as Mom slips past me to the silverware drawer.

She freezes for an instant. "Hmm?"

"The new flowerbed. Right out there." I point through the kitchen windows, past the vegetable garden, to the wavering patch of blossoms. "I like that a lot of things here haven't changed. But that's a change I like."

"Yes." Mom takes two forks from the drawer and hurries away again. "A good change."

"I thought we could make jam today," she says, as we sit down at the table. "I've got currants all picked. Some blackberries."

"Sure."

The word berries pulls the memory of Mina along with it. "Do you talk to any of the neighbors these days?" I ask.

Mom laughs. "We don't have any neighbors."

"Not nearby, I know, but maybe over on Radio Road. Those farms. A few houses."

"No," says Mom. "Why?"

"I just wonder if Mina might have grown up over there. If any of them might know her. If she's still around."

Mom gives something between a shrug and a headshake.

"It's making me crazy that I can't remember her last name," I go on. "That I never knew her address or anything. I mean, I spent so much time with her. And still."

"Sorry I'm no help," says Mom.

I cut a wedge of pancakes. Syrupy juice pools on my plate.

"It all seems so strange now," I say. "That I could know somebody that well, spend every day with her, and then she could just disappear."

I swallow the end of the word.

I shouldn't have said something so clumsy, something that drags so many other thoughts with it.

Of course people can disappear. Simply. Easily. Out of the blue.

My mother puts a hand on my arm. Her grasp is usually gentle. Moth-like. But now, for a second, her hand is a vice. "Sometimes," she says, "you just have to let things go."

Then she pushes her chair back. "More tea? I'll put the kettle on."

After breakfast, my mother gets the kitchen ready for jam-making, hauling out the huge black pot, the rows of jars. I go out to the garden with a mixing bowl to gather the last currants. Only a few bunches are left hiding on the bushes, the tiny bright red berries dangling like glass beads. When I'm done, there's enough room left in the bowl that I might as well gather some bluettes too. We can mix them with currants for jam, turn red and blue to rich violet.

I head down the slope, past the roses, past the flowerbed of nodding poppies and cosmos, into the woods. The bluettes are as thick as dew. I pick quickly, the little blue fruits piling up, and feel a rush of happy greed. Mina and I used to do the same thing, filling our birchbark cups until they overflowed, cramming handfuls into our pockets, like this wealth would make us rich.

When my bowl is full to the brim, I put a handful of berries into my mouth. Then another. And another. I'll eat Mina's share. I'll remember for both of us.

At last, I turn back toward the slope. In the distance, the house waits, pale and quiet. I climb slowly back up the hillside. The taste in my mouth turns me smaller and smaller. I'm a child again. Smaller than a child. Shadows stretch to cover me. The sky pulls back like a tide.

By the time I reach the flowerbed at the edge of the yard, the poppies are taller than I am. The daisies stare at me with their wide insect eyes. Things that are missing, that hide just out of sight, trail after me as I fumble through the kitchen door.

My throat clenches.

Am I going to cry?

Who am I crying for?

Not for him. No.

Maybe for two cold, barefoot girls hiding in the woods. With nothing to eat but wild berries.

I set the bowl on the counter. Harder than I meant to. My hands feel strange, too small and too big at the same time.

My mother glances up from the sink. She looks at me. She looks at the bowl.

Her eyes go wide. Strange.

"What are you doing?" she says.

"I just...picked some berries," I answer. My tongue feels wrong behind my teeth.

"Why?" Mom's voice is soft but sharp. She steps beside me. "Did you eat any of those?"

Of course I ate them. I've eaten hundreds of them in my lifetime. Maybe thousands. Mina and I, with our hands and pockets full...

Haven't I?

Didn't I?

I realize I haven't answered aloud. That I can't.

"How many?" Mom is asking. "How many?"

She holds my face. Stares into my eyes.

"No," she says. "No. No. No."

But this is wrong. This can't be what's making the edges of the room go dark, the tunnel of my throat pinch tighter and tighter.

My left knee gives. Mom catches me.

I try to steady myself. My body is slipping, ready to shatter. I can't breathe.

"Hospital?" I croak.

My mother shakes her head. She shakes it and shakes it.

"No. We can't," she says, but I know she's not talking to me. "Not the hospital. God, no."

She pulls me to the living room. I fall across the couch. The twinkling lights on the dead Christmas tree float and spin above me, drifting higher.

"Stay here. Just a second. I must have something..." my mother says, her voice and face dwindling away.

I lie still.

But I'm not alone.

Someone else sits near my feet.

Someone so heavy that the whole couch sags toward him.

I can smell him. Sweat. Cigarettes. Rotting flesh.

I can't see him. But I follow him anyway. Just like in last night's dream, I move without meaning to, drawn somewhere I don't want to go. I want to scream for my mother, but I have no words, no strength to stop. I'm dragged through the house, across the kitchen, out the back door. Straight through the garden. To the new flowerbed.

Of course.

Of course.

I knew he would never leave.

The flowers ripple and teeter. They shudder on their stems. Petals fall.

Something thrusts up from the ground, from under the dirt where it's been hidden. Something that reaches out and grasps my arm.

His hand. Huge. Pale blue. Slick but dry, like a block of carved soap. Soft with rot on the surface, bones like iron underneath. It pulls me close.

I'm going under. Just like him.

For a breath, I wonder how she did it. Maybe a special jar of jam. A batch of muffins. Coffee cake.

She knew they were poisonous all along.

If she knew, why didn't I? What did I imagine, and what did I know?

Questions lunge to the surface, like the second rotting arm that lashes out of the dirt and clutches my leg. So much that I thought was real, that I needed to be real, was just a little girl's loneliness mixed with poisonous hallucinations. So many days spent in the woods, by myself, nibbling child-sized handfuls of tiny blue berries. Enough to build up a tolerance. Enough to make me feel less alone.

But now it's too much.

So much time has passed, and the pull on my body is too strong.

He won't let go.

He won't ever let us be.

The darkness of loose dirt smothers me. I can't breathe. I can't close my stinging eyes. I can't speak.

But something else moves through the depths.

I can see it, even though there is no light.

Another hand. Small. Dirty. Stained with deep blue.

It catches mine.

Mina.

She's come back for me.

She pulls, and I pull myself, and together, we burst back into the light.

Petals rain around us. Winking fairy lights whirl above our heads. The sky spins. We're both barefoot, escaping again, laughing as we fly out of his reach.

Slowly, the spinning white sky becomes a ceiling. The fairy lights settle onto the limbs of a dead pine tree. The scent of dirt and daisies disappears. Now there is only lavender. Soft dust.

My mother kneels in front of me.

"Drink this," she says, pushing a bottle against my mouth.

And I do.

I wake up to the confetti of sunlight across my bed. I'm achy. Thirsty. Like I always felt after nights spent climbing out the window, running off into the woods. I hold up my hands. Dirt clings around my nails. Blue stains tinge my fingertips.

But these aren't the hands of a little girl. They're bigger, steadier.

Steady enough.

I slide out of bed and open the door. The sound of batter in a skillet whispers from down the hall.

My mother stands at the kitchen stove, flipping pancakes. She turns as I step into the room.

"Good morning," she says. Her voice is so delicate, a breath could break it. Like the wand of a dandelion seed.

"Good morning." I swallow the dryness of my throat. "Can I help with anything?"

Mom shakes her head. "Everything's ready."

I take a seat at the little table, and drink half of the jam jar full of water that's waiting for me. Mom takes the other chair. She serves us each two pancakes with a layer of sliced strawberries between them, as red and perfect as cartoon hearts.

She doesn't say anything. I don't say anything. The flickering anxiety in her motions is different now. It's not some deep-buried dread. It's fresh. Raw. Her hands jerk back, away from the edge of my plate, as though she thinks I won't want them there.

She's not afraid of what I'll learn anymore.

Now, she's only afraid of me.

Whether I still trust her. Whether I'll ever trust her again. Whether I believe that, sometimes, what goes missing should stay missing.

She waits, watching me raise my fork.

I cut a bite of the food my mother has made for me. I lift it to my mouth.

The pancakes are perfect: hot and light, butter-seared at the edges. The berries burst in my teeth.

I find sweetness there.

Nothing else.

Mom's eyes follow me. Her lips start to curve, the seed of a fragile, hopeful smile.

I smile back.

We finish our breakfast at the little round table, just the right size for the two of us.

BURN THE WITCH (RED)
BY LILLAH LAWSON

The rain from the night before still saturates the forest; brown leaves, deadened but damp, give a muted crunch under her feet as she runs down the path. Off, some short distance away, is a burning pyre—she can smell the smoke, acrid but pleasant, stinging her nostrils, filling her lungs with muted gray. It's pitch-black in the forest, but she can see well. Up ahead, over the looming, dark trees, she can almost make out the tendrils of smoke as they billow upward from the roaring fire.

The fire they have made is for her.

As she runs, her inky black hair whipping behind her, her dark blue cloak having fallen down to her bare shoulders long ago, she smiles a little. It is a wolfish smile, all teeth. Red lips curl over those teeth, which are pointed and straight. Her lips are so red that one might wonder if it was lipstick or blood.

Her feet are clad in little ballet flats, satiny and black, and they are now soaked from running through the wet forest. Caked with mud, and a little bit of blood, too. She has forgotten her wolf-skin boots. The gray fur that lines her hood is also damp, brushing up against her shoulders as she runs. She has picked up her pace, ignoring the burning tightness in her legs and the hot fullness of her lungs—she has caught his scent, and she will not let go until she's tracked and caught him.

It's almost imperceptible, his scent, over the smell of the burning trees that make up the funeral pyre. But she can smell him. It is a cloaked, hidden away smell, and were it not for her heightened skills, he might've gone unnoticed beneath the lingering stench of the villagers, with all their hate and judgment, and that incensed desire to see her burn, and the smoke, and the wine, and the heady scent of apples that permeates through the forest. But she is special—she has trained for this, has learned how to stalk her prey, and her olfactory does not fail.

She smiles that blood red, toothy grin again, stopping for a moment to catch her breath. She should hurry, she knows, but she relishes this. The hunt, the waiting. It's glorious bliss, the anticipation. When she meets someone unawares, they are almost always immediately disarmed.

She always catches her man.

Her ears perk up. Off in the distance, perhaps a mile away, she hears the unmistakable sound of boots crunching the damp leaves. Someone is walking gingerly in them, but unable to fully mute their heavy step. It is a man; tall. He wears heavy boots, heavy pants, and holds a heavy load. He is breathing quickly but quietly—out of breath. He smokes. There is a slight wheeze to his breathing, likes he's out of shape, but still cunning and fast, or so he thinks. He is darting in and out of trees, his head covered; he is making good time.

Or so he thinks.

She will still catch him.

She stands still for a few moments, the wind snarling in her hair, billowing her cloak around her, leaving her shoulders bare in the cold. Goose flesh prickles her skin as she listens for him again, catching another whiff of him, intoxicating in its frail subtlety. It fills her with hunger. She closes her eyes to the caress of it—the cold, white air, the damp leaves, the smoke, the dark, him on the horizon, just out of her supernatural peripheral vision. If she focuses hard, she can almost see him there, crouching down, darting through trees, his unnaturally pale blue eyes focused ahead of him, determined to get away.

He won't.

She tastes blood in her mouth, mad, and takes off at a run again, heading in his direction, her feet knowing the way without needing to think. She's on the hunt for this prey, her muscles and nerves working in conjunction with each other, on impulse, on autopilot. It feels beneath her dignity, having to give chase like this, but she enjoys it. It has been too long. The hunt has become too easy for her, making her complacent, too willing to take her prizes as they offer themselves. That he runs is a thrill to her, an enticement. He is giving her a gift.

How good he will taste.

She covers much ground in so little time; it's not a fair fight; how fast she is, how cunning, how sly. But he knew it would happen. When he decided to sell her out, he sealed his fate.

She comes upon him easily in a little clearing, after a time. He has stopped there. She's disappointed—she had anticipated catching him, closing her arms over him, bringing him down.

It's almost ethereal, the scene. Him standing there, his back to her, his long, stocky body clad in all black, down to his boots, except for the bright red hoodie he always wears. It is covered in grass stains, oil, dirt; all manner of muck, but somehow, he's still a picture. He is tall, taller than any man she's ever had before, the cut of him lean but full of hard muscle, his shoulders broad under the red hoodie, the soft cotton clinging to his form, molding him. The hood is pulled low, resting against his gingery brows, stark against the pale, rosy hue of his skin. His profile is all angles; angelic.

He is tense, she sees it in his shoulders; he has sensed her now. In his arms is a bundle—a basket, the handle broken, and he holds the bottom with his large, tapered hands, securing it. The basket, too, is black, and she can see something dripping from it—a cloying sweet smell fills the air, mingling with his scent, the one that drives her wild, makes her blood run hot. Drip, drip, drip. He is as still as a statue, waiting. He is staring up at the moon, waiting for her to make her move.

She opens her blood-red mouth to speak, but then he turns, slow and sure, and looks at her.

His face, pale in the moonlight, is chiseled like something stone. Full lips, a straight roman nose, the eyes wide and such a light, cold blue. Eyelashes so pale they catch the moonlight. Once, before he had betrayed her, she had marveled at those eyes, how they were so like her own, and yet so different. Hers, too, are blue, almost gray, and they sparkle with dark fire like charcoal. His are light—an airy, breeze-colored blue that gives way to powdery silver when he is excited or scared.

It is these eyes that give him away now. The icy-light of them is the only indication that he feels fear, or anything at all.

"Hello," he says finally, his low voice smooth as it ever has been, gravel and silk, like motor oil.

She regards him coldly, feeling her red mouth curl into a sneer.

"It is a beautiful night," he says, baiting her. "A full moon. You see?"

As if she didn't know. She swallows down a snarl. She holds her hands by her side, fighting the urge to claw his angelic face into bloody ribbons. Just to see how the skin would tear, how his blood would taste.

"You already know what it tastes like," he says coolly, putting a hand over his heart. She can imagine how it pulses beneath his fingers. "Don't you remember?"

She remembers. There had been a night, much like this one, when they had succumbed to the darkness of the trees, lying down in a bed of freesia so aromatic she could have drunk it, and they had lain there naked, tangled in each other. She had howled at the wolf moon, big and yellow and bright, and he had thrown his head back, and laughed. Everything had seemed alight with cold fire, and his eyes had been like mirrors. She had plunged her hands into his silky red hair, so bright it glowed orange under the Harvest Moon.

He had succumbed to her willingly. She still remembered the taste of him—musky, salty, deeply pungent. He had not minded; he had not even cried out when her teeth pierced his hot flesh. It took a lot to hurt him.

But she'd find a way.

He nods upwards, toward the fire, the smoke still looming over their heads, cloaking around the trees. The smell is stronger here, downwind. "They're waiting for you," he says in that same low voice, looking at her.

"Oh?" she asks, her own voice dripping honey and fire. "Why should they? Did you promise to deliver me to them?"

"No, of course not." He mirrors her question with a smile, his light eyes wide. "Why would I? You'll walk there willingly."

"Whatever gave you that idea?"

"You said," he replies, holding his basket, shifting his weight from one boot-clad foot to the other, "that you didn't fear them. That they couldn't hurt you. Now could be the time to prove it." His full lips curl into a sensual smile.

"As if I have anything to prove," she says haughtily, throwing her head back, her black hair falling in waves behind her. He stares. Her lips curl back into a smile of their own. He could not resist her charms. No one could. It would be his undoing.

He is here, right in front of her, ripe for the taking. And deserving of justice, too. He has betrayed her, after all. So why, then, does she hesitate?

He turns, looking into the forest, as if waiting for some unseen third member of their party. He tilts his head back, smelling the air, his red hoodie still partially covering his face. She is grateful for it. She'd forgotten how handsome he is, some mix of Botticelli and Elvis; beautiful but rough around the edges. Those lips, the light eyes, and his hair. That red, what some called "ginger", coppery and fine, piled atop his head in waves that had driven her slightly mad once. Now her madness is different, but her appreciation of his exterior qualities are still in effect. Unfortunately.

"If you knew what was good for you," she says casually, stepping forward, pulling her own cloak up over her hair, "you would run."

"I've been running," he replies, his eyes still wide, on her. "I'm tired. And I'm not afraid of you."

"You should be."

"Maybe," he says, with a grin. "But I've always been a reckless man."

"To your detriment."

He shrugs. Smiles.

"What's in the basket?" she asks, aware that she is stalling.

"Apples."

She snickers, he takes no notice.

"I've been picking apples today."

"For who?"

"My grandmother, of course," he says with a laugh. "Who else?"

She does not get the joke. This time her voice does come out a snarl. "I'm bored with you now." She pounces on him, then, leaping forward in seemingly a single movement, landing on him, feeling the hardness of his muscles under her as his long legs buckle and she brings him to the ground. The basket lands on the damp ground with a thud, and flies open. She is too busy enclosing her lips on his warm, salty neck to look, but she can smell the sickly-sweet scent of too-ripe apples, mingled with the woodsy, warm scent of his blood. She doesn't have to look to know they're Granny Smith; green and ripe and ready.

Just as she is.

A high, keening sound comes out of her as she bites down on his skin, nuzzling into the soft area where his gingery hair meets his neckline. He does not fight her; he does not flinch. She does not bite him hard—she won't do that at first—just a graze, enough for the rich, salty copper of him to hit her tongue.

"Yes," he says, though she had not asked a question. His voice is a whisper—not frenzied or panicked, but low and warm. He really isn't scared of her. This angers her and thrills her.

She means to destroy him. But she's going to do it slowly.

"I'm going to ruin your life."

"Please," he pants, his laughter low and musical. "I want you to."

Burning in her memory is the first time she'd ever seen him, in this very forest, at dusk, the dull sky rapidly fading from faint blue to black, the stars just coming out, the moon only a slivery crescent in the sky. He had been cutting wood, then, for a fire. Not a funeral pyre like the one that burned for her tonight, no, just an ordinary fire for his house. She had happened upon him, watching him from behind a cluster of trees, disguised well. She watched him for some time, the way his hands grasped the axe, the way his arms pulsed with the movement of his chopping, seemingly so effortless. The way the sweat shone on his brow, which he'd wiped carelessly off his forehead with the sleeve of that same red hoodie. She wasn't sure how long she watched him.

At some point, he had stopped, leaned on his axe, stared out into the trees, and said casually, "You gonna introduce yourself?"

Stunned, she just stood there, still hidden behind the trees, wondering how he'd known she was there. Could he smell her, in the same way she could smell him? She had licked at her sharp teeth, unsure, the hairs on the back of her neck standing at alert.

Still leaning on the axe, he'd reached into the pockets of his thin-legged black jeans and pulled out a pack of cigarettes. He tapped them on the palm of his hand once, twice, three times, then pulled one out and lit it. His every movement was fluid. His upper lip was firm and begged to be bitten. She had wanted to taste his blood even then, but she had not come out. Even the keenest of predators must put survival first.

How had he known she was there?

After a while, he'd put out the cigarette, stomping it with his heavy black boots, and gone back to chopping firewood. She'd waited until he was turned fully away from her, busy with his work, and then she'd turned herself and fled back through the forest, her satiny ballet flats carrying her as fast as if she'd had wings. Soundlessly, she'd run, and she'd hated herself for the fear she'd felt, wondering if he'd catch up with her, and the hope she felt, too. That he would.

That evening she'd removed her dark blue cloak with the woolen hood, bathed quietly, and blown out the candle. She was hungry and cold in her little, freezing cabin. Afraid to burn a fire, afraid of drawing the stranger to her. She didn't know what he was, who he was, and until she did, she'd better be careful.

She had never been afraid of anybody before. It thrilled her.

Hours later, a loud thump outside her front door woke her. She rolled over, peering out the little window by the bed, but the night was dark as ink. She heard rustling outside, and her heart began to beat hard. She had run her tongue over her teeth again, red lips turning into an angry grimace. She would not fear this—she would conquer it. She'd lit a candle and gone to the door, preparing for a fight. She'd whipped the door open, her face a snarl.

The man was standing there. Looking red as everything, red as blood. He had smiled at her, his teeth as white and sharp as her own.

"Sorry to wake you. I noticed you didn't have a fire going tonight. I thought you might be out of wood. It's cold." He gestured to her stoop, where a bundle of freshly cut logs now lay. "I have plenty. Brought you some."

She stared at him, the hairs on her neck prickling again, her back tensed and ready to spring. She took in his gingery hair, his pale blue eyes, his finely carved features. She growled, "Who are you?"

"Oh," he said, with an easy laugh. "Hey. I'm Red." That smile. "That's what people call me, anyway."

Red. Red. Red.

The color of her blood, burning in her heart. The color of her rage. She's biting down, pulling at him, trying to devour him both with love and anger, and he's not fighting back, he's not doing anything but letting her. It's maddening, this. She wants to kill him, can easily kill him, but she wants him, too. At the very least he could fight back.

His voice is low, and he's laughing in her ear. Laughing. He knows she won't do it.

He knows she can, but that she won't.

I'll rip his heart out, she thinks, and pins him down, straddling him, sitting atop him with her arms over his. Overpowering him easily, she rips at his red hoodie, the zipper flying off into the brush. The shirt underneath is black, because that's all he wears. She rips it, exposes his skin; his chest smooth except for a few stray gingery hairs. She opens her mouth wide, her wolfish grin becoming a bellow, as she leans down to close her mouth on his soft flesh and end him once and for all.

He tastes so good. Unholy water.

"It's time," he says in his wet gravel voice, and her heart crashes to her stomach. "I'm sorry."

Arms are suddenly pulling at her roughly, pulling her upward, wrenching her away.

She kicks blindly at the air, and one slipper-clad foot connects with Red's face. He is still on the ground, a little dazed, and barely seems to feel it. He is watching her, his face a stone, eyes shimmering from silver to blue to green, swimming in sadness, the only indication that he feels anything at all.

She can't see who has grabbed her, but she knows. She can smell them all around, the stench of sweat and hate and judgment. How she didn't smell them before she doesn't know—she must have been too maddened by him—the desire to swallow him whole—to notice anything else.

Red will be her downfall.

She is strong, but not strong enough. There are too many of them. They flank her on all sides, ripping at her cloak, pulling at her hair, scrambling through the forest and dragging her behind them. They are not gentle. Rocks and twigs scrape at her legs, drawing blood; her hair catches on branches, a rock connects with her bottom red lip; it splits and the blood pools.

She can no longer smell Red, or the cloying scent of soon-rotting apples. All she can smell is smoke, sour and gray. It is getting closer and closer, snaking around her legs and arms like a ghostly appendage, and soon it will close around her heart, scalding hot kisses of fire, the only thing that can destroy her.

But before it does, it will singe her flowing black hair, melt her blue eyes, blister her skin and blanch her bones until they hold no color at all.

She raises her head to the sky, but she can't see the moon past the trees from where they are. They jostle her, rush her down the hill towards the pyre. They are laughing, jeering. Her scream turns to a howl, then loses its muster, resigning itself to a low, pitiful growl. She moans, she cries. They are still laughing.

She continues howling, baying, whimpering. They take no notice. These measly sacks of flesh have never bothered her; they are earthly things, and she is of the moon. Tonight, they are real. Their harsh laughter hurts her ears. Their smells disgust her. Her own fear nauseates her. But these are nothing compared to the putrid realization that her heart is broken.

They drag her down the path, roughly. Time passes. She is passed from hand to hand, arms to arms, jostled, kicked and beaten. Finally, they are there.

Hot bodies cluster around, leering and rejoicing, gathered in sweaty groups to watch her burn. The smiles on their faces are wide and delighted. As she's pushed forward, they erupt into a hysterical scream.

"Burn the witch! Burn the witch!"

She could laugh. She isn't a witch. She wouldn't know a witch from a ghost.

She curls her red lips over her teeth, regarding them coldly. They cannot smell her fear; they have no gifts. The fire is hot against her back. Soon they will push her onto the pyre, and she will go up in flames. Her hackles raise. She can feel the hairs as they prickle up and stab through her skin. A low growl erupts in her throat.

They scream again, louder, drowning her out.

"Burn the witch!"

Rough hands grab at her, and she's pushed onto the fire. She feels nothing at first. Then the bottom of her beautiful blue cloak catches a spark and erupts into flame. Her dark black hair whips backward, tangling, catching embers. She begins to moan. She won't scream. She will not scream. The bottom of her dress burns and singes her legs.

The pain begins.

The howl rises up from her throat unbidden, bursting forth from her chest, through her lips and out into the dark night air, as though it would pierce the moon itself.

All the villagers are pushed together in a tight circle, all their eyes on her, alight with orgasmic hysteria. They watch her burn with glee. They do not even notice what she has become.

Her eyes do not see them, suddenly, because he is there.

Dressed all in black, almost, clutching a basket of apples, standing there, in the clearing, pale eyes flashing cold. Red.

He holds the basket of apples high. The jeweled green orbs seem to glow in the light of the fire. He raises the dripping basket over his head, and then it drops.

Through the fire and the maddening wheeze of the crowd, she can hear each apple hit the damp ground. Thud. Thud. Thud. She remembers how they had smelled in the forest—fermented, sweetly sour. She hears them as they roll down the hill, ripening the earth in their wake.

No one has time to scream.

The crowd erupts into green flames.

Their screams fill the air, then fade into the wind, along with the smoke, kissing the mottled brown trees as it goes.

The fire at her own feet has died. She looks down at the tattered, ruined ballet slippers. She is standing on coals, shimmering orange and ruby red. They are not hot. Her hair, her cloak, are free of the burn. There is no pain. She runs a hand down her pale, bare arm, erupted in gooseflesh, but otherwise perfect.

Red walks around the now-burning throng and casually lights a cigarette, passing by a woman whose hair is burning, gingerly nudging at another with his foot, moving around the heaping, smoldering pile of cooked bodies. He takes his time; it seems that he looks at them all, locks eyes with each and every person as they turn to ash.

When his work is done, he looks up, light eyes meeting hers, seeming to dance.

He turns to the throng, raising his arms for attention; ignored, for they are all dead now. He shrugs, then clasps his hands together, like a reverend at a pulpit. "You see," he says, as though continuing a conversation that had been put on pause, projecting his voice among a crowd that can no longer hear, "she's not a witch." He takes a puff on his cigarette. "But I am."

She stares at him, agog.

"You beautiful, terrible wolf," he says, turning to her with a grin. He unties her, helps her down. Her legs shake.

"Whatever will you do with me now?" He reaches up, pulls back his red hood, and winks with one pale, blue-gray eye.

She smiles at him, throwing back her dark hair, regaining her ground. Everywhere it smells like apples and smoke. Green for apples, brown for blood, black for ash.

She leans toward him, keening, pulling him close, and sinks her teeth into his throat; red delicious.

HOPE IN HER DEVOURING
BY TIFFANY MORRIS

Hungry for an orange-colored sky, her stomach knotted acidic with Valencia juice. The cuts on her hands stung as the peel unraveled. As rind separated from flesh, the pungent sweet smell filled her stuffy apartment.

She'd thought, of course she'd thought, the cursed song was just an urban legend. She'd heard of it, but she hadn't paid that much attention. She didn't know when she must have heard "(From Nothing) With Flowers" but she had certainly never sought it out. Now the world was draining of its colors and turning blue.

The song was rumored to change connections in the brain, infecting every listener with a seizure synesthesia. The song arrested the listener's senses and changed how color and sound were communicated. Upon hearing it, so the story went, people went mad, blinding themselves or killing themselves as their world grew dim. She knew the world aglow outside her window must have been gray: Oyster-soft and stretched out over the city, a world painted in shades of dirty late-winter snow. The temperature outside was humid; the weather app said cloudy with a chance of showers.

She swallowed the last orange segment, a pale harvest half-moon. The small piece went down thick and coarse in her throat. The box of fruit now emptied, she threw the shed snakeskin of the peel in the garbage and broke the box down into large, jagged splinters.

This was her hope: Orange was complementary, the opposite of the blue that infected her.

Evelyn peered out the kitchen window. The world outside was indeed blue. Not the beautiful cathedral blue carved into the eye of some god. Not the color of the hour before sunrise, the way it exhaled the calm anticipation of a new day. It was the sadness of your name forgotten. The dry fade of a cracked old house, rotting from within, abandoned by a family who had once laughed within its walls. The navy-tinged black of the body stains silhouetted on its floors.

Oranges. She needed more oranges. Other orange fruits, sliced open at the gut dripping blood-slow down her forearm, gushing down her chin, falling in sticky rivulets onto her chest. She would buy orange fabric to wrap herself in, something in a shimmering chiffon, prom dress bright and gleaming, or maybe something silken-soft or woven, something to grasp onto and sink her fingernails into. She was determined to find an antidote to the infestation devouring her eyes.

Evelyn wouldn't blind herself. She could find a way to live with it, if she had to.

The song, from what she knew, was a disintegrating sound of violin layered on cello. Evelyn didn't know much about music; she liked what she liked, and some of that was classical, but she didn't know any of the terminology. Her playlist history ranged from "classical thunderstorm ambiance" to "melancholic doomwave" and whatever random pieces, usually something droning and slow with reverb that the algorithm queued by itself. It was music to block out the world, occasionally cinematic, but easy enough to ignore if something required her focus.

The dull heat of the daylight warmed her skin. People on the bus were ghostly, sickly, pallid. Their faces wore unspoken lamentations, a choking blue misfortune that had its hands clasped around each of their throats. She shut her eyes to the blue-gray of cancer wards and the sullen beep of life support machines, the flame-bright blue of divorce papers, the corpse blue of a missing ex-lover.

There were always rumors about cursed videos, cursed songs. She should have been superstitious, should have turned off the autoplay function, avoided the possibility of ever hearing it.

At the grocery store, the fluorescent lights hummed. Rows of bright packages that had once screamed neon now looked like a dull knife, the unsubtle geometry of their illustrations transforming into gradient. She squinted her way through the produce section, filling her cart with leafy carrots, apricots and peppers and peaches. The soft skin of the peach puckered under her fingers. She placed it in the thin plastic bag. Her fingertips had left small indentations in its flesh.

There was still hope in her devouring.

The flesh sank soft against her teeth. Tart pulp tore at her mouth as juice dribbled onto her chin. Her lipstick smeared—why had she worn it?—as she closed her eyes, tasting deeply. She hoped the taste would deliver her from this sadness, that the bright searing color of it would somehow transmute into wellness and reverse the infection.

She listened to happy music. Soaring chords, sun-soaked lyrics, words of faith, words of hope, words from every possible source of joy: Love, redemption, nature, beauty—

The colors were still fading, dulling into shades of blue, rotting at the edges, infesting sadness into every pore and pixel. Polychrome to duotone: Hints of bloodred, graying yellows like overripe fruit waiting for the worms to tunnel through their skins.

She'd gone to the walk-in clinic. The fluorescent bulbs hissed and sputtered and the doctor—after a four hour wait and her frantic explanation—the doctor had simply increased her antidepressant prescription. This sort of thing just wasn't possible, he'd said. His skin was the gray of sickness, of putrescence. He'd be turning soon, too.

Evelyn went to the pharmacy and refilled her prescription.

She'd called in sick to work; her paid leave would be ending soon. She didn't know how to go back, how to adjust to the writhing way the colors died before her, their long gasps with no exhalation, the slow drip of how they faded from view.

Evelyn scrolled with dull desperation through scant pages of information on "From Nothing (With Flowers)". Among the repeated search results were a few videos of people trying the challenge and reacting to the song. The best information she could find came from an indie music website devoted to obscure and offbeat music history. Part review and part history, the article read:

"Walter J. Patterson, born January 1, 1927 in Hamburg, Germany, found success late in life as an experimental composer. His twelve full-length albums went largely unnoticed by the public-at-large, but found middling popularity in underground music circles. His most infamous work, the five-track album *Howling // Seascape* (1985), was best known for its hidden tracks that played with subliminal messages and neurolinguistic programming. The hidden first track, a pregap composition entitled '(From Nothing) With Flowers', met with notoriety following the composer's suicide.

While no lyrics have ever been ascertained from the song, the work has been reported to inspire suicide and suicide contagion, emitting frequencies that disturb the processes of color function in the listener. This claim has been widely disputed and is considered to be an urban legend, with provenance springing from the earliest internet forums and independent zines. This phenomenon has been largely attributed to the composer's own untimely death after completing the album. Critics agree that *Howling // Seascape*, while a fine example of the composer's overall aesthetic experimentation, is not among Patterson's best or most complex work. Music historian Leonard B. Kessler has stated that 'the album is a clear journey through the clockworks of an unravelling mind; it is a tribute to the disintegration of an era and a pean to the world that could have been' (New Musique Review, 2005). Renewed interest in Patterson's work has emerged through internet folklore and fakelore, with users daring each other to listen to the track and record their responses. Others have embedded the song in video form on websites, titling the song with a misleading name, hoping to 'infect the listener with despair' (Trollolol ReBoarded, 2017). No related suicides have been reported."

Evelyn tried to find other posts, any indication that someone else had experienced this macular degeneration in earnest. There were scattered reports of people having blinded themselves, having jumped in front of trains and out of windows, having taken too many pills following the challenge. It was always a friend of a coworker, an uncle's best friend. She was unable to find anything as concrete as a police report or news article. Everything could so easily be faked, and no one had even bothered to go that far.

It had been ten days. Everything changed color and dimmed into the writhing despair of blue. The color itself became alive with crushing density, a jagged anguish that stabbed at her chest.

The apartment sweltered with the too-sweet smell of rotting fruit.

Evelyn searched for the song. Maybe hearing the song once again would reverse the impact, would bring the colors back to her.

She found it. Hand shaking, she took a long drink of water. A deep breath.

The background on the video was a sea on fire. Ocean waves crested with a blaze.

She hit play.

The crushing sound of violins swelled and burned. Her pineal gland tingled, a static writhing between her eyes, her whole body tensing and convulsing with the cold horror of cello rising and shrieking against the violin loops and the crackling, the howling seascape.

She closed her eyes and opened them when the song ended. It hadn't reversed it. The blue deepened, sea-dark, everything murky with its underwater gloom. Evelyn sobbed.

She would miss the color of the sky towering infinite into the stratosphere, pregnant with the promise of stars.

No true sky waited for her.

Darkness deepened around her. The sun had set.

There was only one way to dress herself in the orange, the color bright enough to make her clean, bright enough to scour away the blue.

The gas can was red, even if she couldn't see its promise. It hit against her thigh as she went into the backyard. The flames that ripped over her soaked skin would be sunbright. She would be reborn phoenix new, a star burning in the expanse of the dark.

FIVE STARS
BY J.B. LAMPING

He looked like the first bite of ice cream on a summer night, and she wanted him immediately. He had soft brown curls with swirls of caramel highlights. She couldn't help but smile when a chocolate lock fell in front of his eye.

She got a drink at the bar, then did her best to look lonely and appealing. Within minutes he made eye contact. She grinned sheepishly and looked down at her drink. Soon he was at her side, leaning in close to ask her name. Thirty minutes later they were stumbling out to a cab, taking a short ride to a place he'd never leave.

Tito's Bar ★★★★☆
Had the best brownie sundae here! The brownie was soft and warm, even after I got it home. Ice cream was smooth and velvety; the perfect Friday night snack. Can't wait to go back and try something new.

Three drinks in and she still hadn't seen anything worth her time. She was in the mood for something fruity. There were a few guys that might have piqued her interest on any other day. A man with golden blond hair and a warm smile, like the perfect slice of yellow butter cake. Across the bar from him, sat a tanned man with light brown hair. Plain cheesecake, she thought to herself.

Finally, she saw him. He was leaning against the wall, with short dark hair and impossibly pale skin. He looked up at her, his piercing blue eyes stirring up a hunger she hadn't felt in weeks. Lemon blueberry cupcakes.

He watched her approach, smiling as she got closer. They sized each other up for a few moments before he leaned in and whispered, "Your place or mine?"

"Mine."

Perdita's Tavern ★★☆☆☆
Lemon blueberry cupcakes were sweet but too dry. Looked much better than they tasted. Might come back another time even though the food options were pretty limited.

She knew a third trip to a bar this week was excessive, but every other outing had been so unfulfilling. She was looking for something that would truly satisfy her. She hoped for something exotic, like raspberry or caramel. Or even just something fun, maybe a chocolate orange liqueur. The options on this Thursday night weren't very exciting. In other cities, a Thursday night would mean a full bar. Not here. Less than a dozen men milled around the dim-lit bar, and only two of them were worth any consideration. She was getting hungry, so she stared them down and weighed her options.

The first option was tall and muscular. His brown skin looked soft, but maybe too soft. Like he spent too much time on his appearance. A guy like that could be more trouble than he's worth. He was like a beautifully layered trifle. Difficult to assemble, but once it was done it looked like a dream. Unfortunately, trifles were a bitch to eat. The other guy was like a cold cup of vanilla pudding. Dusty blond hair, light gray eyes, pale white skin. Bland but minimal work required.

She watched the two men, who seemed bored by their own conversation. She decided to take it easy tonight. She'd been waiting long enough. She sauntered towards the vanilla pudding man and alighted her delicate hand on his pale arm. "Can I buy you a drink?"

The Olde Lodge ★★★☆☆
Drinks were decent, but very limited dessert selection. Vanilla pudding was a bit boring but not bad. Service was good. Maybe I'll come back on a busier night when there are better options.

Friday was the best night. Every bar was packed with significantly more men than women. She loved having options. She liked to wait until she was in the moment to decide what sounded good. Tonight, there was much more than chocolate and vanilla. She could have a strawberry milkshake, lemon meringue pie, coconut macaroons. The options were endless. She spotted a bachelor party in a private booth in the back. A smile formed on her face before she could stop herself.

"Hey boys," she said from the edge of the VIP area. The men drunkenly cheered her arrival while a bouncer stood between her and the table. She held up her empty glass and locked eyes with the groom. "Who wants to buy me a drink?"

The Mellow Melon ★★★★☆

Picked up a pecan pie here. So delicious and definitely worth the wait. Great service and affordable drinks. Can't wait to come back next week for another mouthwatering treat.

She was so full from her last few excursions that she didn't go out to the bars for a week. On her first night out again, she walked around for an hour simply enjoying her drinks before she even began looking for her next treat.

She found him loitering by the bathrooms. He was holding an empty beer bottle, pretending to take sips from it every few minutes. He had thinning cinnamon colored hair, with a wispy goatee to match. His cold green eyes were positively predatory. She smiled at him, a real smile for once.

He smiled back at her, his thin pink lips parting to reveal sharp yellow teeth. She gently took his hand and led him to the dance floor. He followed her awkwardly, dropping his empty beer bottle on a table along the way. He shuffled behind her as she danced against him. The wisps of his goatee brushed against her shoulders.

"Want to get out of here?" she asked as she turned to face him. The predatory look in his eyes turned confused. This wasn't going as he had planned.

"I figured we could have some drinks here first," he said smoothly.

"We could have some drinks at my place," she cooed, pressing her body against him. He looked conflicted, torn between wanting to control the situation and just giving in and leaving with her immediately. She tried not to give it all away in her smile, but he looked absolutely delicious. The orange of his neatly pressed polo matched his hair perfectly. Pumpkin, cinnamon, ginger— this was what she had been waiting for.

His breathing changed as she touched him. He began taking shaky breaths to control himself. She traced her finger along his chin, brushing over the tan freckles. She felt him stifle a gasp when she got to his thin red goatee. She used her other hand to carefully stroke the front of his jeans until she found what she was looking for. She bit back a laugh at his disappointing display, then tucked two fingers into the front of his waistband.

"You look like you've had a rough week," she whispered, tugging him closer using the front of his pants. "Why don't you let me take care of you?" She leaned her face close to his, almost close enough for a kiss. She could feel the man was breathless. He finally managed a nod, then held onto her hand as she led him out of the bar and down the street.

She walked quickly, holding onto his wrist tighter than he would have thought possible. The rush of cold, fresh air seemed to clear the man's head.

"Do you live around here?" he asked, finally finding the ability to speak again.

"Just another block and we'll be there," she answered, not bothering to look at him. The man had a fleeting feeling that he should be worried. The street was dark and sparingly lit by scattered streetlights. He shook off the feeling. He was taller and bigger than she was. There was no way she could overpower him.

She pulled him through the open glass front door of a large apartment building. She pushed the button to summon the elevator, then slid her arm around his waist to pull him close. The man felt his desire return. The elevator chimed and the door opened to reveal a group of men heading out for the night. The group smiled at the wispy ginger man, all but ignoring the woman on their way out the front door. Before he could think about their curious behavior, she was leading him onto the elevator. Once the door shut, she pressed herself against him again. The man let out a soft moan as she played with the top button of his jeans.

"Sorry for dragging you here so fast," she said sweetly. "I'm just so hungry, and I couldn't wait any longer." The man leaned in to kiss her, but she stopped him an inch from her face. "Not until we get there."

The man barely registered leaving the elevator and entering her apartment. She brought him into the kitchen, giving him a long kiss before slipping out of the room with a promise of a quick return. The man touched his thin lips, wondering if the woman's dark red lipstick had left a mark. He gazed around the room nonchalantly, his mind focused on what they'd soon be doing in a different room in her apartment.

White subway tiles lined the kitchen walls under pristine pearly cabinets. Each cabinet door was outlined in soft pink, with purple flowers painted in the corners. The cabinet handles alternated between blue and pink ceramic pulls. The first word that came to the man's mind was "cute". He reached out to touch the gray and pink countertops, surprised to find such expensive granite in an apartment. A glass vase filled with daisies sat in the middle of the counter next to a delicate-looking tea set. The man smiled at the petal pink teacups. The kitchen looked like it belonged in a dollhouse.

After a few minutes, the man grew impatient and decided to find his temptress. The rest of the apartment was dark, and he was sure she was there waiting for him. Before he could leave the charming kitchen, he noticed a silver tray on the counter. He saw the sharp glinting blades the same time he heard the woman enter the room behind him.

"Sorry to keep you waiting," she purred as she opened some cabinets. The man slowly turned to face her. "I had to find a clean apron. What do you think?" She held out the skirt of the pink apron, which was dusted with white polka dots. She didn't wait for him to respond as she resumed getting mixing bowls and measuring cups out from the cabinets. The man felt a paralyzing fear creep over him. He tried to inch backwards away from the woman.

"You of all people should know that it's a little late for that," she laughed.

Hooligan's ★★★★★

Had the absolute best pumpkin pie here! So creamy and smooth. The fresh ground cinnamon really topped it all off. Can't wait to come back for more!

WHEELS
BY JEANNE E. BUSH

They decapitate her every night.

She is alone on the road as she drives. The evening sky starts to darken, and the headlights seem dim as she scans the empty Kentucky road. The branches of the trees lean in as she follows the winding lane through the woods. The music coming from the speakers changes and "Paint It Black" by the Stones begins to play. This stretch of road is long—she knows this—and she hums tunelessly along, watching the road get darker as the evening deepens.

Suddenly, a silvery gray insect lands on the windshield—is it a fly? She doesn't think so. Then another lands and another after that. More insects gather, landing purposely on the windshield, writhing together as they crawl over each other. Soon it is getting difficult to see the road, the buggy grayness filling the view. She turns on the wipers, smearing dark bug bodies across the glass.

She continues on, almost blindly, talking softly to herself in her horror but knowing that she must keep moving on as the insects continue to gather. Their gray bodies are on every window now, and she can hear the clicks on the glass as their little feet move across the space. She can almost see their thousands of mouths chomping up and down, up and down, and her terrified eyes open wider as a soft horrified "Oh" escapes her lips. She speeds up, desperately wanting to be off this road and among other people.

Then the unthinkable happens. One of the insects emerges from the air vent to her right. She somehow thinks, "Wheel bug?" as she sees the small circular sawblade pattern on its back. It struggles, pushing itself through the vent, then it is up and flying. Frantically, she works the buttons for the air conditioner, panic-stricken as she tries to close the vents. But more insects break through and soon dozens, then hundreds of bugs are in the car flying around her.

The car crashes into a large tree, and her arms flail around her face at the merciless swarm. She feels a sharp sting on her throat, then dozens of little bites. She screams as her hands move to frantically brush the insects from her neck. But they are hungry now, so hungry. They continue to bite her neck until red blood drips, then in a frenzy they continue to gnaw and cut.

Terrified, she opens the door, stumbling from the car, running, but the insects are on her, needing her blood, continuing to bite her at the neck until she falls. She feels them writhing in her shirt, scurrying across her face and arms, scuttling through her hair. But they want her neck. They begin feeding, cutting the veins and arteries and tendons in her throat until her blood pours forth. They continue chewing through to the discs and joints of her neck bone. She is dazed, nearly dead, as the assassin bugs continue to cut the head from her body, feeding, feeding.

She awakens in the gray. The room is small with a high ceiling and empty dingy walls. A long window is in front of her; next to it is a narrow black door. She sits on a dark sofa, but otherwise the grim room is empty. Long sheer curtains hang limply in front of the window and little light is allowed into the room. It is gray and she *feels* gray. Gasping, her hands flutter to her neck, relieved to find that it is intact, whole.

She leans her head back onto the top of the sofa; she is so tired. The heaviness of this gray room feels like a thousand pounds, dragging her body down. She feels lethargic, limp, and so very sad.

Then she begins to hear the sounds coming from outside the window. Moans, high-pitched shrieks, and groans enter the room, frightening in their pain and their sadness. Heartsick and terrified, she watches the darker gray shadows move back and forth outside. The cries and laments mount, growing louder until she feels she will go mad. She leans over and lays her head on the sofa cushion, her hands covering her ears. A moan escapes her lips, mirroring the sounds she hears outside. Her groans get louder, louder, her terror and growing sadness reflected in the gray.

Finally, she rises, forcing herself to her feet. She sighs heavily as she walks to the black door, and with her head against the smooth wood, considers opening it to join the writhing throng outside the room.

The hospital room is dim with only one small side-table light on. The young woman's father sits near the window, watching the labored breathing of his daughter. The ventilator hisses softly but otherwise the small room is deathly quiet.

She has been his life since her mother died twelve years ago. His bright little girl, so curious, so strong. She was never afraid of spiders or of things hiding under the bed. She faced any fears with a fierceness that could only come from her loving mother. In high school, she had a big group of friends. In college she took English, math, and science classes like chemistry and entomology, and absorbed every bit of the information she was given. Now she is here, so weak and fragile. His heart breaks as he watches her.

Her walk through the park on campus that night should have been uneventful, as it had been every night she strolled from her small apartment to the steps of the university library, just on the edge of campus. Her interest in science, entomology to be specific, had not been fully sated by course study this year, so trying to devour every bit of information had been her goal these last few months before graduation.

She heard the pounding of shoes on the concrete walkway just before she heard the laughter erupt. She didn't know how many attackers there were, but they were on her quickly. The smell of crack-stained teeth and alcohol filled her nose as the first attacker held his hand over her mouth and breathed heavily into her ear.

She felt the knife blade, cold on her neck, and was paralyzed with fear. She was turned to face another of her attackers, a shaggy teenager with moppy blond hair. He was wearing a gray concert t-shirt with a crude drawing of a leather-clad skeleton swinging a circular saw blade on a chain. As he turned to his friends, she saw the bug tattoo on his neck. Her attackers' eyes were vacant but angry, high on the illegal substances coursing through their bodies. What possessed these youths she would never know, but they were threatening, and she was terrified.

The young men argued with each other, though in her terror she couldn't make out the words they spoke. Without so much as a warning, the teen behind her pressed the knife blade deeper into her neck and she felt a sharp pain, then a warm trickle of blood.

The door opens and a middle-aged priest enters the hospital room. He looks over his glasses at the father as he walks closer. "Any change with your daughter?" he asks.

"No," the father returns. "Her sleep is so restless but at least that means she's alive."

"It was a close call in that park. I thought you'd want to know that they caught one of the culprits. They think they'll get the others."

The father looks up. "Did they find the knife that..." He falters, then continues, "That did this to her?" He gestures towards the bandages that surround her neck. His eyes fill with tears, and he sobs softly. "They could have killed her, and almost did when they slashed her throat. Now she seems to be in her own purgatory, and I don't know how to get her back."

The priest reaches over to place a hand on the father's shoulder. "Purgatory," he repeats, then asks softly, "Would you like me to say a prayer for her?"

The father shakes his head, then reconsiders the request. "I'm not a believer, but if you want to say a few words, I'll take them."

The priest nods, then folds his hands and begins a short prayer, "Lord, we ask that you watch over this young woman..."

She is in her car again, driving along a deserted Kentucky road. The music coming from the speakers changes and "Gimme Shelter" by the Stones begins to play. She hums along tunelessly as she winds through the tree-lined lane, the leaves close in as she passes. A silvery gray insect lands on the windshield, and then another and another. The scream—a product of knowing this time, knowing what comes next—has no time to escape her lips. The car fills with little bug bodies. The frenzy begins once again.

They decapitate her every night. But this time, she'll fight for these nights to end.

She is in the gray room with the narrow black door and the sheer curtains over the long window. Panicking, she reaches for her neck and is relieved to find it unharmed, shrouded beneath a veil of gauze, but whole. The shadows are gone, as is the heavy sadness, and the images of the insects no longer cause her fear. Replacing the moans and shrieks outside the window is the distant sound of her father's voice and that of a stranger. The gray begins to brighten to white.

ELEGY
BY NU YANG

On cold nights, Death sat on rooftops and peered into the windows that belonged to nameless living souls. Families settled into their beds. Couples made love on clean sheets. Hungry children crept down the stairs for a late-night snack. Like the living was obsessed with death, Death was obsessed with the living.

It was during those nights when he first saw the Outsider. The girl walked like the living, she breathed like one, but she was missing the color of a soul. Time for Death was infinite, and in all his time, he had never once met anyone like her.

The girl was young, still a teenager. Her hair was the color of straw and her eyes, blue, but they were as dark as a storm and outlined with heavy black eyeliner. She walked with a boy her age. Each step she took had a bounce and a skip to it. Their arms were wrapped around their waists. She smiled and laughed, her head resting on the boy's shoulder. The dark-haired boy radiated a mixture of silver and gold. There was so much life there.

Death descended from the rooftop and fell in step with the girl and boy. They walked for a few more minutes before they stopped in front of a house. The boy leaned forward, but the girl giggled and turned her head away. The boy reached out for her, grabbing her arm, and anchoring her to him. She tugged again and freed herself. They separated, and the girl walked into her home. Death followed.

The girl greeted her parents, who were waiting up to hear about their daughter's date. She dismissed them with a wave of her hand and went into her room. There, Death watched as she called someone on her phone. That evening she spent hours talking about the boy, letting the words "love" and "forever" slide easily off her tongue. As she spoke, she laughed. There was enough life in that sound to make Death wonder if her soul was indeed missing a color.

Even though Death knew of the existence of the Outsider, he was not going to let her distract him of his duties.

Death had wings the color of a radiant sunset on a summer day. He wore white like his other comrades, but that was where the comparisons ended. He performed a duty unlike the Guardians: the protectors of life, and the Cherubs: the messengers. He often had to remind himself his duties were just as necessary as theirs.

While he waited for his next assignment, he observed the living souls.

The toddler taking her first steps illuminated a golden yellow. Her proud and smiling mother sparkled like a clear ocean's reflection. The man riding his motorcycle charged down the street. He was a vibrant red; the color streaked past a car that had just run through a stop sign. He had no time to react. He jumped the curb, and his motorcycle came onto the sidewalk. The front tire crushed the toddler beneath him. The mother's screams, sprinkled with colors, exploded from inside her.

Death slid through the colors and emerged on the other side. The little girl's yellow glow began to fade. Her cries were filled with pain and confusion. He granted her wish for mercy by touching her bleeding head. Her chest rose, then fell. The color around her diminished, so did her cries. He gathered her into his arms. Here, she was still golden.

Death never traveled past the gates. After he left behind the souls he collected, he returned to his work without any hesitation or questions. But after meeting the Outsider and seeing her lack of colors, he felt the need to get through the metal bars. Things he had been so certain of were now filled with doubt. Maybe his answers could be found on the other side.

He waited for the gates to open, but nothing happened. When he touched the barrier, a warmth he could not describe filled his body. He rubbed his fingers together as the heated sensation stained his skin. This was the only taste he could ever get of what took place beyond the gates.

When Death shut his eyes, he saw the colors of those he had taken. Many of them still clung onto him, afraid to let go and crossover. Many of them remained because they had to say good-bye first.

Often, he would go visit the living who had been left behind because he was curious as to why those souls did not want to leave.

Each one was different. The young woman sobbing into her pillow, grieving over her husband who died in the war was not the same as the elderly man who lost his wife of over forty years to cancer. Everyone's pain was not the same. Everyone mourned in their own way.

Death guaranteed mercy to everyone, even to the living.

He sat beside the soldier's widow and whispered in her ear. Her tears stopped falling as she felt her husband's bright blue soul comfort her sorrowful spirit. Then, he moved on to the elderly man and stopped him from packing away the memories of the many years he had spent with his wife. In the picture frames, the man could still feel his wife's healthy green glow leap from the image and touch his face—just like she had done on their wedding day so long ago.

It was only after knowing their living loved ones could move on that these souls could continue their journey to the gates with Death.

Another job well done.

Death didn't close his eyes often, though. He had to be able to see the colors changing around him. The man with the failing kidney received a last-minute transplant. The boy who swam to the deep end of a swimming pool gasped for air as oxygen filled his lungs again.

When Death arrived, he found the fragile newborn struggling to live. The doctors were seconds from walking away. The little one's color was still too weak to penetrate the living world.

Death reached out to collect, but a Guardian swooped in, stepping in between the child and Death. The Guardian's white wings opened, expanding to fill the room. Soon, a new color splashed the walls red and pink. The baby's wails echoed, and the parents smiled with tears, relieved to hear the sounds of life.

The Guardian's steel blue eyes turned to Death. This was not a competition, but it was something they both had to understand—each of them had a job to do.

Death left the hospital's delivery room. As he crossed the hallway, a dying drunk driver called out for him.

The Outsider liked to spend her days outdoors. She sat on the green grass with an open notebook on her lap. Her hand moved from left to right across the piece of paper as she drew shapes and figures and added colors to them. Colors she lacked herself.

Death watched overhead, perched on a tree limb. Filled with curiosity, he joined the girl on the ground. The colors on her pages seemed to leap out from the book. They were alive. He snatched them and they escaped through his fingers. The more the girl colored, the more life jumped from the pages.

He heard the flapping of another set of wings. The tiny Cherub stood behind the girl with his arms crossed and a frown on his round face.

The girl was a question not meant to be answered.

Death rose to his feet and nodded at the Cherub. Both of them took off into the sky, but Death did not—could not—follow the Cherub past the gates. Instead, he went to attend to his other business.

Death stepped into the dark room. It was not the lack of light that made the darkness unbearable here; it was the void inside the man who sat in the corner. His teal outline morphed into navy blue before escalating into aqua.

The man blinked back the tears as his trembling hands picked up the gun. Scattered around him were photographs of a dead family. A woman and three children Death had visited when their home was destroyed in a storm. It had been necessary.

What was happening this very instant was also necessary.

The room grew darker as the man pressed the barrel of the gun into his mouth. His finger curled around the trigger and pulled. The only color now in the room came from crimson blood as it covered the wooden floor.

Death lowered his head as shadows became substance. They crawled over his feet and on the man's fallen body. The shadows growled and snarled as they came upon their prey. Death stepped aside as the black shadows transformed into a blazing array of blues leftover from the man. They slithered away when Death spread his wings, and a bright light filled the room. The shadows howled as they were blinded, releasing the man's soul. Cold blue melded with Death's wings. When he shut them, all was quiet.

Despite the Cherub's silent warning to stay away from the Outsider, Death still came to her, drawn to her colorless soul and her vivacious life.

The girl was out again with the same dark-haired boy. They met for food, watched people in a nearby park, and got into his car.

Death sat in the backseat and watched the girl smile and laugh as the boy drove. When he turned down a dirt road, the girl's smile and laughter vanished. She fidgeted in her seat as the boy continued to drive down the strange road. He stopped the car, unbuckled his seatbelt, and grabbed the girl. This time she could not free herself. As the boy she had vowed to love forever lunged at her, she escaped into the dark woods. Both the boy and Death pursued her.

Despite running with all her might, the boy caught up, tackling her to the ground. He clawed at her clothing. No color emitted from her, but she fought for her life, hitting and scratching the boy until his hands wrapped around her neck, the same hands that had caressed her cheek earlier that night.

The girl choked on a sob before her body became still. With a heavy sigh, the boy looked down at the crime he committed. He buried the girl under a pile of yellow-orange leaves and ran back to his car.

For a moment, Death did nothing. This loss of life was something he hadn't seen coming, even though his eyes had been open the entire time.

From the darkness in the trees, an aura filled the small clearing. The girl stepped out, cloaked in white and with wings the color of dead leaves. She approached him and touched his face. He exhaled, letting loose breath that had been contained for so long. The girl showed him a smoky staircase. In the air, fire burned, and flames licked the building. He ran in, dressed in heavy gear carrying a long hose filled with water. Above him, the roof creaked as the foundation began to give away. He turned to the others dressed in the same attire, shouting for them to leave, then continued to do his work. He had a job to do. It was necessary. When the roof collapsed on him, he saw colors—red, orange, and yellow—the colors of a burning fire, the colors of a sunset on a summer day.

When the girl removed her hand, the image vanished, but now he understood. He was no longer Death. He spread his wings, now white. The girl took his hand, and he felt something he thought only he understood. Mercy. Something that had to be learned in the living world and brought into this one.

The girl tugged on his hand and led him to the gates. Unsure if he would be allowed to enter, he kept his hand in the girl's hold, but she let him go and nudged him forward. With a soft step, he moved closer to the gates, and they opened. He walked in as the warmth he had tasted before welcomed him home.

Death followed the grieving man and woman as they exited the cemetery and headed for home.

Once there, she stood in a corner and watched. The man tried to keep busy by rearranging the furniture for the guests coming from the funeral. Meanwhile, the woman sneaked away to an upstairs room and flipped through a family photo album. Each time she came across a girl with blonde hair and blue eyes, tears ran down her face.

Death knelt beside the crying mother and placed her hands over the woman's. The woman looked up, and even though Death knew she could not be seen, she could be felt. Comfort and mercy passed through Death and to the mother. The woman's mouth spread into a small smile and her tears stopped.

Death sat on a bed with her head tilted to one side. In the room was a boy with dark hair and eyes. His soul was a blend of silver and gold. She didn't know why, but she wanted to feel him. Among the living souls, his was the only one she wanted to take the most, but she was never able to find the right time and place.

Today might be different.

She watched as the boy prepared for his night. Empty beer cans were strewn about his messy room. On a nearby table sat a book filled with drawings, all colored in different shades. She touched them and the colors leaped as though they recognized her. The boy walked past her, picking up a set of keys. Outside, he got into his car and started to drive away. Death joined him. The car sped up, weaving recklessly through traffic.

Death only had to wait.

The boy turned the steering wheel sharply as the tires on his car squealed across the pavement and his vehicle slammed into a telephone pole. His body lurched forward before settling back into the seat. The silver and gold began to fade. This was it. The right time, the right place.

As Death reached over for the boy, a white blur fell in between them. The Guardian held up his hand. *Not yet.* She knew this Guardian well, not only from these meetings, but because he was the first soul she had ever led to the gates.

As police sirens approached, Death and the Guardian stood side by side outside the car. The boy took in a hollow breath and moaned. Silver and gold filled him from the inside out.

She turned to the Guardian. *Now?* He gave her a small nod and took off into the sky, his white wings flapping behind him. She turned her gaze back to the boy. Other living souls were coming to his aid now. All around him colors swarmed and danced.

Death did not move. She still had a job to do here.

The gas dripping from the back of the boy's car burst into flames. He struggled to free himself, but as the fire intensified, the ones who had come to help stepped away. They feared death. They feared her.

Underneath the car, the shadows groaned and climbed over the twisted burning metal. They waited as well.

As the fire grew, the boy called out for mercy.

Death did not answer.